M000034280

# HIGH PRAISE FOR BOUNDARY WATERS SEARCH AND RESCUE: BEYOND BELIEF

~~This book is engaging, romantic, spiritual, mysterious, and suspenseful all in one. It grabs your interest right away with surprising plot twists and likeable characters. I found it was hard to put down. The faith aspects of the story are deep and true, so thoughtfully written. The crime-mystery elements keep you hooked. I feel it would be a wonderful read for book groups. The north country setting in itself is wild and romantic, and nature becomes a huge part of the action. The love story that unfolds will touch your heart and leave you wanting more. But don't worry! Book 2 is coming soon! And, ladies, it's not just for you. My hubby loved it too! ~~Mrs. McGregor

~~The action starts from page 1. This is outside my usual genre so didn't know what to expect. Amazing descriptions of Boundary Waters area, medical treatments, and beautiful sewing with beads to build a world I understood—one where it's not all sweetness and light, evil exists, and people are purposely hurt, and we see people coming to God. ~~Lisa H.

~~ I found the author's careful use of scripture and music to be inspiring. Weaving a story of romance, spiritual journey, action, and the natural beauty of northern Minnesota, the author did a great job of creating a page turner. I can't wait for the next one. ~~Dwight E.

~~Action, romance, soul searching, great character development, suspense, nature—this book has it all! I was pleasantly surprised by this gem. Cannot wait for the next book in the series! ~~DKBB

# BOUNDARY WATERS SEARCH AND RESCUE:
# BEYOND IMAGINATION

## BOOK TWO IN THE BOUNDARY WATERS SEARCH AND RESCUE SERIES

BY

## JOY HARDING

ISBN 978-1-63885-743-3 (Paperback)
ISBN 978-1-63885-744-0 (Hardcover)
ISBN 978-1-63885-745-7 (Digital)

All quoted Scripture except where noted is from the New American
Standard Bible, Copyright 1960, 1962, 1963, 1968, 1971, 1972,
1973, 1975, 1977 by the Lockman Foundation—a Corporation
not for profit, La Habra, CA All rights reserved.

This is a work of fiction. Names, characters, businesses, places,
events, locales, and incidents are either the products of the author's
imagination or used in a fictitious manner. Any resemblance
to actual persons, living or dead, or actual events is purely
coincidental.

Covenant Books, Inc.
11661 Hwy 707
Murrells Inlet, SC 29576
www.covenantbooks.com

# Dedication

For this reason a man shall leave his father and his mother, and be joined to his wife; and they shall become one flesh.

—Genesis 2:24 NASB

And with these words God created the family, beginning with a man and a woman. My husband and I both grew up in such families, with a father and a mother guiding our paths. We now recognize that for the blessing it was. To single parents everywhere, we honor you for loving a child enough to be both mother and father.

I dedicate this book to the Author of marriage and family, our great God.

I dedicate this book to our parents, Don and Wanda and Ray and Nancy. Together, they wove family units worthy of God's plan. Thank you from our hearts for your love, your training, and your example.

I dedicate this book to everyone involved in bringing it to market in readable form, including my contract editor (DKBB), my proofreaders and beta readers (Dan, Wanda, Carol, Christine, Donna, Angela, Ruth, and Jean), my publisher (especially my publication assistant, Cindy), and everyone who has been so faithful in praying for me as I write. Thank you all!

Finally, I dedicate this book to my readers. Thank you for investing your time, money, and interest in this work of my heart. May it bring you enjoyment and help you to rest in our wonderful Lord.

*There is a thread*
*running between,*
*the first and the last*
*breath that we breathe.*

*And in this strand*
*of flesh and bone,*
*reside the hopes*
*and dreams we call our own.*[i]

# TABLE OF CONTENTS

# INTRODUCTION

Hello and thank you for choosing to read *Boundary Waters Search and Rescue: Beyond Imagination*. *Beyond Imagination* is the second book in the Boundary Waters Search and Rescue saga and opens five and a half months after *Boundary Waters Search and Rescue: Beyond Belief* (covering the first three years of Jack's story) ends.

The following paragraphs will familiarize you with the characters introduced in *Beyond Belief* who also are in *Beyond Imagination*. I will present them in the order that they appear in the first book.

*Dr. Jack Lockwood* (male protagonist): Jack is a physician, board-certified in surgical critical care and emergency medicine. He is fifty-three years old when *Beyond Imagination* opens, has been married to Elizabeth Joy Lockwood for three and a half years, and lives just outside of Ely, Minnesota. He is also the cofounder of the Boundary Waters Search and Rescue Unit (BWSRU/BWSR), a professional combined service team operating out of Ely and Grand Marais, Minnesota. When not on call for the BWSRU, Jack is on staff with the local hospital—Ely-Bloomenson Community Hospital (EBCH). Prior to meeting Liz, he was a widower for twenty-one years, and his late wife's name was Ellie.

*Dan Harrison*: Dan is the chief of police in Ely, Minnesota, and Jack's partner in founding the BWSRU/BWSR. He is a Gulf War-honed helicopter pilot. He is fifty-four when *Beyond Imagination* opens. He and Jack form the core of the BWSRU's Team 1. They have been friends for over twenty-four years. Dan has been married to Beth Erickson Harrison for almost five years.

*Binx*: Binx is Jack's black cat. She is eleven years old when *Beyond Imagination* opens.

*Elizabeth Joy Lockwood* (female protagonist): Elizabeth "Liz" is Jack's wife and is a textile artist and teacher. Before retiring for health reasons twelve years ago, she was a religious liberty attorney with her own firm. She maintains her license to practice law. She is fifty-four when *Beyond Imagination* opens. Prior to meeting Jack, she was a widow for eight years, and her late husband's name was Eric.

*Sierra*: Sierra is Liz's Maine Coon mixed breed cat. She is eight years old when *Beyond Imagination* opens.

*Eduard Reynoso*: Eduard is the head of a Columbian drug cartel. Liz testified against him in *Beyond Belief*, and now he's incarcerated for life in federal prison. *Beyond Belief* tells the story of Liz, Jack, and Reynoso in detail.

*Brian Stokes*: Brian is the Cook County sheriff based in Grand Marais, Minnesota.

*Nancy Hanley*: Nancy is Liz's mother. She is eighty-three years old when *Beyond Imagination* opens. Nancy is a widow and lives in Duluth, Minnesota.

*Beth Harrison*: Beth is Dan Harrison's wife and owner of the Northern Lights Café, a bakery/coffee shop (open for breakfast and lunch) in Ely, Minnesota. She loves baking, camping, canoeing, and climbing. She and Dan are Jack's and Liz's closest friends. Beth is forty-nine when *Beyond Imagination* opens.

*Gus Walters*: In his midtwenties, Gus is the youngest officer on the Ely, Minnesota, police force and the youngest on-call member of the BWSRU.

*Dr. Zachary Birch*: Zach is a physician, board-certified in surgical critical care and emergency medicine. He serves as the lead physician for Team 2 of the BWSRU. He's on staff at EBCH when not on call for search and rescue.

*Todd Hanley*: Todd is Liz's brother, her only sibling, younger than her by four years. He works for the CIA and is based out of Washington, DC. He is married to Damson, and they have two adult girls.

*Victoria Ruth Jordan*: Victoria (Vicky) is Jack's sister, younger than him by five years. She's an automotive engineer and lives in a suburb of Detroit with her husband Ted. They have two adult boys.

*Walter Mark Beckett*: Walter is Jack's brother, older than him by a year. Walt is a journeyman electrician who lives in Albuquerque, New Mexico, with his wife, Morgan, and their four college-aged children.

*Lloyd Arthur Beckett*: Lloyd is Jack's father. He and Jack have a difficult relationship. Lloyd is eighty-one years old, retired from the pastorate, and lives in Chicago, Illinois, when *Beyond Imagination* opens. Lloyd divorced Jack's mother when Jack was thirteen.

*Frank Bornell*: Frank is an FBI agent that was involved in the Reynoso case.

*Dorrene Rock*: Dorrene is Jack and Liz's family physician in Ely, Minnesota.

*Stephen Lynch*: Steve is the pastor at the Ely Evangelical Free Church where Jack and Liz are members.

*Lazarus*: At two and a half years old, Lazarus is the youngest of Jack and Liz's cats. He is a ginger tabby.

*Christine Anderson*: Christine is an on-call emergency medical technician (EMT) with the BWSRU.

*Dr. Theresa Paschal*: Theresa is a board-certified physician in thoracic and cardiac surgery and practices out of St. Luke's Hospital in Duluth, Minnesota. She saved Jack's life in *Beyond Belief*. She's well-known and well-respected in her field.

*Dr. Andrea Barstow*: Andrea is a physician at EBCH, board-certified in emergency medicine and surgical critical care at the Ely hospital.

# CHAPTER 1

―――――――――――――――✕―――――――――――――――

## PILGRIMS IN AN UNHOLY LAND

Liz Lockwood was in the kitchen starting dinner and enjoying the peace of her surroundings. It was a perfect mid-May afternoon—warm, sunny, and the birds sang exuberantly. She'd had a good day in the studio, her hands cooperating as she'd embroidered beads onto her newest commission. Despite extensive physical therapy, she still had difficulty beading her textile projects. Some days were so bad that all she could do was wet felt background fabric, write, or if her hands were somewhat cooperative, embroider, but today, she'd been able to do the work she loved the most. Finished in the studio, she had one of her favorite playlists on the sound system, and all was right with the world.

Liz looked up in surprise as Jack's car came down their road. He was home from the hospital two hours early. She was thrilled. This was the perfect end to her workday. Wiping her hands on a towel, she went to meet him when she heard the door open. As soon as she saw him, she stopped short. He looked like someone had hit him over the head, hard.

Her heart pounding, Liz moved forward and put her arms around him. "What's wrong, Jack? You look ill."

Saying nothing, Jack embraced her and bent to rest his head on her shoulder.

Liz held him for a long time, rubbing his back and just letting her warmth soothe him.

Finally, Jack took a shuddering breath and straightened. He looked down at her and managed, "I'm okay, love. It was just a bad day all around."

Liz led him into the dining room and motioned for him to sit. "That's horse patootie. You're not okay, not even close. Park it, and I'll be right back."

Liz returned to the room almost immediately, holding mugs of strong, sweet tea. "It's tea, sorry, but at least it's warm. I've got some coffee brewing." After sitting down next to Jack and handing him the cup, she asked, "What's happened?"

Rubbing his forehead, Jack shook his head. "We are pilgrims in an unholy land and never have I been more convinced of that than I am right now."

Liz took his hand and squeezed it. "Jack, tell me what's going on. Did you lose a patient?"

Jack nodded, looking almost despondent. "Actually, I lost two patients, a mother and her child. The mother, who was in her second trimester of pregnancy, had gone in to get an abortion at a regional clinic. Something happened during the procedure, and the twenty-three-week-old baby she was carrying was born alive. A nurse at the clinic called a friend when the doctor refused to do anything even though the mother was pleading with him to help her baby. The friend called emergency services, but by the time they got to the clinic, the mother was hemorrhaging and the baby was dying. Over the doctor's protests, they received permission from the mother to transport her and the baby. Sadly, by the time they got to me, the child was gone, and it was too late for the mother. She bled out within minutes. She kept saying, 'I'm sorry, don't let me die.'"

Jack jumped to his feet. "Excuse me." He ran into the bathroom.

Liz heard retching as soon as the door closed behind him.

⌣

Later that night, as they lay in bed, Liz asked, "Did they arrest the doctor?"

Jack nodded. "Yes, they did, and he won't be practicing medicine again. In fact, he'll be going to prison. As far as I'm concerned, the state should charge him with murder twice over. Minnesota law prohibits abortion after viability—defined as twenty weeks—except when the pregnancy threatens the health of the mother. In addition to performing an illegal procedure on a juvenile, this guy didn't have hospital privileges or a transfer agreement with either EBCH or the Grand Marais Hospital. His facility certainly didn't meet the requirements of an ambulatory surgical center. He left the baby uncovered and pretty much the way he'd delivered her. Apparently, he targeted underage and other at-risk women and offered them a way to have a late-term abortion without any of the safeguards designed to protect expecting mothers from harm or help them make an informed decision. None of this, including his arrest and prosecution, does the baby or her mother I tried to save today any good. Once things started to go sour, that child and her child never stood a chance."

Sitting up, Jack put his head in his hands. "As a medical community, we grievously failed that young woman—she was sixteen—and her baby. I had the privilege of telling her confused, heartbroken parents what had happened. They lost their underage daughter and their grandchild to an illegal abortion they knew nothing about. The mother was a runaway. The father of the baby, who was far older than the girl, gave a false name, posed as the pregnant woman's father, and served as the notification recipient. The clinic didn't require any proof of identification, another felony to add to the doctor's long list. We could arrest the father for falsifying a medical record and for statutory rape, but he took off as soon as the paramedics showed up and the mother died before telling us anything more than he was the father." Putting his arms around Liz, Jack apologized. "I'm sorry for taking this out on you."

Liz snuggled close to Jack. "You're not taking anything out on me. You know I was a religious liberty attorney and believe me when I tell you I understand the frustration. The theory that an 'evolving' Constitution somehow creates a 'liberty right' to abort a child is, sadly, the law, but many accomplished jurists disagree with that interpretation. They believe that the Constitution guarantees the rights it guarantees in plain language and are trying to change or overturn *Roe v. Wade*. In the meanwhile, something benignly called 'choice' kills over a million infants a year and far too many of their mothers."

Shaking her head sadly, Liz continued, "With the kind of abortion law that exists here in the US, there's very little incentive to create programs that would provide alternatives for young women like the mother you cared for today or her baby. Many don't seem to realize that abortion, as used by many, is a very dangerous method of birth control that adversely impacts those women who are low-income, minorities, or who are underage. Today was a case in point, and it's especially dangerous when abortionists don't have a connection with a hospital or a conscience."

Liz sighed. "I wish I could fix it. Particularly when so many couples out there desperately want to be parents, and many don't care about the child's ethnicity or if that child has a disability."

Jack stroked Liz's cheek. "This sounds like you're speaking from personal experience."

Liz nodded. "Yes, although it was a very long time ago. Eric and I had money to raise a child but not to pay a huge amount all at once. He was buying into an architectural partnership and I was just out of law school. At the time, domestic adoption was expensive, and our ages were of concern, particularly with my ongoing health issues. Although my health wasn't such a roadblock with overseas adoption, we simply couldn't afford that option. When we got to the point that we could manage the kinds of fees, official and nonofficial, overseas adoption was known for, my health had deteriorated to a point we didn't feel comfortable adopting. I wish now we'd gone ahead and taken the chance. You want to know something stupid?"

Jack looked at Liz quizzically. "What?"

"I keep hoping that somehow I'll be a mom. I mean, here I am, still health challenged, perimenopausal, fifty-four years old, and I still keep hoping. How's that for silly?"

Jack smiled and kissed Liz. "It's not silly. It's optimistic. Although I'm not sure I could manage a two-year-old at almost sixty, I'd be willing to try. I do know this. Nothing is impossible with our God. Look at Abraham and Sarah."

Drawing Liz to him, Jack held her close to his heart. That night, sleep proved elusive, so he took comfort in her warmth through the long, dark hours. When dawn finally lightened the sky, he got up and sought out his Lord. This morning, for the first time since he could remember, medicine held no joy for him.

Liz found Jack in the library when she awoke. She often found him there mornings, either reading the Bible or praying, but today was different. She could hear his quiet sobs. After getting out of bed, she sat down beside him and put her arms around him. He turned into her embrace, and they held each other close. Praying together, they asked God to show them a path forward and for a way to cope with this particular incarnation of evil—an evil that couldn't rest on the shoulders of a pregnant young woman who felt that she was without options or on helpless babies killed before they could draw a breath. In this case, it was an evil that was all the more terrible because a child had been born alive only to die, alone and in pain.

When they finished, Jack helped Liz to her feet. "Thank you for praying with me."

Liz looked up at her husband's sad face and cupped his cheek. "I love praying with you, Jack. Thank you for caring so much. What's your schedule like today?"

Jack took a deep breath. "Apart from being on call for BWSR Team 2, I'm off for the next few days. I asked Zach to switch details with me before I came home yesterday, and he agreed. I didn't think I'd have the focus necessary for the hospital, and I couldn't take a chance on failing another patient."

Liz made a rude noise. "Jack, you didn't fail that mother or her child! The fault lies with the abortionist and with a society that for fifty years has deemed killing unwanted children a proper choice. As if that's the best solution our 'enlightened' society can manage."

Looking at Jack appraisingly, Liz said, "You know what I think? I think we should go away for the weekend. You can let Dan know where we're going, and if he needs you for a rescue run, he can pick you up in the chopper and I'll drive home. I think it's important we do this to give you time to get your balance back and because nothing helps you sort things through like time outdoors in God's creation. What do you think?"

Jack nodded. "That sounds wonderful."

Blinking in the early dawn light, Liz looked around, wondering what had awakened her. Jack's side of the bed in their suite at the Rocky Harbor Lodge was empty, but she saw light coming in from the living area. She stretched and prayed that this getaway would help soothe her husband's aching spirit. After calling Dan yesterday, they'd driven down Highway 61 along Lake Superior's north shore until they reached this favorite place just south and west of Tofte, Minnesota. When she'd made the reservations, she'd specified a lakeview room, never imagining that the lodge would give them a "regular customer" upgrade to a suite with a fireplace and a large whirlpool tub. They also had a deck overlooking the water, and their long weekend came with vouchers for a complimentary breakfast and dinner. They'd enjoyed the dinner last night and then had gone for a long walk along the lakeshore. Later that evening, after sharing a whirlpool, they lay in the king bed, relaxing in the glow of the fire. Jack had fallen asleep before Liz, and she'd begun to think that her prescription was working.

Getting up, Liz padded into the living area. Jack was asleep on the love seat, his Bible open and face down on his chest. Walking over, she knelt beside him and kissed him awake. When his eyes opened, she smiled and said, "Honey, this doesn't look at all comfortable. It's early, so why don't you come back to bed for an hour or two? I'm lonely in there all by myself."

Jack smiled tiredly, sat up, and wrapped his arms around Liz. Kissing her, he apologized, "Sorry, I hadn't intended to leave you alone for so long."

"When did you get up?" Liz asked curiously. "I know you like the early morning, but it's just after five right now."

"I guess it was a little after two." Jack got to his feet and took Liz's hand. After they snuggled back into bed, he kissed her temple. "Please don't worry. I had a wonderful time with you yesterday, and I'm looking forward to today."

"Jack, I *am* worried," Liz insisted. "You couldn't have gotten more than two or three hours of sleep if you got up at two. I know what happened last Thursday is eating at you. Won't you please let me in? Maybe I can help."

Jack sat up and leaned against the headboard, his face a study in pain. "Liz, nothing in my training prepared me for what happened the other day. I'm used to losing patients, sadly it happens, but this was different. As a trauma specialist, I don't often deal with OB-GYN cases and I certainly haven't encountered abortionists or their not-so-little industry."

Looking at Jack appraisingly, Liz said, "But there's more to all this, isn't there?" Her arms around him, she waited for an answer.

Taking a shuddering breath, Jack began, "When we first met and were having our 'getting to know you' conversation, I told you about Amy. Do you remember?"

Liz nodded. "Yes. She's the physician you dated for over a year in Denver, right?"

"Yes. Do you also remember me telling you that she was the only woman other than Ellie and now you that I'd been intimate with?"

Liz's brows knotted as she tried to figure out where this conversation was going. "I do. You dated for a long time and..."

"And there came a night after we'd gone out that I couldn't—or rather didn't want to—say 'no' or 'wait' to her. Ellie had been gone for almost a decade, and Amy and I had been seriously dating for over a year. She'd been ready to take that step for some time. I loved her and I'd been feeling alone and like half a man for too long. My guard was down, and it just happened. What I didn't know is that when I asked her if she was using some kind of protection and she said yes is that rather than meaning that she was on some form of birth control, she was just playing the odds."

Liz paled. "You don't have to go any further, Jack. I'm sorry that I opened an old wound."

Jack kissed Liz's forehead. "You didn't open the wound. What happened at the hospital did. All you're trying to do is help by listening. I need to finish this, so you understand what's going on with me. After that night, a month went by and Amy and I didn't see each other. We never slept together again. At first, I just passed it off to my crazy schedule, but then I began to wonder if I'd somehow disappointed her. I was serious enough about the relationship that I invited her out to dinner with the intent of asking her to marry me. She had something quite different in mind for that night. When I 'popped the question,' she started to laugh and commented that I really was on another planet. She'd come that night to break things off with me. Almost as an afterthought, after telling me how much she hated my schedule, hated my need for time alone, and called me a prude for making such a big deal about sex she mentioned, with some satisfaction, that it was good she'd taken care of things. That way, she assured me, neither of us would have a ball and chain to carry around as a reminder of a mistake.

"That's what Amy called our unborn child, a ball and chain," Jack took a shuddering breath, "and that's how I found out that our baby, my baby, had been wiped out of existence at four weeks gestation. It seems that fathers have no say in such matters. She never told me. Instead, she just visited a clinic and dealt with 'it.'" Jack was silent for a few moments before adding, "My son or daughter would have been sixteen years old this year, and when that young woman died, in pain and pleading with me to save her, I just couldn't..."

Liz pulled Jack close and rubbed the back of his neck as he slumped against her. She had no idea what she could say to ease his pain. She knew her husband well. He was a moral, honorable man who revered life. While he'd perfected the art of withdrawing behind the physician's mask when dealing with the loss of patients, this loss was different. It hit him where he was the most vulnerable, a place deep inside him where he carried unresolved guilt and pain. She couldn't imagine what last week had put him through, especially when he'd been the one to speak with the parents. "Jack, honey, what happened with Amy wasn't…"

Jack pulled away and looked at her incredulously. "Wasn't my fault? Liz, that child was half mine. I wasn't a believer in any true sense of the word at the time, so I didn't feel bound by what the Bible has to say about sex. Yet I was old-fashioned enough to believe that sex in the absence of commitment and love was an empty pursuit, probably thanks to my father's antics. I thought Amy shared my hopes for the future and making love with her was an extension of that belief. Regardless of what happened later, I was still a physician. I knew that there was a possibility that being with her might result in pregnancy. Yet I never called to ask her. I just got involved in my own little world, and by the time we had dinner that night, I was far too late. It's not like I was seventeen years old and scared stiff. I was in my late thirties, and I would have welcomed that child. I, um, I grieved that child."

"Dear heart," Liz whispered, "I'm so sorry for your loss."

Jack hugged Liz. "Thank you. Needless to say, that ended things between Amy and me. Up until you came into my life, I hadn't thought about that night in years. Even then, I'd never really wondered what that child might be like as a teenager or as an adult. In fact, up until Thursday when I drove home, I'd never really regretted not having children. Now," he stroked her cheek with his fingertips, "I find myself wishing we'd met a decade earlier. I know there's more to it than that," Jack grinned sheepishly, "namely that Eric was still alive, and you were married. Apart from that, I wouldn't have wanted you to carry our child if it would have endangered your life, but you'd have made beautiful babies."

"No, Jack," Liz lay back against the pillows and pulled him down with her, "*we'd* have made beautiful babies. And as you often remind me, nothing is impossible with God." She kissed him with the deep love that was in her heart. "Let's keep praying about this. I know there are a lot of children out there who need a daddy like I know you'd be."

"And a mommy like I know you'd be." Jack put his arms around Liz and closed his eyes. "I love holding you like this."

21

Liz cuddled close to Jack, and as the sun rose, he finally relaxed into sleep. His face was less taut with stress and grief than it had been, and Liz prayed that talking about it had helped with the burden he was carrying. When she was sure he was sleeping soundly, she got up, poured a cup of the coffee she'd brewed earlier, wrapped herself in a blanket, and went outside on the deck. Another glorious day was upon them, and she wanted to begin it by talking with her Lord.

Fifteen hours later, Liz was back on the deck, enjoying the lingering rays of the setting sun reflecting on the water. It was warm, calm, and she was happily settled in the Adirondack glider with Jack's arms around her. It had been a restful day. After sleeping until almost noon, Jack looked and felt better. After he'd gotten up, they'd gone into Tofte, had lunch, and afterward, returned to their bed. Their loving had been slow and healing, then they'd fallen asleep in each other's arms in a puddle of bright sunshine. Later, they'd enjoyed dinner in the lodge's dining room and had just gotten back from another walk along the shore a few minutes before. Cuddling together, they watched as darkness descended over the lake, both of them captivated by the lazy movement of the water and the star-frost glaze on the tree-lined shore.

Liz was almost asleep when Jack shook her gently. "Hey, wake up, I don't think you want to miss this."

Blinking her eyes, Liz extricated herself from Jack's arms and sat up straight. Vertical bands of green and yellow with occasional flashes of red and orange danced across the dark northern sky in an ever-changing spectacle of light and color. Liz had seldom seen such a remarkable display of the aurora and never at this time of year. "Jack, this is amazing. I've never seen the northern lights like this outside the deep winter months. Have you read anything about unusual sunspot activity?"

"I've never seen *anything* like this, apart from one late October night in Lake Louise, Alberta. To answer your question, no, I've not read anything that would explain what we're seeing. It's…"

"Shhh!" Liz whispered, "listen."

Through the deep silence of the midnight hour, came a faraway crinkling sound, like someone rolling plastic wrap into a tight ball. Jack frowned and whispered back, "What's that noise?"

"That's the northern lights, the aurora."

Jack looked at his wife like she'd grown a second head. "I'm serious. What's that noise?"

Liz squeezed his hand. "I'm not making this up. When it's really quiet, you can hear the aurora."

Jack's irritation turned to awe. "You're kidding?"

"No, I'm not kidding. Do you see anything else that would account for the noise you're hearing?"

"No, but I've never..." At a loss for words, Jack whispered, "Wow!"

~⁓~

Liz squeezed Jack's hand as they drove back up Highway 1 late Sunday afternoon. "You're awfully quiet. Are you okay?"

Jack smiled at Liz fondly, lifted her palm to his lips, and kissed it. "I'm fine. I was just thanking God for you and for your wisdom in suggesting our weekend away." He glanced sideways, his eyes meeting hers. "Do you have any idea of how much I love you?"

Liz smiled back at Jack. "Almost as much as I love you. It was wonderful to have some time away from work and to just be alone together." Her smile faded. "Jack, about what happened last week. Are you sure you're ready to go back to the hospital, or should you be taking more time off?"

Pulling over to the side of the road, Jack undid his seat belt, leaned over, and kissed Liz. "Thank you for your caring heart and your concern. Yes, I'm ready to go back to what I do, to what I have loved doing for years. I can't promise that the same thing won't happen if similar circumstances arise, but for now, I can feel the strong pull of the healer inside me clamoring for me to get back to work." He kissed her again, lingeringly. "It's all thanks to you. I don't know what I'd do without you anymore."

"God willing, it will be years before either one of us has to figure out what we'd do without the other." Liz cupped his cheek in
her palm. "Let's go home. I'm looking forward to one more quiet
evening before the hospital figures out you're back. We need to think
of a good way to thank Zach for the peace of this last weekend. Any
ideas?"

"I was thinking that I'd offer to take his place on the BWSR
fast-water rescue training over Memorial Day weekend. It means I'll
be away for most of the weekend, but," Jack smiled, "there's actually
no reason that you can't ride along if you don't mind sharing my tent
and battling a few mosquitos."

"A few mosquitos?" Liz questioned suspiciously.

"I'm not kidding. They start hatching in mid-May, but four
weeks later, about the middle of June, it will take an actual search and
rescue emergency to get me into the woods."

Grinning, Liz nodded. "In that case, tell Zach you'll take his
place, and I'll keep your sleeping bag warm while you're out training
responders to keep the world safe for unseasoned campers, canoeists,
and crooks. Only, don't expend too much effort on that last category,
okay?"

# Chapter 2

## A Milk Run Turns Sour

"I'm going to swing out over the lake and bring us in over Devil's Kettle Falls. It's a sight to see in the springtime." Dan moved the control stick, and instead of flying over forest, the four of them were suddenly looking out over the pristine blue of Lake Superior.

Jack laughed from his seat behind Dan. "Isn't this a little out of the way, Harrison?"

Dan eyed his wife, who was sitting in the seat next to him. "Isn't he the one who keeps saying 'everyone's a critic?' Tell the man what we're doing, okay?"

Beth turned to face Jack. "Jack, our pilot here wants us to see a miracle of nature. He knows where and when we're expected at the staging area for training, but since it's a milk run, he figured we could have a little fun on the way."

Dan turned inland as they passed the mouth of the Brule River, his bank just steep enough to force a gasp out of Liz, who sat behind Beth. It was Liz's first time, well, her first time conscious, in a helicopter.

Jack reached for his wife's hand. "Easy, love. Our pilot's just showing off a bit. Humor the old guy."

Liz slapped Jack's shoulder. "You're terrible! Why in the world would you want to tick off the guy who holds our lives in his hands?" Reaching forward, she patted Dan's arm. "Don't listen to him. He's just jealous."

"Jealous? Of Harrison?" Jack snorted. "Why in the world would I be jealous of him?"

"Because," Beth broke in giggling, "he married the owner of the best bakery in Minnesota, who also happens to make a great cup of coffee."

Jack thought for a moment and said, "Well, there is that. Seriously, Dan, it's a gorgeous day, thanks for thinking of this. Liz and I haven't been up this way in about six months. We snowshoed up the river last January."

Dan pointed out to the left. "There it is. Wow, the water's still high."

Beth and Liz unbuckled their seat belts to get a better look out of the windows. Liz sat in Jack's lap so she could see the foaming water of the falls and the place where most of the flow disappeared into a hole in the bedrock. Jack's arms steadied her as she tried to balance while craning her neck to see more of the landscape.

Beth, unable to avail herself of her husband's lap, leaned forward, using binoculars to help her view the falls. Suddenly, she stiffened. "Hey, there's someone down there, on the bank of the river just above the falls. It looks like he's holding something." Her face paled. "Dan, he's got a rifle pointed at us!"

"Hang on!" Dan yelled, banking sharply as bullets pinged off the canopy. "All of you sit down and buckle in, now! I'm going to…" A red light flashed above him as an alarm sounded. Black smoke started billowing around the aircraft. A few seconds later, the engine noise cut out. Everyone could feel the helicopter begin to lose altitude as Dan tried desperately to level the aircraft and restart the engine. Beth picked up the microphone, her voice calm as she called, "Mayday, Mayday, this is BWSR 1 out of Ely. Complete engine failure caused by ground fire. Mayday, Mayday…" She went on repeating the aircraft call sign and alternating it with their location until Dan shouted, "Brace! We're going in. Brace…"

The rotors windmilled uselessly as the helicopter spun end for end twice, tore through the trees, crashing canopy-down in a small lake, bouncing into the air, then splitting in two before it hit the water again.

～⌒～⌒〜

Liz choked as she inhaled a mouthful of water. Blinking, she tried to figure out where she was, why she was wet, and why she couldn't breathe. She hurt and something was holding her in place, keeping her from moving. Struggling violently, she was suddenly free, and a hand pulled her head above water. Her husband was beside her. He was pale and bleeding profusely from his head and arm.

"Jack," Liz put her hand to her head, "what…what happened?" Then she realized where they were, and the memories returned. She could see flames reflected in the water and realized that what remained of the aircraft was on fire. "We've got to get out of here. Dan…Beth…" She looked around wildly, but the forward part of the helicopter was gone, replaced by a wall of wreckage. She and Jack were alone in the burning aft section, trapped in the mangled remains of their seats, jagged metal, and plastic.

Jack put his shoulder against what used to be a door, and it gave slightly. He motioned for Liz to help him, but when she moved, she felt a stabbing pain in her back. "Ow!" she gasped. Trying again, she managed to move enough to help him. Together, they pushed at the panel, this time creating an opening large enough for their bodies.

Jack groaned as he lifted Liz around him and pushed her through the opening. "In case the guy with the rifle is still out there, stay under the surface of the water as much as you can until you get to shore, then run for the woods. I'm going to grab my bag from behind your seat, and I'll be right behind you. Be careful!" He coughed as the smoke and heat worsened. Giving her a shove, he shouted, "Go!"

Liz squeezed through the sharp, pointed remains of the door, feeling it tear her skin as she moved, but finally, she was free. She swam toward shore, keeping below the surface as Jack had instructed. When she finally reached shallow water, she managed to get her feet under her and slowly stood up. When she looked back, she was horrified to find the wreckage fully engulfed in flames. "Jack!" she screamed, ignoring his instructions and heading back into deeper water. "Jack…"

Emerging from the lake, Jack grabbed her around the waist and pulled her back to shore and relative safety. "Liz, Liz, easy, love, I'm right here."

Liz calmed down enough to quit fighting her husband. Instead, she grabbed him by the shoulders. "Jack, are…are you okay? You're bleeding." She touched his head. "There's a lot of blood. Where are Dan and Beth? The front part of the helicopter wasn't there. Are they…they…"

Liz's voice rose in pitch as she pulled away from Jack. "We have to find them! Come on, we have to…have to…" The ground spun away from her, and she fell into darkness.

&#10086;

"Liz, honey, wake up. Jack's grumpy because you're sleeping on the job when we need your help."

Liz frowned, her eyes still closed. She hurt pretty persistently and she just wanted Dan to leave her alone. "Go away."

"And here I thought you were worried about li'l old me. I think my feelings are hurt."

Liz's eyes snapped open, and she looked into Dan's worried gaze. "Um, Dan…" Her memories returned, and she sat up suddenly, throwing her arms around him. "Thank God, you're alive! Oh!" She smacked his arm. "Don't you ever do that to me again! Are you okay?"

Dan smiled wanly. "I'll live to fly another day. I clobbered my head when we came down and…" he waved at his left shoulder. Jack had improvised a sling and swathed Dan's left hand in gauze. A jagged piece of metal had pierced the pilot's palm and gone all the way through his hand. "There's this. Your husband said it was dangerous to pull the metal out in these conditions, so he shot me full of a local anesthetic and poured disinfectant over the wound." He winced at the memory. "Then he put this getup on me until I get to an emergency room. After he finished, he told me to park it while he examined Beth. He didn't want to move her too much until he knew what was wrong. He also threatened me with severe bodily harm if I didn't bring you around."

Liz hugged him more gently. "Dan, honey, I'm sorry. Where are Jack and Beth, and are they both okay?"

Dan looked worried. "Your husband was bleeding pretty heavily from his head and arm the last time I saw him, but he insisted he was fine. Beth was breathing, and I couldn't see any injury, but she was still out for the count. After we crashed, I checked on her, made certain that the wreckage wasn't going to incinerate itself, then I went after you and Jack. I saw you both come out of the water, and I saw you drop. How are you feeling? Jack checked to make sure you didn't have any life-threatening injuries before he went to examine Beth, but I know he's worried about you. That's why he left me here with his bag." He smiled and teased, "I'm a trained EMT you know, and I'm fully prepared to do anything up to and including field surgery."

Liz smiled wanly. "I hurt, but since your chopper looks a whole lot worse than I feel, I'm going to call it a win and pass on the field surgery. Besides, I think that hand of yours puts anything that's wrong with me to shame." Getting to her feet, she gasped as a sharp pain in her back tore through her, but she managed to stay upright. Waving Dan off as he struggled to his knees, she said, "Look, you're just gonna get in trouble if Jack sees you anywhere but sitting on your rear and you know it. I'm okay, or as okay as one can be after being shot out of the sky. I'm just going in search of my husband and your wife. I need to see for myself that they're both okay, but where are they?"

Dan pointed away from the lake. "Our half of the chopper came down about sixty feet that-a-way. Thankfully, we landed in a bog. The wreckage is almost up to its floorboards in muck, but other than that, it's pretty much intact. Jack left Beth in the remains of her seat, settled me out here on the shore with you in case we needed to flag down a search party, then went back to help her. That was about fifteen minutes ago." Dan paled and collapsed back onto the rocky shore. "Sorry, I need to sit down. Honey," he grabbed her hand with his good hand, "selfish as this sounds, please don't fall on your face so you can come back and tell me what's going on with my wife."

The world had stopped spinning around Liz, and she managed a faint smile. "As Arnold famously said, 'I'll be back,' so don't worry. Just give me a few minutes to find Jack and…"

"Jack's right here." Jack came out of the woods, carrying a barely conscious Beth. Liz could tell carrying her was putting him in a lot of pain. She also saw something she didn't like in his expression—something that only someone who knew him like she did would see. Moving to intercept him, she asked quietly, "What can I do?"

In the same low tone, Jack said, "Walk with me and sit down as soon as we get back to Dan. I've seen your back, and I don't want you to pass out from the pain or to start bleeding again because I'm going to need your help with Beth."

The look on Jack's face brooked no argument. Liz walked with him back to where Dan was sitting, sat down, and watched as Jack laid Beth gently on the sloped granite shoreline. Beth smiled faintly as Dan leaned over her. Liz could hear their murmured endearments. What surprised her was when Jack interrupted them after just a few seconds.

"Hey, you two, the only room you're going to be getting in the near future is a hospital room. If you promise to be good and listen to your doctor, I'll see what I can do about getting you adjoining beds."

Dan looked up, his smile fading when he saw Jack's expression. "What's wrong with her, Jack?"

Beth touched Dan's hand. "Jack and I have already talked. Things aren't good with me, babe, but I'm not in a lot of pain, and I trust Jack with my life and yours. If things don't go well…"

"No, no, don't say that! You're going to be fine." Dan's eyes moved from Beth to Jack. "Tell her she's going to be fine. Jack, please, tell her!"

Jack grasped Dan's good shoulder. "Dan, I don't know that for a fact, but I'm going to do everything I can, you know that."

"What's wrong with her?"

"Beth's bleeding inside, and I'm almost certain she has a lacerated spleen. Our choices are to wait for rescue and, in the meanwhile, try to set up a transfusion of some kind, or for me to operate, using what supplies I have in my field kit. But doing that kind of surgery," Jack waved his hand at the surrounding wilderness, "out here, without a sterile environment, a proper blood transfusion setup, laparoscopy tools, or general anesthesia is a dangerous proposition. She and I talked about this, and I told her that at the rate she's losing blood, I don't believe she'll survive the first option. However, the second option is only marginally better, and I'll be the one holding the scalpel."

"And I told Jack that I want to go for option two because it's my best chance at living to see tomorrow, *especially* with him holding the scalpel. Even if the worst happens, there's no one who I want with me, apart from you, more than Jack and Liz." Beth smiled weakly and touched Dan's cheek. "Don't look so sad, DH, if I don't make it, you know what awaits me on the other side. Please, don't, don't…" Her eyelids fluttered closed, and she lost consciousness.

Dan looked up, fear in his eyes. "Jack, do something. I'll do anything you want me to do. Help her, please."

Jack crouched down beside his friend and said, "You know I'll do everything I can, brother. However, despite your training, I'm going to ask Liz to assist with the actual procedure. With your dominant hand injured, you can't help me with the surgery. There is something I do need you to do if you're willing. Beth told me that her blood type was AB positive, and I know you're type A positive, so I'd like to set up a rudimentary blood transfusion between the two of you while we operate. Are you willing to lie down and help Beth through this?"

Dan nodded. "Whatever you need, whatever I can do. Please don't let her die."

Liz tried to control her anxiety at the thought of assisting Jack as he operated on their friend. Still, she knew that as hard as this was for her, it was even worse for her husband. In a hospital setting, because of their close friendship, he would have turned Beth's surgery over to a colleague. Out here, with Beth bleeding internally, he had no choice but to operate.

Liz helped Jack prepare, and after building a fire and boiling water, she sat down beside him and Dan. "We need to do something before we start." She reached for both of their hands and prayed for wisdom and strength as they worked to save this one that was so dear to all of them. After seeking out their Lord, Liz handed Jack the scalpel and said, "I'm ready, are you?"

Jack nodded. "As ready as I'll ever be. Dan?"

Dan lay on the rock upslope from Beth, pumping a wad of gauze to keep his blood flowing into his wife's vein. He swallowed hard. "Yes. Jack," his eyes met Jack's, "whatever happens, thank you. Beth and I both know the risks and that you'll do your best."

Jack drew the blade over Beth's skin and said to Liz, "I know we gave Beth something to keep her out, but if she comes to while I'm doing this, she's going to be very unhappy and very loud. So keep the sedative handy."

Liz nodded and blotted Beth's blood with a sponge, just as Jack had instructed her. They'd positioned Beth carefully, articles of clothing and pieces of the helicopter's seats supporting her. Thankfully, Jack's field surgery kit, used in his search and rescue function, was intact, so they had the basic equipment needed to proceed with the operation. Jack had started an IV in Beth's arm, trying to keep her circulating blood volume from falling into the cellar, and put her on oxygen to help her breathe.

Jack's scalpel finally pierced the peritoneum and blood from Beth's damaged spleen spurted, flowing out in gouts of deep red. "Liz, I can't see to clamp the arteries," he said tersely.

They had nothing to replace the suction in the hospital OR, so Liz, swallowing bile, pressed a wad of sterile gauze into the wound, irrigated it with the cooled boiled water, then blotted the incision a second time, this time applying more pressure. That gave Jack the window of opportunity he needed to clamp the worst of the bleeders. They repeated this procedure several times before the flow of blood slowed. Once they'd controlled the worst of the bleeding, he proceeded with the surgery.

After Jack finished and closed the incision, he removed his gloves and put his hand on the unconscious Beth's forehead. "Nice job, honey. You came through like a trooper. So did your husband."

Jack was pale, and when he stood up, he staggered. Liz quickly got to her feet and helped support him even though the world was also spinning around her. A few moments passed, then Jack pushed Liz down to a seated position and said, "Thanks, love, I'm fine now. You did great, but stay still, okay? I don't think I can handle another surgery today, especially one that involves operating on my wife."

Moving over to Dan, Jack dismantled the transfusion setup. After bandaging his arm, Jack squeezed his friend's hand. "Beth made it through surgery, her vitals are good, and we stopped the bleeding. Thanks to you, she skirted the worst of hypovolemic shock. The biggest danger now is infection, so I've started her on antibiotics. Here's hoping that the search parties find us before the guy with the rifle. If we can get Beth to the hospital, her chances are good. She's going to be out of it for a long while yet, so for now, you stay down."

Dan grasped Jack's hand. "Thank you. I don't even know what to say, other than that," he choked. "I...I don't know what I'd do without, without..." He turned away, unable to finish.

Late in the night, Jack returned from checking on Beth. She was still unconscious, but her color was better. Her temperature was within the safety zone thanks to the antibiotics. Dan was awake and sat with Jack by the fire. Liz was asleep with her head in Jack's lap, his jacket over her shoulders. All of them were in pain and feverish, but apart from Beth, Liz was the only one able to rest. The two men conversed together in low tones.

"Jack, what's wrong with Liz? I know something's going on from the way you keep pushing her down," Dan looked worried.

Jack frowned. "She's got a large shard of metal buried in her back. I got the top section out, but I don't dare go deeper without imaging. She's in a lot of pain, and if that piece moves or if I dislodge it, it could damage her spinal cord. That's why I'm trying to keep her as still as possible. That's also why I sedated her an hour or so ago. She wasn't happy with me, but I feel better knowing she's resting and not moving around."

"Is she going to be okay?" Dan asked.

"That answer is the same for any of us. It all depends on how quickly we get out of here." Jack looked at his friend. "How certain are you that the Mayday got through before we crashed?"

Dan's expression lightened. "I think our chances are good. Beth started sending it as soon as the engine cut out. That means we had a good minute of uninterrupted radio transmission. The transponder kept sending out signals until we crashed. We came down a bit off our flight plan, but between the Mayday, the transponder, and our being long overdue, I think the troops will not only be out in force, but they should find us pretty quickly." He smiled ruefully. "I never expected that we'd be the objects of our own search and rescue operation on this year's training run—we're never gonna hear the end of this."

Jack smiled. "It's a good thing we're so terrific at what we do. Speaking of which, that was some pretty fancy flying. Four of us survived a crash that should have taken us all out. Thank you."

"You're welcome. I'd say it was nothing, but I don't want to have another few minutes like that ever again." Dan's cheeks reddened, and he changed the subject. "Jack, you didn't say anything about you. I know you lost a lot of blood. You've had a very long day. What's going on?"

Jack shrugged and touched the blood-saturated bandage over his ear. "Nothing too serious. Some lacerations that need stitches, a strained back, and a badly bruised shoulder. I was the lucky one, the rest of you suffered worse." He looked at Dan seriously. "How's your pain?"

Dan waved him off. "I'm fine."

"I know that can't be true," Jack countered. "I need you to be straight with me, Harrison. What's your pain like on a scale of one to ten?"

Cowed by the intensity in Jack's gaze, Dan gave in and answered truthfully, "About a ten, but, Jack, I don't want you to give me something that'll put me out. I want to watch over Beth tonight. I owe her that much. I was piloting the aircraft when we crashed. I should be the one lying there, not her."

"You do know how ridiculous that reasoning is, don't you?" Jack snorted. "Beth would smack you into next Tuesday if she was conscious."

"It's no more ridiculous than you wanting to come with the Hostage Rescue Team when we went after Liz a couple of years back," Dan retorted.

Jack managed a smile. "Touché. But since Beth is right here and I need to disinfect your hand again, why don't we compromise? I'll do the same thing I did before, a local and a topical disinfectant. It's crude but effective, and it will hurt like blazes. That combination won't make you sleepy, but we've all had a heck of a day, so don't blame me if you fall asleep anyway. It's actually not a bad idea if we set a watch since the guy who shot at us is still out there. I'm beat, so if you're up to it, why don't you wake me in about three hours and I'll keep watch for the rest of the night. He pulled the anesthetic and disinfectant out of his bag. "You ready?"

Dan slowly pulled the sling off his arm and held out his bandaged hand. "Can I at least have a stick to bite down on this time?"

❧

Both Dan and Jack woke to the sound of rotors overhead. Despite his assertion that he was wide awake the night before, Dan had fallen asleep shortly after Jack had curled around Liz, and all of them slept through the night. Although chilled by the early morning temperature, they were little worse than the night before. They watched the BWSRU's small, amphibious helicopter settle onto the water's surface and taxi toward the shore. A few seconds later, Zachary Birch, the physician on Team 2, emerged from the cockpit, balanced himself on the pontoon, and jumped into the water, wading the few feet to shore. He was crouching down beside Jack and Dan before the rotors on the chopper stopped spinning. Dwight Beecham, a Cook

County sheriff senior deputy based in Ely and the pilot for BWSR Team 2, secured the helicopter and joined them a few minutes later.

Zach had just finished listening to Jack's injury report and looked up when the pilot joined them. "Dwight, everyone's alive, but we've got casualties. How many can that bird carry in a pinch?"

"I can carry three passengers, maximum, so we'll have to take two trips. There's no way our larger medical evac choppers can land here. It's too swampy, and there's not enough room."

Zach nodded then asked, "What kind of time are we looking at for a round trip to the nearest hospital and back, and is that Ely or Grand Marais?"

"With the wind speed and direction, I'd say we're faster going into Ely and about one and a half to two hours round trip." Looking worried, Dwight added, "That's providing no one uses my bird for target practice."

Looking at Jack, Zach said, "I'll stay here, but who should be the first out?"

Jack shook his head. "Zach, I need you to go with Beth and Dan. I'm too close to this, and after the last twenty-four hours, I don't have the concentration necessary if something goes wrong with either one of them." Jack took Liz's hand. "As long as Liz and I stay fairly quiet, we can wait until Dwight gets back."

Frowning, Zach said, "Are you sure? Neither of you look great."

"Just look at Dan and Beth and tell me if you still question my call," Jack snapped before adding, "I'm not saying that Liz and I won't be happy to see the inside of the ER. I'm simply saying that these two should go first." He waved a hand at Dan and Beth.

Seeing a look of protest form on Dan's face, Jack speared him with a glance. "Quiet! This isn't just for you. It's for your wife, so shut it and behave."

Dan closed his mouth with a snap and bent over a semiconscious Beth. "I guess I've been told huh, babe?"

Five minutes later, Jack and Liz watched the helicopter carrying their friends lift into the sky. Liz looked at Jack, a faint smile on her face. "Thank you for convincing them to go ahead. I didn't want to be separated from you, and I'm guessing Dan felt the same way about being separated from Beth."

Jack put his arm around Liz, gently hugging her close to ward off the chill air. "I wanted you on that first trip out, but Dan and Beth's injuries are more serious than ours and," he looked at her sheepishly, "I don't want to be separated from you, either. Please promise me you'll stay quiet and still."

Liz nodded. Jack had told her about the metal in her back the evening before. "I promise. Let's just sit here by the fire until the cavalry returns because Zach was right, you don't look so great either."

Jack chuckled. "Practicing medicine without a license again, are you, *Dr.* Wife?" He kissed her, easing them both back onto the pile of clothing and seat cushion remnants. "I'm sure not going to argue with your prescription."

They rested together that way for close to an hour and were almost asleep when something whistled past Liz's ear, kicking tiny splinters of granite into her face when it hit the rock beside her. Both of them were instantly awake when they heard the sharp report of another shot. Shielding her with his body, Jack took her hand and pulled her along for several strides until she could get her feet under her. After that, she needed no prompting to run for the cover of the trees as the sound of another gunshot whistled through the quiet morning.

By the time they reached what remained of the downed helicopter, which now sat tilted at a fifteen-degree angle to the ground, both of them were breathing hard. Jack jumped in, dragging Liz with him when she struggled to make the same low jump. He eyed her with concern. "I know this is a stupid question, but are you okay? None of those bullets hit you, right?"

Liz managed a smile. "Relax, I'm just winded. My back hurts, but I'm not hit, and my arms and legs are still working fine. Did you see whoever is shooting at us?"

"Not close enough to establish anything other than the fact it's an older Caucasian male with a rifle."

"That's pretty good since I was too busy dodging bullets to see anything." Liz stretched her back, keeping low. "What now?"

Jack forced open a crumpled compartment in the pilot's side door and took out a pistol and a flare gun. He loaded the flare gun, and gave it to Liz. "Here. If you get into trouble, point the business end at the center of mass and fire. Don't hesitate, because the element of surprise is probably your only ally with the kind of firepower this guy has." Then he loaded the pistol, keeping it for himself. "We stay here for now. If he finds us, at least we can defend our position and ourselves. I know this probably goes without saying, but stay low and out of sight of the woods. I'll keep watch."

Liz nodded. "You be careful too. I don't want you to get shot any more than you want me to get shot, and I don't have the training to dig a bullet out of your backside, front side, or whatever side gets hit."

Jack never ceased to be amazed by Liz's resilience. Someone was using them for target practice, and she still found a way to make him smile. He reached over and squeezed her hand tightly. "No one's going to be digging bullets out of either one of us. Stay still. Our run for cover probably moved that shrapnel in your back, and I don't want to take a chance that we won't be able to tango together on our next vacation."

"I don't know how to tango in the first place, but I'll stay down so you can give me lessons." Liz eyed Jack. "Do you remember that first night at your house when you told me you were a physician working with the Boundary Water's Search and Rescue Unit?" Seeing him nod, Liz continued, "You might have mentioned that, unlike all those doctors on television that walk around in a climate-controlled building in white coats, you run around in the woods, wearing jeans and flannel shirts, and get shot at on a regular basis."

Jack leaned over, put his arm around Liz's waist, and kissed her. "That would be boring, and to be fair, I did tell you that crime was on the uptick in the BWCA. Besides, sometimes I do walk around in a climate-controlled hospital wearing a white coat." He raised his head. "I think we lost this guy. I..."

A bullet whistled over his head and buried itself in the plastic resin above their shoulders.

"You were saying?" Liz gasped as she dove for the floorboards. She watched as Jack fired back. "Can you see the guy?"

"Yes, he's in the trees about forty feet away. Older guy, at a guess, he's the same one who was shooting at us before. At least I hope he's the same one that was shooting at us before. I'd hate to think there were two people that I managed to tick off so badly before noon."

"You're crazy, you know that?" Liz giggled. "We're being shot at again and you're cracking jokes."

"You want to see me get good and angry, just raise your head another inch." Jack put his hand on her shoulder and pushed her back into a seated position. "Stay down!"

Liz ducked obediently. "What about you?"

Jack aimed and fired again. This time, they both heard a cry of pain, followed by the crashing and crackling of someone moving through the undergrowth. Jack listened intently for a few minutes. "It sounds like I hit him." Starting to get to his feet, Jack stopped when Liz grabbed his shirt.

Looking at him grumpily, she asked, "Where are you going? He could still be out there."

Jack squeezed her hand. "He could be, but it's more likely that he took off. Liz, he could also be in the woods bleeding out, and since I'm the one who put the bullet in him, I can't take that chance."

A stubborn look formed on Liz's face. "Okay, fine." She got to her knees, grabbed the flare gun, and said, "Let's go."

Jack pushed her down again. "Where do you think you're going?"

"With you," Liz announced crisply. "Wither thou goest and all that. You're not going out there alone."

"Liz, I don't have time to argue with you. You need to stay still."

"That may be, but I need to watch your backside more. You know you'd do the same thing if you had the metal in your back and I was heading out to find the bad guy with the gun. So stop arguing and let's go. I promise to sit down as soon as we figure out if that guy's still out there." Liz lifted her head to peek outside. "I don't see him."

"You are the most maddening…" Jack clenched his teeth to avoid saying anything else he would regret and instead took Liz's hand and led her to the other side of the crumpled aircraft. Jumping the three feet to solid ground, he lifted her to his side after he was certain no one was going to start shooting at them. He crouched and looked around, keeping her close. "Liz, stay low and follow me. If I wave you back, please just go, and don't turn it into a filibuster. I'm trained for this, you're not."

Ten minutes later, they stood in the underbrush just inside the tree line on the shore of the lake. It was quiet, and no one was in sight. No one had intercepted them or shot at them as they'd made their way around the chopper and back to the lake. Jack found a blood trail leading away from the crash site, but rather than follow it, he'd led Liz to where they stood. Sitting, he gently pulled her down into his lap. "Liz Lockwood, I adore you, but there are times I wish you didn't have all that legal argument training." He kissed her tenderly. "Since we seem to get shot at more than your average couple, I just want you to stay safe, stay out of the line of fire, and let me do my job."

"That's not fair, Jack," Liz protested. "I didn't run into the line of fire. I was behind you the entire time, and besides, no one shot at us. This is all I wanted, you and I together, safe for the moment, and well-hidden."

Wincing, she shifted in his embrace. "Well, I also want Dwight, Zach, and the helicopter to hurry back." She looked worried. "What if that guy starts shooting at them?"

"I'm guessing that they'll bring reinforcements and…"

Jack stopped talking as two choppers came in low over the lake. They could see Dwight piloted the smaller of them. The other was clearly a National Guard bird. It was larger, heavily armored, well-armed, and from all appearances, it was going to stay in flight and cover those on the ground. Ten minutes later, Jack and Liz were in the chopper, and they were all heading back to Ely.

# Chapter 3

## Fallout

Jack shrugged out of his robe and knocked on the bathroom door. "Liz, may I come in? I just want to brush my teeth."

Getting no response, Jack opened the door and smiled at the steam in the air. Liz liked her showers hot and didn't like the noise of the exhaust fan. She'd wanted to take a bath in the deep, free-standing, soaking tub, but he'd recommended against it because of the still-fresh wounds on her back. Instead, she was relaxing in the walk-in steam shower that he'd treated himself to when he'd built the house. He could see her sitting on the built-in bench under the rain showerhead.

Taking a deep breath, Jack relaxed against the white subway-tiled wall, just soaking in the normalcy of the moment. Somehow, what was supposed to have been an easy, predictable weekend of train-ing and togetherness had gone terribly wrong. Thankfully, they were all safe. At Zach's insistence, Jack and Liz had both spent the night following their rescue in the hospital. Zach had stitched up their wounds and performed minor surgery on Liz to remove the jagged sliver of metal from her back. This was their first night home since the crash, the hospital would be releasing Dan tomorrow, and Beth a day or two after that. Her recovery would take more time, but she was doing well.

Thinking about the could-have-beens, Jack suddenly wanted to do more than brush his teeth. Walking over to the shower, he rapped on the glass enclosure. "Hey, do you have room for one more in there?"

Normally, Liz's response to a question like that was immediate and enthusiastic, but tonight, she was quiet. "If that's what you want, honey, that's fine," she finally responded.

Jack wiped the steam from the glass so he could see his wife clearly. To his surprise, her eyes were red-rimmed and brimming with tears. "Hey, love, what's going on? Are you in pain?"

Swallowing hard, Liz stammered, "No, not really. It's just, well, a lot of things. You know what last weekend was like."

Jack noticed something else strange. Liz's towel, which usually hung on the warming rack until she was ready for it, covered the elegant cheval mirror he'd given her for her last birthday. He frowned. "Liz, tell me what's bothering you. Or if you'd rather not have me in the shower with you, I can wait until you're finished for us to talk. I just thought it would be nice to be close because you're right, last weekend was pretty awful. Regardless of where, we do need to talk, I think."

Sniffing, Liz attempted a smile. "No, it's fine, Jack. If you really want to join me, I'd love it."

Shedding his pajama bottoms, Jack stepped in behind Liz and pulled her against him. Nuzzling her neck, he said, "Now why don't you tell me what's upsetting you."

"I'm fine, really." Liz turned in his arms and planted a kiss on his chin. "Hi. Shall we get clean together or," she grinned, "whatever else you have in mind?"

Jack rested his cheek on the top of Liz's head. "Hi, and yes, in a minute. I think I want to pursue our conversation a little further first. Did you throw your towel over the mirror, or did the maid forget to hang it up?"

"We don't have a..." Liz stopped talking. "Oh, uh, I'm sorry, I'll put it back on the rack when I'm finished in here."

"Liz, I don't care a fig where you hang your towel. I don't care if you drop the thing on the floor, but I'm thinking that there's some significance to the fact that it's covering your mirror. Am I wrong?"

Liz flushed pink. "I don't..." She blew out a frustrated breath. "Can't we just drop this conversation and enjoy our shower?"

Kissing her, Jack murmured, "If I thought you were enjoying this like you usually do, we wouldn't be having this conversation in the first place."

"Honey, it's not a question of me enjoying it, it's..." Liz shook her head. "Never mind."

Jack put his arms around his wife and asked her the three questions that were on his mind. "What's going on, Liz? What does it have to do with the mirror? What were you looking at?"

"I was just looking at my back. It's no big deal."

"Oh, but I think it is. I just don't know why."

"How can you say that, Jack?" Liz turned her head and looked at him, tears spilling from her eyes. "You could have anyone you want."

Finally starting to understand what was going on with Liz, Jack looked into her eyes. "I have the one I want. It took me twenty-one long years to find her. You know that."

"Look at me!" Liz sniffed.

Jack grinned broadly. "I am." His grin disappeared when Liz burst into tears. Nonplussed by her response, he said nothing until her sobs faded to hiccups. He stroked her back and finally asked, "Love, do you think I'm that kind of man? One who would lie to, cheat on, and hurt a woman who's done nothing to him but make him feel cherished?"

"No! I never said any of those things about you. *You're* not the problem."

"Then why are you crying? Liz, is this about the lacerations you suffered when we crashed?"

Liz blinked. "You make it sound like it's nothing, Jack, but after Reynoso, and now this, my body is..."

"Beautiful. Liz, my love for you has nothing to do with the scars you have on the outside and everything to do with who you are on the inside. Please don't interpret that as meaning that I don't find you attractive. Our physical relationship wouldn't be what it is if I didn't find you and your body beautiful. I'm not blind. I know that neither of us is twenty-five anymore, but do you find me less attractive because of this? He pointed to his forehead where a scar was all that remained from the night when he'd tried to stop a home invasion targeting Liz. Then he pointed to his chest and the scars from both the bullet wounds he'd suffered and the subsequent surgery that saved his life, and finally, he pointed to his arm, and a jagged, barely closed wound from the helicopter crash. "Or these?"

Liz looked at him, outrage in her eyes. "Of course not, Jack, but what I'm talking about is different."

"How?"

"By an order of magnitude."

"Oh, so you're telling me that if I get another scar or maybe two, then you'll stop loving me."

Looking confused, Liz shot back, "Of course not, but Jack…"

"Okay, so maybe you won't stop loving me, but you'll no longer find me attractive, is that it?"

Liz just stared at him, tears in her eyes. "That's not fair! I…"

Jack put his palms on either side of her face and traced her cheekbones with his fingertips. "Liz, listen to me. Satan's feeding you a pack of lies from the deepest part of Hell. This has happened before, and I don't want it to haunt you for one more second. Just as you love me at my age with all my imperfections, I love you in exactly that same way."

He gently touched one of the healed marks on her back. "I'm grateful for these scars because they mean you lived through an experience that should have killed you. Because they are part of you today, I am holding you—alive and warm in my arms—and not hanging on to a memory while I sleep alone."

Jack lifted her head until her eyes met his. "Liz, I love you more than life itself. I love your warmth, your humor, and your intellect. I love that you can make me laugh, even when things are going wrong. I love you beyond any hope of walking away. If you believe nothing else I say, believe this, I am yours, heart, body, and mind." He bent his head and kissed her deeply.

By the time they returned to their bed, Liz barely had the energy to move. Rolling over, she rested her head on Jack's chest. "How can I be so tired and so wide awake? Is that some kind of stupid middle-aged medical condition?"

"Mmph." Jack's arm tightened around her, but he didn't open his eyes or say anything intelligible.

Liz pushed on Jack's shoulder, her sated, happy mood fading. "Wake up! If I can't sleep, nobody should sleep."

Jack opened one eye just long enough to look at her and looped his arm around her waist, "C'mere, love. Just relax."

"Of all the stupid…do you think if I could 'just relax' I wouldn't have already done it?" Liz looked at Jack and was frustrated to find him asleep again. She decided to change her tactics. Propping herself on one elbow, she feathered light kisses down the side of his face, over his chin, and when she got to his chest, she noted with some satisfaction that she had his attention.

Jack rolled over and put his arms around Liz. "Wench." He kissed her, teasing her with the same light touches she'd just used to wake him. Squirming, she finally freed herself and sat up. "Again? I don't think I have the energy."

Jack sat up next to Liz in bed. "Then why in the world did you start something like that?"

"Because that was the only way I could think of to get your attention. I didn't want to be awake and alone right now. I can't sleep," Liz said sheepishly. "I'm sorry."

Hugging her close, Jack quipped, "Feel free to wake me up like that anytime. Tell me what's bothering you."

"You mean other than the facts that a few days ago someone shot our helicopter out from under us, two of my best friends are lying in hospital beds, and we just made love like a couple of twenty-somethings on a bender? I'm confused, my body is confused, and I don't want you to go tomorrow, um, later today, but I know you have to, and I know it's the right thing to do, but I'm just…"

Chuckling, Jack put a finger under Liz's chin and tilted her face up so she was looking at him. "A mess? Liz, I have an idea that might help you worry a little less when we head out to find the guy who fired on us last weekend. Would you like to ride along with the backup crew? That way, you'll know everything as soon as we do because we're in constant radio contact. And there might just be a good surprise for you in the morning."

Liz nodded. "I'd like that. It's better than waiting for you to come home or for a sad-faced officer to arrive and tell me the bad news."

Jack ran his hand down the side of his wife's face. "Love, what's got you so spooked about all this? I'm trained for this kind of work, and you have to know that, just like always, I'm going to be very careful because I want to come home safely to you."

"I know," Liz looked miserable. "I don't know what it is about all this, but I'm scared."

"Yet you followed me into the line of fire the other day after we crashed."

"That was easy. There was no way I was going to let you go out there alone without some backup."

"Liz, honey," Jack said soothingly, "I'm not going to be alone when we go looking for this guy. Gus, Sheriff Stokes, and our department's sharpshooter, Gary Gibbs, are all going to be with me, and they're a great group. Besides that, you, Christine Anderson, and Dwight are our backup crew. I think we stand a pretty good chance of locating our guy and coming home alive to talk about it, don't you?"

"I do, and I never said my fears make a lot of sense. I thought I was over this kind of unreasoning dread. Yet this whole evening except for," Liz smiled, "well, you know, has been one emotional fight after another for me. It feels like that time right after I came back to you in the hospital a couple of years back," she finished sadly, her smile fading.

Jack paled. "Please tell me you don't plan to leave again."

Liz cupped his cheek in the palm of her hand. "Dear Jack, I will *never* leave again. I know where all this is coming from, and it's not from God. I just need you to be with me for a little while until I get this all sorted. I'm sorry for being so selfish. I know you need to get some rest."

Putting his forehead against hers, Jack whispered, "Love, I'm happy to be with you, even if it takes all night. You're first in my world, and if you really need me to stay behind in the morning, I will."

Liz shook her head and said sharply, "Don't offer me that out, Jack. This is your job. It has been your job since we've known each other. You are going to go do that job tomorrow, well, later today, and I'm going to ride along with the team, but let's leave enough time to pray together in the morning before we head out, okay? I need that grounding. Plus, I'll be praying for you the whole time we're apart."

"Thank you. We'll get this done, and then I'll be back in my climate-controlled hospital in my white coat for a while." Jack smiled. "Will that make you happy?"

Liz kissed him. "What makes me happy is you doing what you were born to do, what God has equipped you to do. I'm very proud of you. My heart just needs to catch up to my brain. For some reason, I tend to go all 'mother hennish' when someone starts shooting at you."

"They were shooting at you too, Liz, so I know exactly how you feel." Jack lay back, pulling her with him. "Turn over."

After Liz rolled onto her stomach, Jack straddled her backside and rubbed her tense shoulders, slowly moving his hands down over her back in a relaxing massage. At first, he could feel her warm skin tense beneath his touch, but as he worked deeper, he felt her relax. He carefully skirted the areas covered by gauze dressings and massaged the tight muscles in those areas that had been compensating for the injuries. When he finished, he leaned forward and kissed her neck. "Hey, you still with me?"

Liz's only response was a sleepy "Mmm, love you."

Jack lay down next to Liz, put his arms around her, and they finally slept.

# CHAPTER 4

## AN UNEXPECTED DISCOVERY

"Hey, Jack," Brian Stokes, the Cook County sheriff, raised his hand in greeting as Jack and Liz pulled Hildy II—their large four-wheel-drive SUV equipped for search and rescue—to a stop and got out. Jack took his wife's hand, and they went over to greet the sheriff, Liz shivering a little in the early morning chill.

"Hey, Brian, glad to have you with us," Jack replied. "You know the offer's always open for you to join the BWSRU on a permanent basis."

Brian smiled. "Thanks. One day, I may just do that, but for right now, I've got my hands full serving the good citizens of Cook County. This morning, I'm serving those good citizens by trying to catch one of our not-so-good citizens. How are you both after your encounter with this guy?"

"We're much better than we were last weekend." Jack looped his arm around Liz and pulled her closer. "Brian, this is my wife, Elizabeth Lockwood. She's going to be riding along with our backup crew. Liz, this is the Cook County sheriff, Brian Stokes."

Liz extended her hand. "It's good to finally meet you in person, Sheriff Stokes, and please, call me Liz."

Brian shook her hand. "Good to meet you, Liz, and I'm Brian. Welcome aboard."

Liz knew it was a great compliment to her husband and Dan that Sheriff Stokes was here with them and was considering their offer to join the BWSRU. He was a very busy man, dedicated to law enforcement and his constituency. She smiled at him. "Thank you for allowing me to ride along."

"Aw, that's nothing, honey. I just told him I wouldn't go unless you could come with us, and we all know how indispensable I am." Dan jumped out of the BWSRU's van and gave her a one-armed hug. "Good morning, sunshine."

Liz laughed delightedly and hugged him close. "Dan, you're the surprise Jack talked about! It's great to see you up and around. How's Beth?"

"She's home a day early, and her sister is at the house with her. I think I was driving them a little crazy, so here I am." He punched Jack lightly on the arm with his good hand. "This guy won't certify me as fully fit for duty, but figured I was good enough to provide back up if they need it."

"You know, if you weren't a few days out of some pretty fancy surgery on that hand and if you were able to handle a firearm, I'd want you with us," Jack said, sounding a little vexed. "Since you're still recovering, I sure feel better knowing that you're on our six. Thanks for coming out."

Dan waved him off. "I know why you made the call you did with me, and part of my job has always been to watch your six. Be careful out there." He lifted his gaze to encompass the entire search team. "That goes for all of you. As Sheriff Stokes emphasized in his briefing, this guy has shown himself ready to shoot first, and we know he has some pretty fancy firepower in his possession. Wearing your vest isn't a suggestion this morning. It's a requirement. Don't be a hero and let's get this guy. Do you have any questions for the sheriff or me?"

When no one spoke up, Dan said, "Okay, let's do this—radios on and be careful."

Dan held a rifle out to Jack, who shook his head. "No, let the others take the big guns." He held up his medical bag and the external defibrillator unit. "I've got my hands full." Seeing the look of protest in Dan's expression, Jack reassured him, "Don't worry. I have my 9 mm and will stay with the others. You know as well as I do that

I'm not here to shoot unless I have to. I'm pretty sure we're going to find at least one casualty, and I'm the one who put the bullet in him. Let me do my job while your professional law-enforcement types watch my back."

Seeing Liz frown, Jack reassured her, "Don't worry, love, we prayed about this, remember?"

Liz made a face. "Yes, I remember. You remember that 'unless I have to' part and don't leave it too long before you shoot back." She gave him a light shove toward the others. "Go on. Find your guy. I love you. Please be safe."

Jack winked at her before turning away. "I love you too. See you soon."

She watched until the search party was out of sight then turned to Dan. "Okay, what do you want me to do, Chief Harrison?"

Dan put his good arm around Liz. "Honey, Jack's going to be fine. They're all going to be fine. Come on, Wanda and Dwight already have them on the radio and are tracking them. Oh, and," Dan grinned, "lose the 'chief' thing. Otherwise I'm going to start calling you Elizabeth Joy Hanley Talbot Lockwood, Esquire, every time you address me, and then listen while you try to explain that handle to everyone else."

～◦～

"Something's wrong, Simon. We gotta get help!" Pete looked up at the grizzled man who was limping around the kitchen area of the rustic cabin. "It's taking way too long. Please, lemme go for a doc."

Simon took a swig from the can he was holding. "No! I told ya, no outsiders. Women have been pushin' out babies without docs or hospitals for centuries. Besides, she's your girlfriend, so the kid is your problem. I told ya both to get rid of it a long time ago."

"Uncle Simon, I told you she's not my girlfriend. She's my wife. Doug married us on his boat. He's the captain so he can do that."

"Oh yeah? You gotta piece of paper that says that, do ya?" the older man sneered. "'Cuz if you don't, then you ain't married. This country don't allow fifteen-year-olds to get married, so it don't matter what Doug said or did, you ain't married."

The young girl writhing on the dilapidated sofa cried out in pain. Simon poked Pete in the chest with his finger. "You keep her quiet, ya hear? Otherwise, I'll find a way to keep her from shoutin' like that. We probably got people hunting for us. Besides, I got my own problems with this leg of mine, and I need ta lie down. You need ta leave because this ain't what I bargained for when I took ya in," He waved toward the living area. "Take her with ya and don't bother comin' back."

Simon limped away, muttering imprecations as he went and slamming the door to the one bedroom in the cottage behind him. Peter, a fifteen-year-old runaway, returned to the sofa and put his hand on the girl's forehead. "Mary, I'm sorry. I don't know what to do anymore. Can you feel the baby?"

Mary, Pete's fifteen-year-old girlfriend, had tears sliding down her cheeks. "No. Why is it taking so long? There's so much blood. Please, Pete, I need a doctor."

Peter nodded. "Yeah, I know. Do you think you can stand? We can try to get into town, and if you can't make it, I'll hide you in the woods so Uncle Simon can't hear you and then go for help."

Mary nodded and sat up slowly. "Let's go quick before those pains start again." She put her arms around his shoulders and stood up. Blood stained the towels where she'd been resting and the back of her maternity dress.

Pete helped her out of the house, grabbing a blanket and two bottles of water. They'd barely gotten into the cover of the trees when Mary's next contraction hit and she fell to the ground. Pete knelt beside her, gripping her hand and counting as she writhed and cried. Never had he felt so helpless. How was he going to get her help, and why was she bleeding so badly? Slowly, the contraction faded then stopped.

Mary looked up at Pete. "I can't walk out, Pete. Leave me here and go get some help. Please don't let the baby or me die."

Pete spread the blanket down off the trail and helped Mary move on to it. He handed her a bottle of water. "Here, drink this.

Mary, I can't leave you alone. What if something happens or if Uncle Simon comes looking?"

Mary looked at him, wisdom beyond her years in her eyes. "Pete, we need help. Otherwise, it's not going to matter. Look at all the blood. Please, please, do this for me. For the baby. For our family."

Pete stayed with her for one more contraction. They were coming about four minutes apart. Then he kissed Mary's forehead. "I'll be back soon, and I'll find someone to help. I swear. I'm so sorry for this."

<hr>

The search party paused when a high-pitched scream split the air. Brian Stokes held up his hand, listening intently. They'd been walking for over an hour and had not seen or heard anything. They were still following a faint trail, leading away from the area on the Brule River where Beth had spotted the man who'd shot at them. They were now well within the BWCAW boundaries.

The scream sounded again, and Brian pointed to their right. "This way." They ran on for several hundred feet before stopping again.

Jack listened but couldn't hear anything besides birdcalls in the quiet morning. Then a noise caught his attention.

Brian motioned him over. "Come on, Jack, we're going to backtrack to where we first heard that cry and try again."

Jack nodded. "I'll be right behind you. I just want to check on a rustling I heard back in the brush over there. I'm sure it's nothing, but I don't want to take a chance."

"You're not going by yourself. Gibbs," Brian motioned the sharpshooter over to his side, "take the rest of the team and head back to our last position. Jack and I are going to check on a noise he heard, likely an animal of some kind. We'll join you in just a couple of minutes."

"You got it, Sheriff." Gibbs saluted casually.

Brian and Jack watched the rest of the team move off, then Brian turned to him. "Lead on, Jack."

They hadn't walked more than forty yards in the direction that Jack took when a loud crashing disturbed the heavy brush in front of them. Brian drew his weapon and waited. Suddenly, Jack knocked the gun out of Brian's hands and tackled the teenaged boy who'd appeared out of nowhere. Both of them rolled over on the ground, then Jack grabbed the boy by both arms and pulled him to his feet. "Who are you, and what are you doing here?" he asked.

"Lemme go! I gotta get to town or a telephone fast," the young man shouted.

Jack tried again. "What's your name, and what's wrong? We can help."

"No, I need a doctor! Please, it's important."

Seeing that Brian had retrieved his gun and was now moving toward them, Jack waved him back. Focusing on the young man he held, Jack said in a quieter tone, "I'm a doctor. Tell me what you need and how I can help."

"No," the kid shook his head, "that's the sheriff. You guys are cops. I didn't do nothing wrong, but I got to get a doctor, please, my wife's in trouble."

"Your wife?" Jack was confused, this kid couldn't be over sixteen years old.

Struggling to free himself, the young man shouted, "Lemme go! Please."

Jack motioned Brian over. "Tell this kid who I am and then hold him while I get my ID."

Brian eyed the boy, then said, "This is Dr. Jack Lockwood of the Boundary Waters Search and Rescue Unit. We're out here looking for whoever shot down a search and rescue helicopter last weekend. You wouldn't know anything about that, would you?"

Tears running down his cheeks, the boy pleaded with them, "I don't got time for this. I didn't shoot no one. I wouldn't. Please," he looked at Jack, "if you're really a doctor, please help me, please help my wife and baby."

Turning to Brian, Jack said in a low tone, "Let the kid go. I want to go with him." Then turning back to the boy, Jack showed him his hospital ID. "Take me to her, okay?"

The boy nodded, and Brian let go of him. The boy started to run back in the direction he'd come, and the two men followed him. Jack ran up alongside the kid and said, "It would help me to know your name and your wife's name, so I don't have to keep saying 'Hey, you.' You know my name's Jack. What's yours?"

"Pete," the young man gasped as he ran. "We're almost there."

"She's out in the woods and pregnant?" Jack asked, still confused.

"She's havin' our baby, but something's wrong. The contractions started last night, and Mary, that's my wife, she's bleeding a lot. My uncle kicked us out of his cabin 'cuz she was too loud and he's got a bullet wound in his leg. I thought maybe Mary and I could walk out, but she…she couldn't walk that far. I went ahead to find a doc."

Jack was silent for a moment, concentrating on keeping up with Pete. He was suddenly very worried about both mother and baby and what he'd be facing at the end of wherever Pete was going. Jack was also concerned because he was pretty convinced that the uncle with the leg wound was the same heavily armed man he'd put a bullet in the weekend before. Until they stopped running, he could only hope Brian was thinking the same thing. "Pete," Jack pulled the kid to a stop again, "how much further?"

"Not much. I left her under those aspens." Pete waved at a copse of trees just ahead.

Jack nodded and turned to Brian. "I don't want to scare the girl if she's still conscious, but I think we need to gather the troops because I have a bad feeling that this uncle isn't too far away. The cabin where Reynoso held Liz isn't very far from here, and at a guess, the uncle's been using it as a place to live. Back off just a little and let me follow the boy. Get in touch with Dan and he can guide you to the cabin."

"I'm not leaving you alone, Jack," Brian insisted.

"Fine, I'm not going far. Just get the team here."

Turning back to Pete, Jack motioned ahead. "Take me to Mary. The sheriff's going to stay back so we don't scare her."

By the time they got to the girl, she was unconscious. Jack dropped to his knees beside her, felt for a pulse, and nodded reassuringly to the boy. "She's alive."

"What...what about our baby, sir? And why is Mary so still? Why won't she wake up?"

"I'm not a sir, Pete, I'm Jack, and I'm going to try to help them now, okay?" Jack put his hands on Mary's abdomen, trying to determine the position of the baby. "I need you to go hold Mary's hand, tell her you found a doctor, and that everything's going to be okay."

Pete scrambled, sat down by Mary's shoulder, and took her hand. "Dr. Jack, she's not awake, so it won't matter if I talk to her since she can't hear me."

"She can hear you even if she can't talk back," Jack assured the boy. "I need you to talk to her, so I can help her and your baby. Can you do that?"

Pete nodded. "Okay. Please." His hazel eyes brimmed with tears. "Please, they're all I got. Don't let them die."

# CHAPTER 5

## WHOSE FAULT IS IT ANYWAY?

Liz looked up as Jack came through the double doors of the Grand Marais Hospital surgical suite. He carried a small blanket-wrapped bundle. Watching as he sat down beside Pete, she knew that something was wrong. Taking one of Pete's hands, she squeezed it gently and looked at Jack. "Hey. We've been praying for you and for Pete's loved ones."

Jack smiled. "I know. I could feel it." Turning his attention to the teenaged boy sitting in front of him, Jack said, "Congratulations, Pete, you're the father of a baby boy." He held out the bundle that he carried so Pete could see the tiny form.

Pete reached for the baby. "Wow. Can I hold him?"

Jack gently laid the newborn in Pete's arms. "Of course you can hold him. He's your son." Moving Pete's arm so it supported the infant's head better, Jack said, "Your baby is healthy and came in at a whopping ten pounds, eight ounces."

"He's perfect, isn't he?" Pete said. "Can I see Mary now? Has she seen our boy?"

Jack's smile disappeared, and he put an arm around Pete's shoulder. "I'm sorry, Pete, but Mary didn't make it. She lost too much blood."

"What...what do you mean didn't make it?" Pete's eyes filled with tears. "Mary didn't die. She couldn't." His eyes moved from Jack to Liz and back to Jack. "She was talking to me in the helicopter, so how could she be…be dead?"

Liz took the baby from Pete's arms as Jack tried to explain, "I'm so sorry. She'd lost too much blood by the time I got to her. The baby was too big for her to deliver normally. I delivered your son by cesarean section after Mary passed. Do you know what that means?"

Peter sniffed and looked at Jack. "It means you had to cut him out of her, right? Is that why she died?"

Jack took a deep breath. "Pete, I know this is so hard, but Mary had already died when I did the surgery to deliver your boy. I had to do it. Otherwise, the baby would have died too. I'm so sorry, son."

"I'm not your son!" Tears rolling down his cheeks, Pete lashed out. "I'm not nobody's son, and that baby that killed my Mary isn't really mine! I don't want it."

Abruptly, Jack realized what Pete had said. "Pete, you told me this was your baby, that you and Mary wanted this child. What do you mean he's not yours?"

"My baby wouldn't have killed Mary! But I had to help her, and we could still be a family if she's not really dead. Please, Dr. Jack, don't let her be dead. Otherwise, this is all messed up."

An hour later, Jack, Pete, Dan, Ann Nolan—a representative from social services, and Liz sat in a conference room in the Grand Marais Hospital. The baby was in the nursery. There wasn't a dry eye in the room as Peter haltingly told his story to those gathered. Close to a year ago, Pete and Mary went to Simon's apartment in Grand Marais as runaways seeking shelter from Mary's abusive father, her custodial parent. The first time they'd stayed with Simon for close to a month before Mary tried to go home. Her father had convinced her that he wouldn't touch her again. That promise lasted almost two weeks. Then he'd beaten her so badly that he'd put her in the hospital. The sheriff had arrested her father and then started the process of working with social services to assure a place for Mary. But before the hospital could release her, Pete sneaked her out of her room and they'd gone back to his uncle's place.

What Pete didn't know until about three months later was that Mary's father had also raped her. The baby they found out she was carrying was her father's child. Pete didn't want Mary or the baby to live with that kind of legacy, so they'd told his uncle that the baby was Pete's. Late in the fall, an adult friend, Doug, who had a boat, took Pete and Mary out with him on a sunny Sunday afternoon and, at Pete's urging, had performed a wedding ceremony for the two under-age teens. Doug didn't tell them that the marriage wasn't legal. He just pronounced them husband and wife.

The two of them lived with Simon for several more months before Simon's landlord evicted him for nonpayment of rent with winter coming on. It was then that Simon heard a rumor about an abandoned cabin inside the BWCA that criminals had once used. He'd found it, and the three of them moved in just before it got really cold.

For a while, all was peaceful. Simon had a job in town that paid enough to keep them in groceries. But as the weather got colder, the snow deepened, and his drinking problem worsened, the older man had begun to hate the long trek into Grand Marais. More and more often, he'd just stayed in bed, until one morning, when he'd actually made it into work, a pink slip and a final check were the only things that awaited him. From then on, they lived on what the state assistance programs gave him.

Mary went through her pregnancy with little prenatal care and worked hard to keep up the cabin, what there was of it, did other chores, and cooked for herself and the two men. Peter also worked around the cabin, clearing snow and chopping wood. Then on most days, after he finished his chores, he snowshoed into town to do day labor for employers that were willing to hire a minor and pay him under the table. The work was backbreaking and underpaid, but Pete used his wages to bring home groceries that Simon didn't care about, like fresh fruits and vegetables. When he wasn't working, Pete used the computers at the public library to learn about childbirth.

By this time, Simon had convinced himself that the cabin was his—or at least should be his. However, on the Friday before Memorial Day weekend, while Peter worked on getting a garden set up in a sunny area that he'd cleared, Simon heard a helicopter overhead. He didn't want anyone to kick him out of the cabin, so he'd grabbed his semiautomatic rifle and headed out. By the time he returned home the following morning, he'd confirmed he'd brought the chopper down, but also that at least some of the crew had survived, as evidenced by the bullet wound in his leg.

Pete had dug the bullet out of Simon's thigh, being as careful as he could, but had received no thanks. After yelling at his nephew and Mary, Simon had gone to sleep. He woke when the BWSR team walked into the bedroom and was now in custody. He was unaware that his nephew and Mary had gone, that Mary had died, or that her baby was alive.

Jack motioned Ann and Dan out of the small room, leaving Liz to try to bring comfort to the young man who was, once again, alone in life. When Ann checked on Pete's social service status, she'd found out that the couple who'd fostered him and who'd wanted to adopt him had backed out of that agreement once their doctor had confirmed the wife's diagnosis of MS. They'd felt it was unfair to Pete. They'd continued to foster him until Ann could find a suitable home for the boy, but he'd run away before that had happened.

Jack looked at Ann sadly. "This kid, who has tried to do the right thing all along, doesn't deserve to be left alone now. Despite what he said to me earlier, it's clear to me that Pete still thinks of the baby as his. I'm not saying that he's got a right to custody of the infant, but what I am saying is that if you take that child completely away from him right now, it will be another loss piled on this fifteen-year-old boy's shoulders. How much of that do you think he can take? Just because he's underage doesn't mean that his love for Mary was any less real, and that child is his only remaining link to her."

Ann nodded. "I know, Jack, but since the baby isn't Pete's, all we're set up to do is to find families to take them in as individuals."

Dan nodded and said, "I agree with Ann. It's all we can do. Pete's done nothing to warrant arrest, but as of now, with his uncle incarcerated, both the kid and the baby are wards of the state and it's up to social services."

Jack frowned at Dan. "Well, that's convenient. Let's all abdicate responsibility for the two of them and let them suffer."

"No one is abdicating responsibility for those two boys, Jack, and no one wants them to suffer," Ann said defensively. "We'll find them a place. It may not be perfect, but at least they'll have someone looking after them. Then we can get Pete back on track for high school. He's a bright kid. He was never really married to that girl, and he's not that child's blood relative, so he has no legal claim over that baby. What do you expect us to do?"

Jack thought back to the whispered conversation he'd had with Liz just before stepping out into the hallway. He eyed the two people standing in front of him and said, "I don't expect *you* to do anything, and I'm sorry if I was out of line, especially since I'm the one who wasn't able to save that young girl's life and delivered a child that no one seems to want apart from a teenaged boy. This has been a bad month for that sort of thing.

"Ann," Jack fixed his eyes on the social worker, "Liz and I talked before I came out here, and we would like to foster both of them, maybe even adopt them together. We're gainfully employed, we have a home in Ely large enough for all of us, and unlike some stranger, we already have a connection with Pete. We can provide references and are willing for you to come any time to do a home study. Right now, we'd like to take Pete with us when we leave. He can stay with us in our hotel room here in Grand Marais tonight, and tomorrow, we can bring both him and the baby home with us to Ely. Can you help me make that happen? Dan here or Brian Stokes, the Cook County sheriff, can vouch for us until a full-scale investigation can be done."

Ann looked doubtful. "Jack, I know enough about you and Liz to know you're qualified to do this, and getting you certified to foster should be no problem, but have you thought about the commitment you're making? I know how busy you both are, and as much as you might feel a connection to the boys after today, none of this is your fault."

Smiling sadly, Jack said, "Why does this kind of thing always come down to fault? That boy in there and the baby lying in the nursery need someone to think of them, to advocate for them, and in this case, that happens to be Liz and me. We care, and we want to do something to make two young lives better. No, I'm not experienced as a father, but I am a physician, and I do have nieces and nephews, as does Liz. Those things ought to count for something."

Ann patted his arm soothingly. "Jack, I'm not telling you that you shouldn't do this. I was just asking if you're sure about doing this. As for tonight, I can't make that happen. Pete's signed into my custody until tomorrow, but if this is what you and Liz both want, then I'll do the paperwork, run a quick criminal and background check, and I should be able to release them both to you and Liz late tomorrow afternoon. We'll be calling to schedule a home visit as soon as possible." She focused on Dan. "Chief, do you have any comments or objections?"

Dan shook his head. "No, those kids couldn't be in better hands until we can get this all sorted out. Brian and I have one more charge to add to the girl's father's rap sheet. Simon Patterson, the uncle, is being arraigned in the morning on charges stemming from the helicopter incident, his harboring of two underage kids, and anything else we can think of. He may not be directly responsible for Mary's death, but he was certainly culpable in it. Anyway, I've no objection to releasing the kids into the Lockwood's custody. If you need any other information, just let me know."

Later that night, Jack and Liz collapsed onto the bed in their hotel room and for a few minutes did nothing but breathe. They were both exhausted. Their morning had started forever ago when the search team had headed into the woods. By noon, Jack had delivered a baby while grieving over yet another young mother. By 3:00 p.m., they'd found out they were about to become surrogate parents for a fifteen-year-old and an as-yet-unnamed newborn. In the five hours since, they'd been buying supplies and working with a convalescing Beth and her sister up in Ely to get someone to move furniture in their home and to accept the delivery of new furniture that would be at their place by noon the next day.

Finally, Jack opened his eyes and elbowed Liz. "Hey, you awake?"

"Sorta," Liz opened her eyes and looked at Jack, "maybe I am too old for this parenting thing. Even if it's only temporary."

"I'm hoping it won't be a temporary thing," Jack confessed as he sat up, "but for right now, I'd settle for dinner. Why don't I order a pizza from Sven and Ole's[1] and go get it? It's not the healthiest meal in the world, but I don't feel like going out to dinner. Besides," he looked at his watch, "our choices are kind of limited at eight in the evening."

Liz looked at Jack gratefully. "That would be great. Would you please get me a large iced tea too?" Seeing a look of censure start to form on his face, she waved him off. "Don't get your knickers in a knot, Jack. I'm gonna need the caffeine just to stay awake while I chew. So as you once told Dan, just shut it and behave." She grinned and patted his knee. "I love you."

"I love you too, and I'm shutting it, but if you're up all night…"

Liz kissed him, a sultry look in her tired eyes. "I promise to make it worth your while."

Later, as they were eating their pizza, Jack smiled and took Liz's hand. "You know, I still lose my breath when you look at me like you are right now with love in your beautiful eyes."

"Wow!" Liz's eyes glistened. "What brought that on?"

"I don't know," Jack admitted. "I was watching you—sitting cross-legged on a bed in a two-star hotel room, a slice of pizza in your hand, and looking like you're having the time of your life. I know you're dead tired and that you may have some reservations about what we're doing, but you're still here, still supporting me, and still trying to make everything just right for those kids we're bringing

---

[1]    Sven and Ole's restaurant is located in Grand Marais, Minnesota, but their reputation for great pizza is famous throughout Minnesota (https://www. svenandoles.com/).

home tomorrow. I guess I'm amazed by how good God has been to me."

Liz ran her fingers down Jack's cheek. "Honey, you make it sound as though being with you is some kind of penance or something. I love you, and I'm having the time of my life just because we're together. While we didn't have a lot of time to talk about whether or not to foster these particular kids, we've talked a lot about parenting in general for several weeks now. I want that as much as you do. My only concerns about this particular situation are the issues I know poor Pete will be facing in the days ahead. In addition, I may also have a concern or two about fostering and more particularly about adopting a newborn at my age. Still, that's pretty silly because when we came home from our weekend away in the middle of May, I spent an entire afternoon online, trying to figure out if there was a way for me to get pregnant at my age."

"You never told me that," Jack said in a surprised tone. "Why didn't you just talk to me?"

"Because I knew that if there was any danger, like maybe the large doses of estrogen I'd need to carry a child if I'm in menopause, that you probably wouldn't be totally forthcoming with me. I get that, but I wanted to do the research and see for myself."

"And what did you learn?" Jack asked curiously.

"I learned that it might be possible for me to carry a child, but if I'm in menopause, something that it's late onset and my irregular cycles make difficult to determine, my eggs have all basically turned to dust. That means using in vitro conception between your sperm and donor eggs. I also learned that to carry a child after menopause requires aforementioned doses of estrogen, and given the cow that Dorrene had when I asked her about hormone replacement therapy, I figured that pumping that much estrogen into my system was like playing Russian roulette with my life. As much as I'd love to be a mom to our child," Liz squeezed Jack's hand, "I want to live out my life with you more. I don't want to leave you alone again, to hold a memory in your arms instead of a living, breathing woman."

Jack grinned. "Didn't I say that to you in the shower the other night?"

"Yep, you did, and I listened well. Anyway, getting pregnant is even more out there for a woman my age than fostering or even adopting a newborn. Since we're doing this, you'll just have to keep harping on me to eat all that healthy stuff and to exercise."

Aware of the irony, Jack swallowed a mouthful of pizza before replying, "Count on it, and you'll just have to keep harping on me to stay healthy too."

After they finished dinner and were in bed, Jack put his arms around his wife. "Are you really okay with this? I need an honest answer, Liz, not one colored by your sense of humor or what you think I want to hear."

"Jack, honey, you know me well enough to know that if I truly objected to bringing those kids home with us, I would tell you. We prayed about it this afternoon."

"Yeah, but that was after the fact," Jack interjected.

"God isn't bound by a time line. You know that. You also know that if we called Ann in the morning and told her we couldn't do this that she would say 'thank you for telling me' and find those kids other homes. I think we're meant to be doing exactly what we're doing, and I look forward to sharing this adventure with you. I pray that we will make a difference in dear Pete's life because he is the one who's so grievously impacted by all this. I've never met a fifteen-year-old who's as polite as that kid is, even when his world is falling apart. I wonder what happened to his birth parents."

"Ann said that his father was a minister and his mom was a teacher. Pete was a twelve-year-old only child when the three of them were in a head-on collision that killed everyone in the two cars except for him. After he got out of the hospital, social services placed Pete into his one and only foster home, and he was there until he ran away to help his girlfriend, Mary, get away from her abusive father. You know the rest. Apparently, some of the lessons Pete learned from his birth parents stuck, despite the influence of his uncle and Mary's situation." Jack looked at Liz, embarrassed. "I'm sorry, Ann told me Pete's history earlier, after we went out into the hall this afternoon, and I forgot to tell you."

Liz cuddled closer to him. "Jack, it's been a really long day for you. You certainly don't need to apologize because you forgot to tell me something that Ann mentioned sometime in the middle of everything that's happened. I'm the one who should be apologizing because it sounds like I've communicated to you that I have reservations about all this. I need you to know that's simply not the case. I think God may be answering our prayers in a way that neither of us could have foreseen. It's going to change our lives, but I'm okay with that, if you are, and I know you are."

Jack held Liz close. "I know it's going to change things, but it's going to add a new dimension to our relationship, one that I never thought we'd be blessed to share." He smoothed her hair away from her face. "You're going to be a fabulous mom. I know that, and I hope I can be a great dad too."

"You'll be a great dad, Jack. You have a huge heart and a great capacity for love. Those kids will be blessed having you for a surrogate dad—or dad—whatever the future holds."

"Does that mean you'd be willing to consider adopting these two and not just fostering them?"

"I wouldn't have gone along with any of this if I didn't think that was a good possibility. I want those two children to feel like they have something permanent with us. Frankly, my heart's already involved, and if we have to let them go, it will be so hard. I guess I'm already thinking of them as ours. I know that's stupid, but I can't help it, especially after the time I spent with Pete today while you guys were out in the hallway." Liz yawned. "I hate to say this, but I'm beat and we have an early call. I love you."

"I love you too, Liz." Jack pulled the covers up around them. "Sleep well."

# CHAPTER 6

## WE ARE A FAMILY

*Sleep, my child, and peace attend thee,*
*All through the night.*
*Guardian angels God will send thee,*
*All through the night.*
*Soft the drowsy hours are creeping,*
*Hill and dale in slumber sleeping,*
*I my loved ones' watch am keeping*
*All through the night.*
*While the moon her watch is keeping*
*All through the night.*
*While the weary world is sleeping*
*All through the night.*
*O'er thy spirit gently stealing*
*Visions of delight revealing,*
*Breathes a pure and holy feeling*
*All through the night.*[ii]

Liz blinked her eyes, awakening from a half doze when she finished singing the only lullaby she knew. She'd fed, changed, and rocked the newborn, and he was finally asleep. She'd never experienced motherhood, so when the baby kept crying after having his needs attended to, she'd done the only thing she could think of, the thing that calmed her when she was upset, she sang. Getting up from the rocker in the library area of their room, she put the infant down in the crib, smiling when he stayed asleep. She was almost ready to join her sleeping husband when she heard a noise outside their bedroom door.

She opened the door to find Pete curled up on the floor. "Pete, honey, what are you doing down there? Are you okay?"

To her surprise, the gangly teen got to his feet and hugged her. "I…I woke up, it was dark, and no one was there. At first, I didn't know where I was, but then I remembered everything. Mary's dead, isn't she?"

Liz rubbed Pete's neck gently. "Yes, Pete, she's with Jesus now. I'm so sorry for your loss."

Pete sniffed. "You don't think it's just a stupid kid thing?"

"No, I don't. Pain is never stupid, and love isn't something that only adults feel. I know you loved Mary, and I'm so sorry."

Resting his head on her shoulder, Pete stood still. Liz simply held him, rubbing his back until his tears stopped.

After a while, Pete pulled back and said, "Please don't send me away. I won't bother you and Dr. Jack again."

Liz stopped him before he could walk away. "Pete, I know this has happened really fast, but you need to know that Jack and I want you with us. We care, and we want to know how you feel, what's making you happy, what's making you sad, what's scaring you, and how we can help. May I ask you something?"

Pete nodded. "Yeah."

"Do you really want to go back to your room right now?"

"I, uh, I really like my room. It's nice."

"That's not what I asked, Pete. I asked if you want to go back there right now."

Hanging his head, Pete whispered, "No. I don't wanna be alone, but I know that's babyish."

"No, Pete, it's not babyish. When I'm feeling sad or afraid, I don't like to be alone either. I want to be with Jack." Liz took his hand, leading him into their room. "Come on. The baby's asleep in his crib, and I'll make up the love seat into a bed."

"You mean you'll let me sleep in here with you and Dr. Jack?" Pete looked at her, surprise and something that looked like hope in his eyes. "Really? I'm not a baby anymore."

Liz smiled. "I know you're not, Pete, but it's not just babies who don't want to be alone. I sleep with Jack because I want to feel him close. For tonight, anyway, I'd worry about you a lot less if you were in here with us, just in case you need something."

Pete nodded. "I'd like that too, but you don't need to make me a bed. I can just lay down on that couch by the crib."

Pulling sheets, a blanket, and a pillow from the closet, Liz quickly made up a comfortable resting place on the love seat. "There you go. I'm sorry, it might be a bit short in length for you."

When Pete lay down, he fit, barely. Bending over, Liz kissed Pete's forehead. "If you need something, please ask Jack or me, okay?"

Pete looked worried. "I don't want to wake you up."

Laughing quietly, Liz patted his shoulder. "I'm up with the baby every couple of hours anyway, so I'll probably be the one waking *you* up. I hope you can sleep. Good night."

Liz watched Pete close his eyes then crawled in beside Jack. He turned over, pulled her close, and whispered, "Thank you. I love you."

<hr>

"Is Liz okay, Dr. Jack?" Pete asked when he came to the breakfast table. "I saw her sleeping on the couch in the living room. Why didn't she just come back to bed?"

Jack smiled up at Pete and patted the chair next to him. "Sit down, Pete. Liz is okay. She has an illness called fibromyalgia, and some days, she hurts a lot, especially if she didn't get good rest the night before. She's on the couch because she didn't want to wake you."

Pete hung his head. "I woke Liz up in the middle of the night, so it's my fault."

Patting Pete's shoulder, Jack shook his head. "It's no one's fault, Pete. Liz got up to feed the baby every few hours, and that's what kept her from sleeping well. That's probably on me because I forgot to tell her I'd taken some vacation from the hospital and wasn't going into work this morning. When she got up earlier, I encouraged her to get some more rest." Jack smiled and pointed to the sound asleep infant, resting in the swing next to them. "While Liz sleeps, you and I are on baby duty. Is that okay with you?"

Pete nodded. "I'd like that. Is he a good baby, Dr. Jack?"

"You know, Pete, I don't have a lot of experience with babies because I never had one of my own. He seems to be sleeping and eating really well, so I'd say yes, he's a good baby."

Looking genuinely pleased, Pete smiled. "I'm glad. Thank you and Liz for helping me take care of him. I don't know much about babies either."

"Thank you, Pete, for trying to do the right thing and for giving that baby such a good name." Jack thought back to lunch the day before. The four of them had been in a restaurant awaiting their food when Liz had brought up the subject of naming the little boy, resting in the infant carrier at her side. They'd asked Pete if he and Mary had talked about a name for the baby, and they'd named him Lucas John Lockwood, honoring his mother's final wish.

"It's okay to call him Luke, right?" Pete asked. "I know it's not his formal name, but I'd like it to be his everyday name."

"I think it's a good thing for Luke to have an everyday name. Almost everybody does. Your full name is Peter, but you like people to call you Pete. My full name is Jackson, but people call me Jack. Liz's full name is Elizabeth, and people call her Liz. So Luke is a fine everyday name," Jack said. "In fact, the apostle Luke in the Bible was a doctor and was one of Jesus's best friends. Is it okay that we gave Luke our last name, at least for now?"

Pete nodded slowly. "I guess. I mean I don't want him named after Mary's dad even though he's the real dad. That would only make people think bad things about the baby and Mary. And he's not really mine even though I was gonna use my last name for his last name, and I guess you're the ones who are taking care of both of us, so yeah, it's okay." Pete looked up, a shy smile on his face. "I really like you and Liz."

Jack squeezed Pete's shoulder again. "And we really like you. Thank you for coming home with us. Are you hungry?"

⁓

With eggs, bacon, and toast in front of them, Jack and Pete were eating when Pete put down his fork, looking uncomfortable.

Jack noticed the teen had stopped eating long before his plate was empty. "What's the matter, Pete? Don't you like eggs?"

"Nothing's the matter, Dr. Jack. I like eggs a lot. Thanks for making them."

"Well then, is something else wrong? Otherwise, go ahead and finish your breakfast."

Pete looked worried. "I don't have a job right now, and I can't afford to pay you for this food and all the nice stuff in my room and for the baby's stuff. I'd rather you use part of my share for Luke, if that's okay. Once I can get some work or do some chores around here, maybe then I can eat more."

Jack caught a glimpse of Pete's former life, and it made him terribly sad. He got up and crouched beside the teen's chair. "Hey, Liz and I asked you to come live with us, remember?"

Pete nodded. "Yeah, but..."

"Pete, we want you here. We want to provide for you so that you can have a life like most teenagers. You've taken on so much responsibility that God intended for adults, not for their children. Liz and I are hoping that you'll let us carry some of that responsibility for a while."

"But we're not your children. We're just someone else's kids," Pete said miserably. "You don't have to do all this."

"Pete, you and Luke are here because we chose you. Doesn't that count for something?"

Pete's eyes went wide. "You mean, you didn't take us because you had to?"

Jack shook his head. "No, we asked you to come and be a part of our family because we wanted you both here with us."

Liz walked into the dining room, knelt by Pete's other side, and took his hand. "Pete, you don't know us very well, so take your time, but please let us help. We want you and Luke here with us, and we're beginning to love you both."

Pete looked from one of them to the other, pushed back from the table as tears started to roll down his cheeks, and ran into his room, slamming the door behind him. Liz got up to follow him, but Jack held her back. "Love, let's give him some time to absorb all this. We'll go check on him in a little bit, okay?"

Just then, the baby woke and started to cry. Jack put his arms around Liz, kissed her, and said, "I've got this. Will you rest for a while longer? Please."

⌒⌣⌒

Later that afternoon, Liz raised her hands in the air and clapped, "Way to go, Pete! I never thought I'd see anyone beat the reigning world champion!"

Pete, who'd come out of his room, dry-eyed, just before lunch, smiled and held up the tweezers. "Sorry, Dr. Jack. It looks like the funny bone isn't so funny for you."

Jack did his best to look sorrowful. Resting his head on his cupped hand, he said, "Well, it's been a long time since I've been handed a defeat like this." He surveyed the game board in front of him and winced at the recollection of the loud buzz he'd just caused trying to remove his patient's broken heart. Extending his hand to Pete, he shook the teen's hand. "Congratulations, Dr. Pete."

Pete's face lit up. "Thanks, Dr. Jack. This was fun."

Liz, who'd been an observer only, grinned. "Anybody want to celebrate Pete's victory with some strawberry shortcake? I made it this morning after I woke up from my long nap."

Jack nodded. "Yum, I'm in!" He kissed Liz on the end of her nose. "Thank you for making it."

Pete looked at them strangely but raised his hand. "I'll have some too, please, if there's enough for all of us."

Liz laughed. "Pete, when I bake, I do it right. There's always enough for everybody, even if you want seconds."

Pete's eyes went wide at Liz's words and then abruptly filled with tears. He pushed back from the table so rapidly that his chair fell over as he ran into his room and slammed the door so hard it rattled the windows. Liz looked at Jack, baffled. "That's twice in one day. What did I say this time?"

Jack shook his head. "I'm not sure. Maybe he doesn't like strawberry shortcake?" He put his arms around Liz. "No one ever said this was going to be easy. I just wish I knew what to do to help. Fixing broken bones is simple compared to this."

Luke let out a thin cry and squirmed uncomfortably. Liz got to her feet and picked up the now-squalling infant. She wrinkled her nose and said, "Well, this is one problem even I can diagnose. Excuse me while I go change this little guy."

Leaving Jack, she disappeared into their room, where they'd set up the baby's changing table next to the crib. Jack sat for a moment then went over and knocked on Pete's bedroom door. "Hey, Pete, can I come in?"

"It's your house, Dr. Jack," Pete's muffled voice was scarcely audible. "Do what you want."

Jack opened the door. Pete was lying on his stomach on the bed, his face buried in the pillow. Sitting down beside the teen, Jack put his hand on his shoulder. Pete flinched away from the contact, so Jack pulled back and said, "You know, Liz is sad because she doesn't understand what we did to make you run away from us. Can you help me understand so I can tell her? What did we do wrong?"

Pete threw the pillow across the room and sat up. "You didn't do nothing wrong."

"Okay, if we didn't do anything wrong, then why are you in here rather than enjoying strawberry shortcake with us?"

"Why are you guys being so nice to me? I'm just a kid with no parents. I can't tell you nothing more about Simon or Mary's dad. You know Luke's not mine, so why?" His hazel eyes filled with tears. "Why don't you just let that foster lady take care of us, or if you want Luke, she can just take me."

Jack looked at Pete sadly. "Pete, there's nothing we can say to you other than what we've already said. If you don't believe Liz or me, then there's little more we can do to convince you. We want you to be a part of our family, but if you want to go back to Ann, I'll take you to her in the morning. It's up to you." Jack got to his feet and squeezed Pete's shoulder. "Thank you for trusting us enough to at least give it a try. I'm sorry if we aren't the right home for you."

Jack held Liz and sighed morosely, "I was sure he'd open up after I talked to him, but he hasn't come out of his room since this afternoon. He didn't eat dinner, and all he said when I asked him to come out to eat was to 'leave him alone.' What did we do, or what didn't we do, or what more could we have done?"

They'd gone to bed several hours before, and Liz had just gotten back from changing and feeding the baby and found that Jack was awake. Cuddling closer to him, she said, "Jack, you know that Pete is hurting. We've done everything we know to do, but we can't force him to believe us or to stay with us. I'm so sorry. What did Ann say?"

"She said to bring him over in the morning. She's arranged a placement for him with a family in Tofte. He'll have two brothers and a sister."

"What about Luke?"

"The family can't or won't take him. Ann would like us to continue fostering Luke, at least for a time, if we're willing."

"How do you feel about that, Jack?"

"If you're okay with it, I'd like to do it. He's a connection to Pete and Mary, but he's also a little boy who needs a family." Jack looked at Liz intently. "Can we do this?"

Liz smiled and kissed Jack, her lips moving over his, until both of them had to come up for air. She stroked his face gently. "We *can* do this, Jack. I want to raise Luke with you."

Jack caught his breath when Liz kissed him again, this time with both tenderness and passion in her caress. Pulling her closer, he lost himself in her touch, his hands skimming her body. "I love you."

Their loving was a sweet, familiar place, but the door to their room suddenly opened, interrupting them. Pete stood there, his eyes wide. Liz was grateful the blanket covered her and Jack as she whispered, "Pete? Is something wrong?"

"I want to talk to you and Dr. Jack about staying here."

Jack sat up carefully, making sure the blanket stayed where it was. "Pete, we're really glad about that. Still, around here, we knock before walking into someone's bedroom."

Hanging his head, Pete apologized, "I'm sorry, Dr. Jack. I didn't mean to do something wrong. I just wanted to be with you and Liz."

Jack nodded. "We want to be with you too. Will you go into the living room please so we don't wake the baby? Liz and I will be right out."

As soon as Pete left the room, Jack chuckled and rested his forehead against Liz's. "Sorry, love. Talk about bad timing."

Liz smiled. "Five minutes later would have been worse, right? Come on, let's put our robes on and see what the young man has to say."

# CHAPTER 7

## WHAT ARE THE ODDS?

"Jack, have you seen my wrap?" Liz asked as she fastened the sapphire necklace he'd given her the Christmas before around her neck then slipped into her silver pumps. "It's not in my closet."

"I already put it out by the door." Jack came into the room, wearing his tuxedo. He took Liz's hand and whistled appreciatively. The sapphire-blue silk dress she wore was one of her creations with tone-on-tone embroidery stitched in dark blue thread. She'd embroidered a stylized wave pattern on the front of the bodice that ran seamlessly down the long sleeves and circled the deep cuffs. Silver beads in different shapes and sizes defined the waist and connected starburst patterns on the back of the bodice with those flowing down the back of the skirt, where Liz had layered silk dupioni and silk chiffon for texture and fullness. The effect was almost ethereal, like she was walking on water. The beads sparkled when she moved, and the color was perfect for her, complementing both her eyes and her salt-and-pepper hair, which she now wore in a smooth chin-length cut. Kissing her, he whispered against her lips, "You look fabulous."

"You do too," Liz whispered back, holding Jack close. "I'm so proud of you."

Tonight, the hospital was hosting a benefit dinner and ball to raise funds for a new emergency room and trauma wing. Jack was one of the key architects of the building drive, knowing that this area of Northern Minnesota badly needed a regional trauma center. Duluth and Thunder Bay, Ontario, were often too far for patients with injuries that needed immediate care. EBCH often acted as a trauma center, and it was time to make that function a formal one. They needed more room, more and newer equipment, and they needed to hire additional staff, including another trauma specialist. Right now, Zach Birch, Andrea Barstow, and Jack were the board-certified emergency medicine and surgical critical care specialists on staff, but with Zach and Jack both splitting time between the BWSRU and the hospital, Andi was often overloaded and that needed to end. Tonight was the kickoff of the funding drive, and Jack was the keynote speaker, his speech and dessert coming right before the band started off the evening's entertainment. He hoped the donations would flow as freely as the wine, conversation, and song.

Jack reluctantly let go of Liz and, taking her hand, led her into the great room. Ann stood in front of the woodstove, enjoying its warmth on this early September evening. She was holding Luke, and Pete sat on the couch petting Sierra. As soon as he saw Jack and Liz, he got up and draped an arm across Liz's shoulders. "You look really pretty."

Liz smiled and hugged him close. Since talking with them that night back in June, Pete had been a different young man. He was a teenager, and things weren't always easy, but he was a light in her and Jack's world. The four of them had become a family. Luke was growing, and at three months, he was a happy, healthy baby. Pete had taken over some of Luke's feedings and loved rocking the baby to sleep. Pete was also working on catching up with school assignments, and in a week, Liz and Jack planned to start homeschooling him. He would be starting his junior year in high school. They'd offered him the option of attending the Christ Academy private high school in Ely, but when they'd talked about it, he'd grown anxious. He'd seen more of the dark side of life than your average teen and was most comfortable at home. Rather than rock the boat this first semester, the decision to home school had been an easy one. He was involved in the youth group at church, so at least he got to spend time with kids of his own age.

Squeezing him tightly, Liz kissed Pete on the top of the head. "Thanks, Pete. I love you. Please help Ann with Luke."

Pete nodded, let go of her, and hugged Jack. "I will. Love you guys too. I hope your speech goes good, Dr. Jack."

Jack leaned down and kissed Pete on the top of the head just as his wife had done. "Love you, Pete. I hope my speech goes good too."

Straightening, Jack looked at Ann and said, "Thank you for doing this. Dan and Beth have always been able to watch over things when we needed to be gone, but tonight, they're going to this shindig with us. We're really grateful you were willing to drive over. I'm glad you're staying the night since driving back to Grand Marais in the wee hours is not a great idea what with the deer, a dark, twisty road, a drunk or two, and no place close to get help if you have car trouble."

Ann smiled. "Thanks for inviting me to stay. It will be good to spend time with the boys again. Have fun tonight, and best of luck with the fundraiser. In fact," Ann reached into the pocket of her jeans and pulled out a check, "here's my contribution for your trauma center. Thank you for doing this."

Jack pocketed the check and said, "Thank *you*. We'll be home about midnight. If you need anything, call or text. Our cell numbers are on the counter."

<hr />

"Hey, brother, your wife and I are going for a spin around the dance floor." At Dan's nod, Jack bowed to Beth and took her hand. Dan sat back in his chair, enjoying the picture his petite silvery-blond wife and Jack made as they danced. Theirs was a mismatch in height, but they still moved together well.

Dan had spent most of the evening sitting at their table or standing around talking to friends. He wasn't much of a dancer, so he was happy to see Beth smiling as Jack whirled her around the floor. When Liz sat down beside him, he grinned at her. "You guys having fun?"

Liz nodded. "We're having a great time. Actually, *I've* been having a great time all evening. Jack's having more fun since he got through his speech. He doesn't like asking people for money, even when it's for a good cause."

"I don't know why he was worried," Dan said. "His speech was great. He had me convinced three paragraphs in, and we've already given the powers that be a check. Of course, we all have very personal reasons to be grateful for the trauma experts that are already on staff here." Dan took Liz's hand and squeezed it gently. "Very grateful, for you, for Jack, and for my wife."

Liz knew where Dan's thoughts had strayed—at least insofar as she and Jack were concerned. Those dark days, now several years in the past, were mostly a blur for the two of them, but Dan and Beth had lived through it all, staying by their sides and doing their best to support them through the horror.

Not wanting to think about that tonight, she smiled at her friend. "We are blessed. How about you guys? Are you having fun?"

Dan shrugged, "Yeah. This isn't really my thing, and left to myself, I would probably have just donated on-line. But I wanted to be here to support my brother because as you said, he's not big on making money-related speeches. Besides, Beth wanted to come, and it's great to see everyone."

He studied Liz carefully. "How are things at home? Are you two getting used to being parents?"

Nodding enthusiastically, Liz said, "Thankfully, Luke's finally sleeping through the night, so Jack and I are getting past our zombified phase. That's just in time because we're also getting set up to home school Pete this fall. Dan," her eyes sparkled, "this isn't for public consumption yet, but we're filing the papers next week to officially adopt Pete and Luke."

Dan hugged Liz. "Congratulations, honey. I know you've wanted to do that for a couple of months now and you two will be terrific parents—you're already terrific parents. You're braver than Beth and me, adopting a teenager and an infant at our advanced age. Still, Beth and I have decided to join the party and adopt—a mixed-breed dog, that is—from the local rescue." He grinned. "Somehow, it seems like the thing to do."

Liz laughed as Beth and Jack returned to the table. "Congratulations to you two, too." Liz took Jack's hand as he helped her to her feet and led her back to the dance floor.

As soon as the waltz started, Liz relaxed into Jack's arms. He was a wonderful dancer and they'd had a lot of practice dancing together. He knew how to lead without making her feel like she was being driven in a bumper car rally. As the music continued, he drew her close to him, so close that she could rest her head on his shoulder. "Mmm, I love dancing with you. You make me feel like I'm moving on air." She turned her head and kissed his cheek. "Thank you for this beautiful evening and for a wonderful summer. I love you."

Jack stopped in the middle of the dance floor and kissed Liz tenderly. "I love you too."

Less than a week later, Liz was sitting at the dining room table, working on the last of the adoption papers. Luke was asleep in his swing next to her chair, Jack was on his way home from the hospital, and Pete was working on the homework she'd assigned him. It was peaceful and quiet until her phone rang. Five minutes later, she sat gripping the now silent instrument, stunned beyond belief. How could it take so little time to shatter her world?

Liz looked around their bedroom; it felt so empty every time she walked through the door. Wrapping her arms around herself, her tears came, trickling one by one down her cheeks. Unexpectedly, familiar arms slid around her waist, as Jack drew her back against his body. Turning her in his embrace until she faced him, he gently wiped her tears away with his fingertips. He kissed her forehead and whispered, "I'm so sorry, love. I know it's hard."

"It's nothing you did, Jack, you know that. It's just going to take me some time to adjust, that's all. I'm sorry for you too," Liz said sadly.

"Liz, it was my idea to foster those kids in the first place. I wish now I hadn't pushed for it." Jack's voice was low with pain as he rocked her against him.

Liz pushed Jack away. "Don't you ever say that, Jack Lockwood! That's like saying you wish we'd never met Ellie or Eric because all we can remember is the pain their deaths caused us. That's wrong on so many levels. Our late spouses helped to change us into the people we are—and we are the better for having them in our lives. Pete and Luke changed us for the better too, and I'm determined to find my way back to a place where what I remember is the good. I just, um, just can't...I can't, not yet..." She buried her head in her husband's shoulder and sobbed.

Pulling Liz close again, Jack blinked away his own tears. A week ago, they'd been so excited about adopting the two boys. Jack had been looking forward to planning outings into the BWCA for the four of them or guys' outings with his teenage son. Then, out of the blue, Ann had called Liz. The Albertsons, the couple who'd started the adoption process for Pete the year before, had found out that the wife's diagnosis of multiple sclerosis had been in error. After undergoing numerous tests and consults with specialists in the field they'd changed her diagnosis to, of all things, fibromyalgia. Imaging of the woman's brain now showed nothing but healthy tissue, and no one could explain how, in the absence of a miracle, reading a simple film had been so badly bungled.

After digesting that news, the couple had called Ann, and when they'd found out that Pete was still in the foster care system, they'd reinstated their adoption request. After finding out about the connection between Luke and Pete, they'd also filed adoption papers for the infant. When talking with Pete on the night of the hospital benefit, Ann discovered that the teen remembered his former foster family and still missed them. In a short court hearing, the judge gave the Albertsons immediate custody of both boys. There was no reason not to allow the adoptions to proceed. Ann had apologized to Jack and Liz. She'd explained that the new adoptive parents were of a better age to raise the two boys and they'd already cared for Pete for several years.

Two days before, Ann had come to pick up the kids, creating a dreadful scene as Pete was torn between his desire to see his former foster parents who were now his legal guardians, and his love for Jack and Liz. Even Luke, normally a happy baby, screamed for the hour or so it took to pack up the two kids, their belongings, and put them in the van. The last thing that Jack remembered seeing was Pete's sad face looking at him through the van window. Jack had all he could do to keep it together as he watched them leave and waved. Past images of Liz driving away down that same road, leaving him, battered at him as he'd held his crying wife close. Now, two days later, all he could do was the same thing, hoping that his warmth would soothe Liz's hurting spirit.

# CHAPTER 8

## A Very Mixed-Up Lord's Day

"Do we want a boy or a girl?" Jack looked over Liz's shoulder at the photographs she held. It was Compassion Sunday at their church, and they were looking at the children available to sponsor all over the world through Compassion International.[2]

"You choose, Jack. I chose Colombia for the country, so you pick the child we foster, okay?"

Jack reached down, selected the photo of a three-year-old girl from the six cards in Liz's hand, and held it up in front of her. "Meet our new foster daughter, Mrs. Lockwood."

After church, Jack and Liz drove home in one of the first heavy snowfalls of the season, a snow that had waited until the middle of November to come. It was beautiful and peaceful at home. Sierra, Binx, and Lazarus were all curled up on the end of the sofa nearest the woodstove. Jack took Liz's coat, hung it in the closet, and then came to stand beside her, idly scratching Binx when she jumped onto his shoulder. "What's your pleasure, love? A nap, a game, or we could call the Harrisons and see if they want to do something."

Liz smiled. "It's so pretty outside, Jack, and it's not terribly cold for the middle of November. Why don't we have some lunch, and

---

2   Compassion International's mission is to help children develop into who God intends them to be through a holistic approach to child development. They carefully blend physical, social, economic, and spiritual care together—in Jesus's name (www.compassion.com).

after that, we can go for a walk? When we get back, we'll take a nap, then do some research on the little girl we just agreed to sponsor. I bookmarked most of the information on the kids we were thinking about fostering, and now that we've decided, we can get to know Gabriela better. They have information on her family and where she lives. We can write to her online, send photos, and, of course, see more photos of her."

A half hour later, Liz and Jack walked hand-in-hand on one of their favorite trails behind the house. They owned twenty-five acres of land, and the house sat close to the front of their acreage. Most of their property was undeveloped boreal forest and included several streams, wetlands, and part of a small lake. The rear property line abutted the BWCA.

Once they reached the lake, they skirted it to the right, following the faint trail leading to the wetlands. It was a beautiful walk. Just before starting back toward the house, Liz sat on a sloped granite outcrop and pulled Jack down beside her. Taking off one of her gloves, she gently brushed snowflakes from his face and kissed him, her frosty lips an elegant counterpoint to her heated kiss. When they came up for air, Liz grinned. "Hi."

Jack chuckled. "Hi. Having fun?"

Nodding, Liz leaned into Jack. "Yes, especially that last part. If I wasn't on the downhill slide to sixty, I'd suggest something my mother would consider naughty, especially for an old married woman."

Jack lay back on the granite, pulling Liz with him. He proceeded to kiss her breathless, his gloved hands moving over her body. "You mean like this kind of naughty?"

Jack sounded as breathless as Liz felt. She wrapped her arms around his waist. "Yeah, that kind of naughty. I'm sorry that I've been so out of sorts the last couple of months. I know Pete and Luke are in good hands. I've just been stuck in a rut, but today feels like a new start. I feel ready to reach out again and to let God work in His ways, not mine. I wish He didn't have to keep teaching me that lesson. Honey," she kissed Jack's cold lips again, "thank you for putting up with me and helping me back to this place of peace and comfort."

"Liz, you don't need to apologize. It's been a rough two months. I've felt it too, but the truth of the matter is, I'm a happy man just because I have you in my arms and in my life. I've never been with anyone who is more in sync with me and with what I consider important. As I've said before, it's hard to find the words to tell you how much you mean to me." Jack sat up, pulled out his phone, and snapped Liz's picture. He showed it to her and said, "This will always be my definition of beautiful."

The simple sweetness of Jack's compliment caused tears to well in Liz's eyes. "I'm a happy woman for those same reasons, honey. Thank you for making me feel so cherished." She took a photo of him as he lay back on the rock. "Now we'll have matching 'beautiful' photos for our album."

On the walk home, they took more photos to send with their first letter to Gabriela—photos of the two of them together and apart. By the time they got back to the house, they were laughing as they walked, holding hands, into the yard. It took a few moments for them to register that there was a dark sedan parked in the drive. Their smiles faded as Agent Bornell of the FBI got out of the car and walked toward them. Nodding at them, he showed his ID, as if they could ever forget him, then asked if they could all go into the house for a few minutes.

They were sitting in the living room, looking uncomfortably at one another when Jack finally broke the silence. "Agent Bornell, why don't you just tell us whatever you came to tell us. We assume this has something to do with Reynoso."

Bornell nodded. "Yes."

"Has he escaped again?" Liz asked, fear in her eyes.

"No, no, he's still buried deep in federal custody." Bornell looked at Liz. "I'm sorry, Liz, I didn't mean to scare you."

Jack put his arm around Liz's shoulder. "I don't blame her for that assumption. That same question was next up on my list. Look, Frank, it's seldom good news when a federal agent shows up unannounced at the front door. So why are you here?"

"Eduard Reynoso has been diagnosed with pancreatic cancer and is dying. He's in the secured hospital wing of the prison and is refusing chemotherapy and palliative care options. He's asked to see you and Liz before he dies. The prison chaplain appealed to the FBI to get this message to you. However, I'm telling you that you don't have to do this. We have no idea why he wants to speak with you or if this is merely a ploy to get you somewhere where his people can make an attempt on your lives. Frankly, we don't even know for certain if he still has people like that since all his assets are frozen and he's been without outside contact for over two years."

"Where is he being held?" Jack asked.

"At the Grafton Federal Facility in Utah."

"I've never heard of it," Liz said, looking confused.

"I'm not surprised." Frank Bornell smiled grimly. "It's in a very desolate part of the state that makes you think that colors other than brown, tan, gray, and maybe a little sage green are figments of your imagination. The nearest population center is over one hundred miles away, and those one hundred miles are nothing but salt flats and high desert, adding to the security of the facility. There's one road in and out and no cover for any inmate foolish enough to attempt escape. No one has ever successfully broken out of their custody."

"That sounds awful," Liz said, the attorney in her coming to the fore. "What about their rights to communicate with family and counsel?"

"You've heard of Gitmo, I presume?" Bornell asked.

"Of course," Liz replied.

"Well, the same rules apply to Grafton, only it's far more, um, off the map than Gitmo has ever been, and the only people incarcerated in this penitentiary are foreign nationals who have seriously ticked off the US government. You've got no cause to bleed over Reynoso. In fact, the opposite is true. He has shelter, medical care, and three squares a day, and that's far more than he deserves in my opinion. However, that's not what I'm here to discuss. I've delivered the message I was asked to deliver, and personally, I would urge you to ignore it." He looked at Jack. "There's little sense in putting Liz or you through more hell at Reynoso's hands. You know what he threatened the last time you spoke."

Jack pinched the bridge of his nose between his fingers, "Frank, Liz and I need to talk about this. Can you give us until tomorrow morning, and do you have a place to stay up here? It's snowing pretty hard, so I wouldn't recommend going back to Duluth for the night."

"Tomorrow is fine, Jack. I'll just get a room in town."

Liz shook her head. "Please don't do that. You're staying overnight at our request, and we'd like you to stay with us. You're a friend as well as a federal agent. We have a freestanding guesthouse just behind the main house. It's all ready for you, and please join us for dinner, about six, okay?"

Frank grinned wryly. "Yeah, sure, I'm a friend who strikes fear into your hearts when I arrive unannounced." He must have seen the looks of protest on his hosts' faces because he held up his hand. "Seriously, thank you. I'd very much like to stay here with friends. I'd also like to contribute to dinner tonight." He looked at Liz. "What are you cooking?"

Liz grinned. "Jack is making his world-famous baked ziti. Believe me when I tell you it deserves the moniker 'world famous,' and you don't need to bring anything. I know you drove up here for us, and we'd love to have you as our guest."

***

"Wow, that was fabulous." Frank groaned. "I'm so full." He finished the last of the wine in his glass, a wine that he'd purchased in Virginia, Minnesota, the day before. He'd planned to bring it home with him but instead had presented it to Jack and Liz in thanks for having him. As it turned out, it was a perfect complement to the meal. Standing up, he looked at the couple in front of him and said, "Thank you so much for dinner and for having me overnight. I'll leave you two to talk, and I'll see you in the morning."

Jack and Liz got to their feet. "You're welcome, Frank," Liz said. "If you need anything tonight, just give a call or come on over. Otherwise, we'll see you at about nine for breakfast. Good night."

Frank left, and Jack and Liz watched until the lights came on in the guesthouse. After cleaning up the kitchen, the two of them retired to their room to talk. Jack lit a fire in the fireplace and sat down beside his wife on the love seat. Putting his arm around her, Jack said, "Well, this was an unexpected turn to our Sunday."

Liz nodded. "I was pretty frightened to see Frank again, and I never expected him to tell us that Eduard is dying. What are you thinking, Jack?"

"I'm thinking that the timing could be better. We're just getting our balance back after losing the boys, and now this. I know that's selfish, so yes, I think that we need to pray and give it some time. How about you?"

"I agree about the praying part because I was ready to say 'let's go' when Frank told us about Eduard. We've been praying for Eduard Reynoso for almost two years, praying that he would come to know the Lord, and Jack, we told him that we forgave him for what he'd done to us, but have we really? Both of us assumed the worst when Frank showed up. Is that really consistent with true forgiveness?"

Jack opened his mouth and closed it. It was several seconds before he replied, "No, it isn't. Liz, it's easy to tell someone you forgive, but the truth is, after what he did to you, the words are all I can manage. I've no desire to see the man again or to hear his final statement of hatred, and I sure don't want to expose either of us to danger from anyone he's managed to buy while in prison. My answer right now would be to let him die, alone, in pain, and bound for Hell." With sadness in his expression, Jack shook his head. "I know that's wrong, but right now, it's how I feel. That's why I need to pray with you because the kind of bitterness I'm feeling isn't from God."

Liz put her arms around her husband. "Then let's pray. Let's not give Satan a foothold in our lives or our home. God knows what Reynoso did, He knows what's in our hearts, and He knows what the right answer to Frank's question is, so let's talk to God and listen for our answer. We've got all night."

"So," Frank began after they'd finished breakfast, "did you decide on what you're going to do about Reynoso?"

Jack nodded, his eyes tired, but his heart considerably freer. "Yes. Frank, we need closure, so we need to see Eduard one final time. He's facing his end without his family or friends, and we can't say no, even if the last thing we are is friends. How do we do this?"

# CHAPTER 9

===================================⟨X⟩===================================

# A LAST VISIT WITH A LOST SOUL

Three days later, Jack and Liz stepped out of the helicopter and into the blazing sun of a cold high-desert day. The only visible sign that they'd arrived at their destination was a small building directly in front of them. They'd flown over a series of razor wire enclosures and other small structures, but nothing that suggested a large federal presence on the surface. Frank was with them, had been since very early that morning when he'd escorted them to a private jet in Duluth. From there, they'd flown to an isolated field just outside Salt Lake City, Utah, where they'd boarded the helicopter. Needless to say, Liz hadn't been thrilled about another helicopter ride, but she'd kept her mouth shut and tried not to break Jack's hand as they lifted into the cerulean sky.

When Jack and Liz entered the building, they blinked, waiting for their eyes to adjust. It wasn't dark, but it was still a huge change. When they were able to focus, they saw a perfectly ordinary-looking office, with perfectly ordinary-looking people, working on perfectly ordinary-looking computers. What happened next was not so ordinary. After the three of them showed their identification, a uniformed officer escorted them through the office and into a back room. There they presented their credentials again, this time undergoing biometric scans. Once they passed through the documentation area, they entered a body scanner, after which officers conducted a thorough physical search. When they finished, they entered an elevator that took them down more floors than they could count.

When the doors opened, they were in what Jack and Liz later described as an underground garrison. Spectrum-corrected light fixtures mimicked direct sunlight. Frank smiled as they stopped and stared. "Sorry, guys, I know this can be a bit much your first time here."

"Uh, hopefully, our last time too," Jack muttered, putting his arm around Liz's waist. "This is where Reynoso is being held?"

Frank nodded. "After Reynoso's escape and subsequent recapture, he was brought here, and he won't leave here alive. This is home to a lot of very bad people who are the reasons for the security you just went through. Not many visitors come down here, so you are both something of an anomaly."

Liz frowned. "That kind of hopelessness must..." She didn't finish, just shook her head sadly. "That's not what I would have wanted for Eduard, no matter what he did to Jack and me. Where are we meeting him?"

"I'm to take you to the hospital facility," Frank said quietly. "You will visit with Reynoso there, with him shackled to the wall and under guard." Frank must have seen something in Liz's expression because he added, "Liz, whether or not you agree, these are all sensible precautions designed to keep you both safe. This man has made numerous threats against your lives even while here. Please don't demand something that will force me to cut your visit short before you see him, okay?"

Liz nodded, gripping Jack's hand more tightly as they walked down the hallway and entered another elevator. This one took them further down, making her ears pop uncomfortably. She prayed silently that sometime soon she would see the outside world again. Just when she was about to ask Frank to cancel their visit and take them back to the surface, the doors opened into what appeared to be a normal hospital nursing station. Thanks to Jack, this was an environment familiar to her, and she breathed more easily. Looking at Frank, she asked, "Are we here?"

Frank nodded. "Yes, this is where they're holding Reynoso. They're preparing him for your visit as we speak. These good folks," he waved at the personnel at the desk, "will let us know when he's ready."

It was as Frank spoke that Liz saw something that she hadn't seen at EBCH or for that matter in any other normal hospital. In front of every door was an armed guard and in the back of the nurse's station and in front of the elevators were four more armed guards. She swallowed hard and shrank back against Jack. "Honey, this is..." She couldn't finish.

Jack pulled Liz into his arms, ignoring everyone around them. He kissed the top of her head and whispered, "I know, it's intense, but it's kept us safe for over two years. Take a deep breath, then tell me if you don't want to go through with this. It's okay if you don't. You can go up top, and I'll talk to Reynoso alone."

Liz did as Jack suggested, thought for a moment, then shook her head resolutely. "No, I'm okay. As an attorney, I've been in prisons before, although nothing quite like this one. I'm not going to let you do this alone. I need closure as much as you do." She stood on her toes, kissed his cheek, and said, "Thank you."

"Dr. and Ms. Lockwood, please follow me." A male nurse in scrubs motioned to them. "Please stay close to me so we avoid setting off any alarms. I'm cleared into prisoner Reynoso's room."

Liz gripped Jack's hand, hoping that after today he could still move his fingers to do surgery. She kept repeating in her mind why doing this was important, kept praying the same prayers for strength and peace that she and Jack had prayed since they'd agreed to see Reynoso. The walk to his room was short. When they arrived a guard searched them one final time before escorting them down a short corridor with a biometrically locked door on either end. Liz looked around and was relieved to see Jack and Frank close behind her. The guard unlocked the last door, and she walked into the room where Reynoso lay. When she saw the frail figure in the hospital bed, instead of fear, all she felt was pity. That must have shown on her face because Reynoso started on the offensive.

"Ms. Lockwood, how secure and proud you must feel seeing me like this. I must confess some disappointment in not being able to order your deaths as easily as I would have been able to do some years ago. How are your hands? And your fragile psyche?"

Liz stopped Jack from responding with a gesture and said, "Hello, Eduard. I still have good and bad days with my hands, and my psyche isn't nearly as fragile as you presume. If you think secure and proud is how I feel, then you're a really lousy judge of character. If you think that finding out about your illness brought Jack and me joy, then you simply have no idea of who we really are, which is no surprise. We're here because you asked for us. What is it we can do to help you?"

"Besides die, you mean?" Eduard's voice seemed to grow stronger with each hate-filled statement.

Jack took Liz's hand and as one they turned to Frank. "We're done here," Jack asserted tersely.

"Wait, Dr. Lockwood. I can make this visit worth your time," Reynoso insisted from the bed. "It's simply a matter of getting through the preliminaries."

Jack turned and walked over to the prisoner's bedside. He could see the shackles that bound Reynoso to the wall. He could also see the toll that pancreatic cancer was taking on the prisoner's body. There was no question that he was a dying man and that death was only a short time away. "I don't think much of your 'preliminaries,' Eduard, and I would think that you, of all people, wouldn't want to waste time. You are aware that there are treatments that might help extend your life and ease your pain?"

Reynoso smirked. "For what purpose, Dr. Lockwood? There's nothing for me here, and here is where I will die. I will face it like a man, not in a drug-induced stupor while I wait for your chemo to poison me. I don't think that anyone here has any interest in seeing me survive, and even if they did, this particular devil of a disease takes no prisoners. Death will free me."

Jack and Liz shook their heads sadly and Jack said, "If only that were true, Eduard. Death will only set in stone the choices you've made in life."

Reynoso sneered again. "Ah, the preacher Lockwood returns. Once again, I say look to your own fate first. I may go on ahead of you, but you will die just the same. Perhaps not at my hand, but death will take you one day, then the two of you will be separated, and you will finally know the kind of pain I wished on Ms. Lockwood when we last met."

～⌒✕⌒～

Liz's faint smile returned. "Unless God decides in His mercy to take us home together or unless the Lord Jesus returns for His own before we die, in which case we will rise together. In any case, you're wrong. You see, Eduard, Jack and I know that even if God calls one of us home before the other, we will meet again. I knew that even when you were torturing me, and that's why my psyche survived. You couldn't beat me hard enough to break me because all I wanted was to be with my Savior and see my beloved Jack again—because I believed him dead. If I'd died at your hand, or out in the woods, or the cave that night, it would have been okay. However, you made the mistake of underestimating my strength. Once free of you, I wasn't going to give in to your hatred, especially once I knew that I was going to live long enough to see my loved ones again. That was the power of love, Eduard, and love always trumps hatred. I truly hope you come to realize that before the end."

Reynoso was silent for a few moments after Liz finished speaking, and she prepared herself for him to spew more hateful words. She had just about reached the conclusion that taking his final shots at her and Jack, their beliefs, and their lives together was why Reynoso had called them here. Looking inside herself, she couldn't find any anger at that thought, just a deep, profound sadness at a life wasted.

"You sound as though you actually believe that, Ms. Lockwood," Reynoso said quietly.

"I do."

"And you, Dr. Lockwood. Do you also believe that love is all-powerful?"

"If we're speaking of the kind of love that's sourced in God, I do."

Reynoso stared at them appraisingly, then nodded. "Good. Now that we've finished the preliminaries and had the useless, but I suppose inevitable, conversation about my soul's final destination, we can get to the point of your visit. I asked you here because there's something I'd like you to do for me."

Jack and Liz were both astonished. Frank just looked dazed. It was close to a minute before Liz managed to respond. "What would you like us to do, Eduard? If it's within the law and within our power, Jack and I will do our best to help you."

Reynoso frowned as though disturbed by her answer, but he continued, "I have a daughter. She turned five last August. Up until last week, she lived with her mother in Tumaco, Colombia. I haven't seen them since a month before my arrest in Minneapolis several years ago. Last week, a group of armed men forced their way into our house, raped and then shot my girlfriend, lover, whatever you'd call her here, and left my daughter, Gabriela, alone. Gabriela was hiding in the closet when the group broke in, and the group tried to leave in a hurry when several of my people showed up. Sadly, they were too late to help my Manuela."

Liz had tears in her eyes and couldn't believe Eduard's calm. "I'm so sorry, Eduard. I truly am."

"As am I," Jack added. "Where's your little girl now?"

"On her way to this part of the great United States in the care of one of my people. I hope to be able to see her once more if the powers holding me here carry through on their promise to allow it." Reynoso's voice was rock steady, and he showed no sign of emotion.

"Who will care for her after you die?" Jack asked.

"Now we come to the point of our visit. Perhaps my failure to kill you and Ms. Lockwood was providential. You appear to be at a good place in life and, with me gone, a relatively safe place. You seem to be well-off financially and somewhere I heard that you regret not having children. My question is this, will you raise Gabriela as your own daughter once I'm gone?"

His request stunned Jack and Liz into silence. Just a few days ago, they'd agreed to sponsor a Gabriela in Colombia through Compassion. Now the man who'd almost killed them—a dying man—was asking them to parent his only daughter, also named Gabriela. Finally, Liz replied, "What about your extended family, Eduard? Don't you want her with them?"

"If that's what I wanted, I wouldn't have asked you here. Many places in Colombia are very dangerous and have been for a long time. I don't want Gabriela to grow up surrounded by guards or to end up like her mother. Then there's the problem with my competition. With me out of the way, the business passes to my daughter, and that makes her a target and forces her into a life I don't want her to experience. That brings me to my request. I want you to adopt Gabriela and give her your last name."

"Why us? Two years ago, you tried very hard to kill us. Five minutes ago, you were saying how disappointed you were that we weren't dead, and now you're asking us to raise your child?" Jack was clearly confused. "Why would you ask us to do this if you feel such hatred for us?"

"Dr. Lockwood, as you Americans are wont to say 'desperate times call for desperate measures.' As much as I dislike the idea of involving you, Gabby is the central figure in all this. I'm dying, her mother is dead, and I don't have a lot of time, so I thought of the two of you. After all, Manuela wouldn't be dead if I'd been able to be in Columbia with her or if word was out that I'd escaped from your prison. Unhappily, thanks to your testimonies, they locked me away here and I wasn't there to protect my loved ones."

"I'm sorry, but you're the one who tried to kill us," Jack pointed out angrily, "and tortured Liz without regard for *her* loved ones."

"As I told you at the time, that was nothing personal."

"It sure felt personal." Jack exhaled sharply. "So that's what this is about? Using your daughter as some kind of pawn in a game?"

"Calm yourself, Dr. Lockwood, this is no game. Manuela's life ended because of your interference in my life, my life is ending because of cancer, and, by default, Gabby ends up without parents. Clearly, I needed to make a decision and so I thought of you. I'm certain she would be reasonably safe in your care, since I don't believe that either of you is cruel enough to visit the sins of the father on the child. What I'm proposing is a life for a life. My life ends, and you care for my daughter so she can have a life. You owe me that much."

Jack opened his mouth, but Liz put her hand on his arm again. "Is that all, Eduard?"

Reynoso steepled his fingers and continued, "In your care, Gabby would grow up free of the violence that taints my world. While I've no regrets insofar as my own life is concerned, it's not what I want for my daughter. I don't want her involved in the business of the drug trade, and that brings me to another request. You are not to tell Gabby about my family business or our history. She's only five, and you, Dr. Lockwood, will be the father she remembers. If she asks about me, you may tell her the truth about how I died, as she may have some memory of this place. If she asks about her mother, you may tell her that her name was Manuela and that she was very beautiful and a good dancer. If she has any memory of the morning of her mother's death, you may tell her the truth. The fact of the matter is, Tumaco is known for outbreaks of gang violence in its neighborhoods." Reynoso smiled a scary smile. "However, the city will be plagued with one fewer gang going forward.

"Beyond what I've asked of you, you may raise her as your own, in your faith, and perhaps she will be the apology I cannot give you. My last requests of you are that you meet her when she gets here, be witnesses as I sign custody of her over to you, then complete a 'Termination of Parental Rights' petition. I believe Ms. Lockwood is still a licensed attorney, so she should recognize the validity and legality of what I'm doing and what I'm asking you to do. I have also requested the presence of a third-party attorney from the overabundance of US government types who occupy the penthouse floor of this facility.

"Before I finish and you make your decision regarding these requests, you should know that Gabby comes to you penniless. Your government was very efficient when they froze my assets."

"That doesn't matter to us. If we agree to do this, the child will have everything she needs," Jack assured Reynoso, then added, "Liz and I are both in our fifties. That's on the older end for parents, and while we would make provisions for guardianship and her financial stability should something happen to both of us, Gabriela would still have to cope with the stigma of having an older mother and father."

"At least she will have a mother and father," Reynoso snapped. "I grow tired of this sparring. I've offered you a proposition. If you say yes, I want Gabby to leave with you today. She speaks both Spanish and English quite well but sometimes uses them interchangeably."

He looked up at Liz and Jack, and for the first time, they got a glimpse of a frightened, dying father trying to do right by his only child. Liz put her hand to her forehead, turned to Jack, and smiled weakly. "I need a minute or thirty."

Jack turned to Reynoso. "Liz and I need to talk about this. Will you give us thirty minutes?"

With a benevolent wave of his hand, Reynoso replied, "By all means, take thirty-five minutes if you wish, Dr. Lockwood. Gabby isn't due for another hour, and I'm not going anywhere, chained to the wall as I am."

~ ~ ~

Jack was worried. He and Liz were alone together, had been for almost five minutes, and she hadn't said a word. She just sat in a chair, staring at the beige walls. This silence was very unlike her, and he wished he knew where her head was at with all this. She was the one who'd pushed him to make this trip, feeling in her heart a compassion for Reynoso that he still hadn't managed to cultivate— although seeing him this morning had gone a long way toward help-ing Jack see Reynoso's life through his wife's eyes. Kneeling in front of her, Jack took her hands. "Liz, you're awfully quiet. What are you thinking?"

Liz blinked and squeezed his hands. "I'm sorry, Jack, I didn't mean to zone out. I was just trying to sort through everything in my head." She sighed deeply. "I have to admit, I was completely unprepared for what he's asked of us."

Jack kept Liz's hands folded in his. "Me too. Can you tell me what you're thinking about all this? Do we just get on that helicopter home and forget this ever happened?"

Liz looked Jack in the eyes. "Could you really do that? Walk away without another word and just move on with our lives?"

Jack was still for a moment. Never in his life had he wanted so badly to lie to Liz. Finally, he took the hard road and shook his head. "No, at least not for a long time."

Liz bowed her head. "Me either, so I guess that means we're going to have to go back in there and tell a dying man that we're leaving without granting his final request or we're going to leave here with a new daughter, a lifetime commitment for better or worse."

Remorse washed over Jack at Liz's words. He took her in his arms and held her close. "I'm so sorry."

"Sorry for what?" Liz whispered, her lips moving against Jack's ear.

"Sorry there's been so much 'worse' in our lives since I married you. This wasn't what I wanted for you or for us."

Liz stroked Jack's back. "I love you, honey, and I love our life together. Every couple has ups and downs, but through it all, my love for you has only grown stronger. And I think we've had an awful lot of fun."

Jack attempted a smile and almost succeeded. "Me too, but today and all this, it's hard. What do you think?"

Liz smiled wryly. "I think that I wish I had nine months to prepare for welcoming a child into our home. What happened with Pete and Luke is still pretty raw. I've no love for Reynoso as you well know. In fact, there's a part of me that still hates him, especially after the way he greeted us. Because of that hatred, I wonder, will that change how I feel about the little girl that he wants us to parent? Will it make me a less loving and fit mother if we do this? Besides all that, the age thing still lingers as a question in my mind. I'm fifty-five, you're fifty-four, and Gabby is five, that means that when she's twenty, we'll…"

Jack chuckled. "Liz, I've done the math."

Liz looked at Jack, her cheeks pink. "Uh, yeah, I suppose you have."

Taking Liz's hands again, Jack asked, "So is this a 'no' I'm hearing?"

Liz shook her head. "No, just the opposite in fact. Where are you with all this?"

Jack was determined to be honest and to hold nothing back. "I don't have the mixed feelings about Reynoso that you do, Liz. I don't have your great heart, and as hard as I try, I can't wipe my memory of the pain he caused us. While I can say I no longer hate the man, there's no compassion in my heart for him, either."

"Are you sure about that, Jack? I saw the look on your face when you were standing by his bed."

"Okay, so it's complicated. As a physician, I know what he's going through, especially because he's refused treatment or palliative care. I hate that because of that choice, his physicians can't even ease his pain. I know that, barring intervention by God himself, Reynoso's going to die within a week or two. Perhaps my only sadness when I think of him, is that he's going to meet his Lord unprepared. If I could change that, I would. But the idea of doing the man a favor, especially a favor of this magnitude, doesn't sit well with me."

"But..." Liz began.

"Please, let me finish, before I chicken out completely. Liz," Jack looked her in the eyes. "I love our life together. It's better than I'd ever dreamed and I could happily live out my life with just the two of us walking the path together. However, the time when Pete and Luke were with us was something so special and not just for me. I saw you bloom. I saw new happiness and deep fulfillment in your eyes. We've been praying about this for six months now, and a part of me wonders, at our age, how many more chances we're going to get at parenting. We lost Pete and Luke, in part, because of our ages. Now Reynoso is offering us the chance to raise a little girl who really needs us. Yes, it's difficult to trust him, but he's dying, Liz, and barring a miracle, he's dying a lost soul. Maybe we can prevent that tragedy with his daughter." Jack took a deep breath. "So yes, I'd like to do this. I know that challenges lie ahead, I know how old we are, and I know Gabby's background, but I'm still ready to do as Reynoso has asked. You?"

Liz squeezed his hands tightly. "Yes, I am. Providing the legalities are in order."

Jack frowned. "To that point, what exactly does what Reynoso said about the legalities get us? Will we have full, uncontested, and unbreakable custody of Gabby? I will not risk a repeat of what happened with the boys."

Liz nodded slowly. "I've yet to see the papers, but if I'm interpreting what Reynoso said correctly, yes, we will. I'll let you know immediately if the arrangement is something other than advertised. If it's as advertised, we wouldn't have to do anything more, but I would recommend that, when we get home, we do as Reynoso has asked and formally adopt Gabby in our court system. That way she will, legally, be a Lockwood." She raised her eyes to meet Jack's. "Are we crazy?"

Jack shrugged. "Probably, but we've prayed over this numerous times, and it appears our great God has an equally great sense of humor where we're concerned. Are you ready?"

"Not quite, Jack. What you just said reminded me that we have one more thing to do before we go back in there." She took his hand. "Come on, let's talk to God about this again before we decide anything this important. We have the time."

Keeping hold of Liz's hand, Jack knelt beside her, and together, they bowed their heads.

# CHAPTER 10

## FELIZ NAVIDAD Y PRÓSPERO AÑO NUEVO

Jack and Liz led their daughter Gabby out of her room on Christmas morning, holding her hands. When they walked into the living room, Gabby's eyes widened when she saw the gifts under the tree. "Mama Liz, Señor Papa Jack, look, more presents! I got presents last night before church. Who are these for?"

"They're for you, dear Gabby, from Niño Jesús," Liz said.

The little girl looked up, her brown eyes dancing. "Can I open them now, por favor?"

Jack and Liz let go of Gabby's hands and stood with their arms around each other on this Christmas morning. It had been more than three weeks since they'd returned from the Utah desert with the little girl, a little girl who was now an orphan, or would have been if Jack and Liz hadn't honored her father's last request. On their way home with Gabby asleep in Liz's lap, they'd vowed to do everything they could to make her life a safe and happy one. Since then, it had been a bumpy ride. The little girl was confused and often woke up screaming for her mama. But the last three days had been better, especially with the festivities of Christmas upon them.

They'd filed adoption papers in Minnesota Juvenile Court, had received documentation that all was in order, and that the process wouldn't take much time. They didn't have a court date yet, but Liz expected to receive that notification any day. Eduard had kept his word in all respects, signing over custody of Gabby to Jack and Liz, and then terminating all his parental rights. He'd even told his daughter that Señor Jack and Señora Liz would be her new mama and papa and that she would be living at their home. He'd hugged her long and close and then let her go without another word. Turning to the wall was his way of telling them all that the interview was at an end. He'd died just over a week later without saying another word to anyone.

Jack and Liz had not told Gabby her real papa was gone. Reynoso had reminded them just before greeting Gabby that, after today, he wanted his daughter to have nothing more to do with him or his way of life, and they'd agreed. Right now, Jack didn't want to do anything that would stand in the way of Gabby's adapting to her new environment, and he also didn't want anything to wipe away the joy he saw in Liz's face this morning as she sat with the little girl under the tree and helped her open her packages. He breathed a prayer of thanksgiving before he joined his wife and daughter.

⁓⸪⁓

"Gracias, Tio Dan and Tia Beth. It's my favorite doll ever!" Gabby cradled in her arms the doll that Dan and Beth had given her for Christmas. They were all sitting around the Christmas tree later that same evening, having enjoyed Christmas dinner together at Jack and Liz's home.

Beth held out her arms. "May I have a hug, Gabby?"

The little girl ran into her embrace and, before backing away, gave her a loud kiss on the cheek.

Smiling Dan asked, "How about me?" He held out his arms, but Gabby backed away. "No, Tio Dan, no."

"That's okay, Gabby. I'm pretty new to you," Dan said soothingly. "Feliz Navidad."

"Feliz Navidad, Tio Dan." Gabby climbed into Jack's lap. "Papa Jack, look at my doll. Isn't she pretty?"

Before Jack could answer, Binx jumped up on the chair they sat in, lying down on the arm. Gabby reached out to touch her fur. "La gata Binx."

Jack looked at Dan and Beth. "La gata Binx has joined the party. Can the other two be far behind?" Jack was slowly acquiring an extensive Spanish vocabulary thanks to his Colombian daughter and his bilingual wife.

His comment proved prophetic. It was just a few minutes before la gata Sierra curled up in Beth's lap and el gato Lazarus was batting wrapping paper balls around the living room floor, adding to the hilarity of the evening. Liz got her guitar after they finished opening gifts and smiled at Gabriela. "This song is for you, honey. It was my favorite Christmas carol when I was your age."

Gabby bounced up and down on her tiptoes. "Yea, Mama Liz, sing for me!"

> *Away in a manger, no crib for a bed,*
> *the little Lord Jesus laid down His sweet head;*
> *the stars in the heavens looked down where He lay,*
> *the little Lord Jesus asleep on the hay.*
>
> *The cattle are lowing, the Baby awakes,*
> *but little Lord Jesus, no crying He makes.*
> *I love Thee, Lord Jesus, look down from the sky*
> *and stay by my side until morning is nigh.*
>
> *Be near us, Lord Jesus; we ask Thee to stay*
> *close by our dear Gabby and love her, we pray.*
> *Bless all the dear children in Thy tender care,*
> *and fit us for heaven, to live with Thee there.*[iii]

Dan cleared his throat as Gabby clapped delightedly at hearing her name in her mama's song. "Uh, wow, Liz. That was beautiful," he managed after a while.

Liz smiled as she hugged Gabby. "Thank you. I took a few liberties with the lyrics on the last verse, but with our little one listening, I couldn't resist."

The four of them went on to sing every Christmas carol they could think of, continuing long after Gabby had fallen asleep in

Jack's arms. The music didn't seem to bother her, nor did the adults' quiet conversation after Liz put down her guitar.

"How's it going?" Beth asked.

"Some days are diamonds, and some days are stone," Liz said, "but I wouldn't trade a minute of it. Gabby's a wonderful little girl."

Beth looked curious. "Are you going to enroll her in school after the first of the year?"

Jack shook his head. "No. While Gabby had started school in Colombia, neither Liz nor I want to give her another major change to make right now. English is her second language, and to put her into an American classroom when she's still adjusting to living here is too much to ask of a child who's been through what Gabby has in the past few months. Liz and I will teach her and help her adapt through the first part of the year and enroll her in the Christian elementary school in town next fall."

"Any second thoughts?" Dan asked seriously. "Or rather, any surprises, since it was Reynoso who engineered all this?"

Liz looked at Gabby to make certain she was still asleep, then at Jack, who nodded. "We've had second, third, and fourth thoughts, Dan," Liz smiled, "none of which are serious, and all of which are felt by parents everywhere, especially parents who are doing this for the first time at our age. As for surprises, there've been none. Apparently, Eduard was sincere in his request that we parent Gabby."

"That's hard to believe," Dan muttered. "I would have bet that the man didn't have a sincere bone in his body. Still, we're glad for you both or, rather, for you all. Count on us for all honorary aunt and uncle duties, including babysitting," Dan gazed sadly at the sleeping child, "if she'll have me. I didn't mean to scare her earlier."

Liz reached out and squeezed Dan's hand. "Don't let her reticence bother you, Dan, she'll come around. Gabby is shier around men. It even took her a couple of days to warm to Jack enough so she'd let him hold her. I think it's because her mother was her primary parent. Reynoso spent a lot of time out of Colombia, and he hadn't been home in almost three years when he died. We know you'll be a wonderful uncle and godfather to her."

Dan smiled broadly at Liz's words. "Good, because I have another Christmas gift for my honorary niece and goddaughter, albeit something that she's not quite ready for yet. When she's ready and when her mom is ready, I want to take her on a helicopter ride, maybe even let her help me fly the thing."

Liz paled a little but managed to respond, "Um, thanks. Let Jack and me talk about it and we'll get back to you. Personally, I'm thinking when she turns fifty-five will be good."

"Uh, Liz, that would mean your daughter would be in the air with a one-hundred-ten-year-old pilot. Does that really seem like a good idea to you? You had a bad experience your first time out, so I can't really blame you for not being terribly excited. Next time we go up, it's gonna be perfect, I promise."

"Dan, honey, you're one of my very best friends and I trust you completely, but can we not talk about this right now? I'm getting airsick." Liz touched his hand. "I'm grateful that you fly my husband all over the Boundary Waters with great frequency, and you always bring him back in one piece, but I'm just not ready to send my daughter up with her crazy Tio Dan just yet."

"That's wonderful," Jack murmured absently.

"What's wonderful, buddy?" Dan looked at him askance. "Your wife's casting aspersions on me personally and worse, on my flying skills, and you're sitting there grinning. Aren't you going to come to my defense?"

Jack snickered. "I'm afraid you're on your own with that one, Harrison. My credibility was shot the moment we crashed back in May because before we left that morning, I told Liz that you were a great pilot and there was nothing to worry about."

"Okay, at least I know how things stand between us," Dan grumbled. "So what's so wonderful?"

"My daughter."

"Huh?" Dan looked baffled as if trying to figure out what Jack was saying in the context of the sentence they'd been talking about.

"I just love when Liz says something like that—you know 'my daughter' or 'our daughter.'" Jack made a face at Dan. "Yeah, yeah, I know, they just revoked my membership in the real men's club again.

I don't much care. I never thought I'd have a daughter, apart from Binx, so sue me if I'm a little sappy."

His sarcastic grin mellowing into genuine joy, Dan laid a gentle hand on the sleeping Gabby's head and squeezed Jack's shoulder with his other hand. "I'm really happy for you and Liz, brother, and so glad that God has answered all our prayers like this. Merry Christmas!"

⁓

"Happy New Year and Happy Anniversary, mia bella Liz." Jack lifted his glass filled with bubbly cider. He and Liz snuggled together in bed, watching the fire. The clock read 12:01 a.m. While tired, Jack was completely content.

"Happy New Year and Happy Anniversary to you too, mi guapo Jack." Liz sipped her drink then set it on the nightstand. "Just think, we're back here where it all began four years and a little less than two months ago. Gabby is asleep, the monitor's quiet, and we're alone to start this wonderful day." She kissed him tenderly. "Te quiero mucho. Thank you for saving my life that night."

Jack set his glass on the nightstand and wrapped Liz in his arms, lying her back into the nest of pillows. Kissing her breathless, he whispered, "Thank God I found you in time. My life would have been so empty if I'd been too late to save you." He grinned. "Thank you too for teaching me how to whisper sweet nothings into your ear in Spanish. I know it's not very useful when talking to our daughter, but it sure is a lot of fun in our private time. 'Te quiero?'"

Liz wrapped her arms around Jack's neck. "It means 'I love you.'"

Relaxed and joyful, their loving was a perfect celebration of their wedding anniversary and the New Year. Afterward, resting in each other's arms, no words were necessary. Gratitude to God for family, for dear friends, for each other, and for Gabby filled their hearts. They could not have scripted the events of the past year or the way a child would come into their lives, but God had moved and, in His time, had worked a miracle. Life was good.

# CHAPTER 11

## FAMILY MATTERS

"Dad's going to what?" Jack whirled to look at Liz who was just emerging from the bathroom later that morning.

"Well, his text says that he'll be arriving sometime today so that he can preside over Gabby's dedication service tomorrow." Liz's brow knotted. "From the time stamp, I'd say he's already on his way."

Jack took a breath. Then he took another, deeper breath, trying to quell the frustration rising inside of him. He didn't want to feel that way today. It was the first day of the New Year and his fourth wedding anniversary. All he wanted to feel was joy. Wiping his palm over his face, Jack muttered, "Okay. So he's coming for Gabby's dedication, but there's no way he's taking over for Pastor Steve. No way."

Liz came over and rubbed her husband's shoulders. She knew that despite Lloyd's coming to know the Lord, two years before, Jack's relationship with his father was awkward at best. She couldn't blame her husband for feeling the way he did, particularly since Lloyd still had his selfish moments. "Easy, honey. We'll get the guesthouse ready, Gabby will charm him, and then we'll tell him, or rather I will tell him, that he's going to have to settle for standing with the family, just like Mom will be doing. It'll be okay."

Jack groaned. "It's never okay when Dad gets an idea in his head. He needs to grandstand for someone now that he's retired from the pastorate. It's not like this is his first grandchild. He's got six others."

"Jack, honey," Liz said soothingly, "it's been a long time since any of them were children, and the only two of them he dedicated and later baptized were Vicki's kids because Walt and his family aren't believers," she smiled, "yet. I'm not saying that announcing his plans rather than asking is appropriate, but it's very Lloyd. I have a great idea. We'll let Mom handle this. She's meeting his flight in Duluth today, and you can bet Lloyd will lose the argument."

Jack's morose expression lightened. "Do you think she'll do it?"

Liz nodded. "I know she will, and she won't even feel like she's being blindsided by our request. You know she likes your dad."

Jack made a face. "Yeah, I do. I don't get it, but I do."

Slapping at her husband playfully, Liz said, "Lighten up. It's not like we didn't invite your dad in the first place. And to be honest, he's a good-looking, energetic guy for someone going on eighty-one years old. Besides, Mom's an eighty-three-year-old who can hold her own. Just relax, everything will be fine."

The next day, holding Gabby on the platform of their church, Jack had to admit his wife had called it. Liz was standing next to him, Beth and Dan were by their sides, and Lloyd stood with Nancy off to one side as Pastor Steve dedicated Gabby. Dan and Beth, her godparents and designated guardians, along with Jack and Liz, promised to raise Gabby in a Christian home with Christian values and to do everything possible so that Gabby, when she was of an age to understand, would seek out the Lord on her own. Then, as Jack and Liz had arranged earlier that morning, the grandparents closed the ceremony in prayer. It was a beautiful addition to the private service, and Jack found himself grateful that his father and Liz's mother had made the trip. Even Pastor Steve had tears in his eyes as he congratulated them all after the closing prayer ended. He smiled at Jack and Liz and said, "Congratulations, I know God will use you mightily in Gabby's life and," his eyes twinkled, "happy anniversary a day late." He shook everyone's hand and gave Liz the *Certificate of Dedication* for Gabby's memory book.

Gabby was in her glory when everyone came back to the house for dinner. She ran from one adult to the next, giving hugs, showing off her Christmas presents, and basking in the glow of being the center of attention. Dan looked thrilled when she bounced into his lap, gave him a kiss on the cheek, and proclaimed to one and all that this was her Tio Dan.

It wasn't until much later, after spending several hours getting one overly excited five-year-old to bed and then saying good night to Dan and Beth, that Liz and Jack sat down with their parents in the living area. Stroking the sleeping Binx, Jack looked Lloyd in the eyes. "Dad, thanks for coming. I know it's a long trip and not as easy as it used to be for you. You and Nancy really made today something special, not only for Gabby but for Liz and me too."

Lloyd smiled at Jack then at Nancy. "It was good to be here, and Nancy and I enjoyed our time together on the drive up from Duluth." He bowed from the waist in an old-fashioned courtly way to her. "Thank you, my dear."

Liz's mom blushed. "You're welcome, Lloyd. It was my pleasure, and I'm glad you decided to come. After all, it's been a long time since either of us had a new grandchild to celebrate." She looked at Jack and Liz. "Thank you for inviting us. Gabby's a beautiful little girl, and it will be such fun to watch her grow." Getting to her feet, Nancy said good night and disappeared into the master bedroom.

Lloyd got up and also said his good nights before putting on his coat. He always elected to stay in the guesthouse when visiting. Jack was by his side in an instant. "I'll walk you, Dad. It's a bit slippery out there."

When everyone left, Liz laid back against the sofa cushions and cuddled with Sierra. What a wonderful day it had been, but she was exhausted and could feel tendrils of fibro pain tugging at her muscles. She took a deep breath and let it out, practicing the pain-control techniques that Jack had taught her. Kitchen cleanup could wait for a few minutes.

Shaking Liz gently, Jack said, "Love, why don't you go to bed rather than napping on the couch?"

Liz opened her eyes sleepily. "Hey, I was just waiting for you to get back. I need to clean up the kitchen and then I'll go to bed."

Jack sat down next to her prone form, putting his hand on her shoulder. "I already cleaned up."

Making a face, Liz said, "Thanks, but I would have helped. Why didn't you wake me?"

"Because you looked so peaceful, lying there with Sierra in your arms. Besides, you cooked, so cleanup was my contribution to the party." Jack lay down next to Liz on the sofa, drawing her into the curve of his body. The woodstove and the Christmas tree provided the only illumination in the darkened room. All was quiet. Kissing Liz's neck, Jack relaxed, enjoying this peaceful benediction on the day. "I love you, Liz. Thank you for being my voice of sanity about today."

The only answer was Liz's quiet breathing. Jack closed his eyes. He was comfortable and relaxing here, holding his wife to his heart, for just a few minutes, felt right.

***

"Good morning, children."

Liz's eyes snapped open as she looked up at her smiling mother, who was holding a wide-awake Gabby in her arms. "Uh, hi, Mom, sorry. I guess we fell asleep out here last night. Good morning." Elbowing Jack gently, she said, "Hey, wake up. We need to be about making breakfast."

They'd just gotten to their feet, and Nancy had just handed Gabby to Jack when Lloyd walked through the front door, rubbing his hands together. "Brrr, it's cold out there. Good morning, children." Walking over to where Nancy stood, he put his arms around her and kissed her. "Good morning to you too, sweetheart."

It was a credit to Jack's self control that he didn't drop his daughter on the floor. He knew he was staring at his father and Nancy with the same look on his face as his wife had on hers—utter astonishment to the degree that Jack kept forgetting to breathe.

Both Nancy and Lloyd were standing there with patient smiles on their faces. Finally, Nancy broke the silence. "Children, we, um, Lloyd and I, have something to tell you."

Jack set his squirming daughter down so she could go play with her toys and put his arm around Liz's waist, before responding, "Clearly." He noticed something else. Nancy was wearing a diamond on the third finger of her left hand. "Why don't we all sit down? I'll brew some coffee."

Nancy smiled. "It's already brewed. I'll get it, Jack, since I think you both need to sit down more than I do."

Jack just nodded and took Liz's hand, leading her into the dining room. He had to give her a gentle push on the shoulders before she plunked into the chair behind her. Once they were all seated, Jack prompted, "You mentioned having something to tell us, Dad, Nancy?"

The older couple twined their fingers, and Lloyd spoke up, "Yesterday, I asked Nancy to be my wife, and for a wonder, she said yes. We decided to wait until today to tell you so that Gabby could have her special day all to herself. Nancy and I have seen a lot of each other in the time since I was here for Christmas a couple of years back." He smiled. "She's the light of my world and is still working to turn me into a true man of God."

Lloyd's smile faded. "Speaking of that, I apologize for the way I announced my intent to come for Gabby's dedication. It was wrong of me to show up unannounced, and I certainly had no right to usurp Steve's role in yesterday's service. He's your pastor, and it was perfect just the way you planned it. Nancy blistered my ears on our way up here until I, um, saw the light."

"But married, Dad? Again?" Jack couldn't help it, that's what came out of his mouth.

Patting him on the hand, Nancy quipped, "Fifth time's the charm, Jack. And because your father became a new man in Christ just over two years ago,[3] I prefer to think of myself as number one."

---

[3] "Therefore, if anyone is in Christ, this person is a new creation; the old things passed away; behold, new things have come" (2 Corinthians 5:17 NASB).

Nancy looked at her daughter, concern in her eyes. "Liz, do you have anything to say, honey?"

"Married, Mom? To Jack's dad?"

"Nana, I'm hungry." Gabby pulled on Nancy's robe, clearly recognizing the soft touch in the group.

Lloyd patted Nancy's shoulder and said, "I'll get Miss Gabby some cereal while you try to bring these two back to earth."

"Mom," Liz said after a few seconds, "are you sure about this? I didn't even know that you and Lloyd were seeing each other."

With a wicked gleam in her eyes, Nancy said, "Didn't you and I have this same conversation when you and Jack announced your engagement after knowing each other for an entire month? At least Lloyd and I have known each other for several years. And yes, we've seen and spoken to each other often over those years."

"But married? To Jack's dad?" Liz still sounded flummoxed.

"Yes, Liz, married, to me." Lloyd put Gabby in her chair and set a bowl of cereal in front of her before sitting down. "Maybe you'd have preferred it if I'd asked her to cohabit." He winked at Nancy.

"Well, um, that might have been more in character for the man I grew up with, but no." Jack extended his hand to his dad. "Congratulations, Dad, and you too, Nancy." He elbowed Liz. "Come on, wife, join the party. Our convoluted family relationships just got more convoluted." Smiling, Jack looked at the couple in front of them. "I'm really happy for you both."

Liz took her mom's hand. "Me too, Mom, Lloyd, really. This was a surprise but a really good one."

Picking up on the smiles in the room, Gabby clapped her hands, knocking cornflakes and milk all over the table and the floor. "Alegre, Nana and Señor Pop-pop."

"Um, she's saying something like 'happy, jolly, merry,' Grandma and Mr. Grandpa," Liz said as she ran for a towel.

Four days later, in the presence of God, friends, and most of their children, Pastor Steve Lynch married Lloyd and Nancy at the Lockwoods' home church. Afterward, Dan and Beth hosted a wedding brunch at their home. Gabby enjoyed all the people in attendance, but she was most interested in Buddy, a six-month-old standard schnauzer poodle (schnoodle) mix, who added to the joy and confusion by running around and barking nonstop. Much to Gabby's disappointment, Dan finally had to quarantine Buddy in the basement with food and his toys.

"A toast." Jack stood and lifted his glass. Giving the toast was part of his duty as his father's best man. "To my father and his new bride, congratulations. May you have many years of joy together. May your friends and family ever be supportive and loving, and may God richly bless the covenant bond you sealed today. We love you!"

Liz stood and lifted her glass. It was part of her duty as her mother's matron of honor. "To my mother and her new husband, congratulations. May God bless the union His love enabled. May you ever feel secure and blessed in your love for one another. May joy greet you each morning and lie down with you each night. We love you!"

Those gathered applauded then applied themselves to the wonderful food in front of them. Liz found it hard to get anything down, so instead, she watched her mom. Liz hadn't seen Nancy look this happy in years. She wore a dress the color of old lace but far more contemporary in its cut and style. She looked beautiful. Lloyd, wearing a black European-cut suit looked very handsome, especially with his tall, slender build and mane of white hair. For a moment, Liz had trouble breathing because she was so happy. Looking up at Jack, she whispered, "I love you, and I love them, and I love our daughter, and our friends, and our families, and I'm so happy I can't stand it." Tears spilled down her cheeks. "What did I do to deserve all this goodness?"

Gently wiping the moisture from his wife's face, Jack put his arm around her shoulders. "Love, neither of us did anything to deserve this. It's a gift from our great God. Just breathe and let's celebrate the miracle of today with our parents."

# CHAPTER 12

## ONE HECK OF A DAY

Freshly showered, Jack emerged from the bathroom and sat on the bed next to Liz. "Wake up, love. It's a beautiful February morning. The sun's shining, and it's above freezing."

Liz opened one eye and frowned. "If I'd wanted a cheerful weather report at this hour of the morning, I'd have married Willard Scott or whoever took his place." She groaned and sat up. "I'm sorry, Jack, I don't…"

A look that Jack recognized crossed Liz's face, and he quickly moved, freeing her to jump out of bed and run for the bathroom. He followed her and crouched by her side as she bent over the stool. Nothing much came up because nothing was in her stomach, but she still gagged violently to bring up each mouthful of bile. Soaking a towel in cold water, Jack held it to her forehead. "Easy, don't fight it."

When Liz finished, Jack held out a paper cupful of mouthwash, watched as she swished and spat, then walked her back to bed. "What do you want to take for it, Liz?"

"Until I get something in my stomach, just aspirin." She swallowed hard and sank back against her pillow. "And could you bring me an ice pack, please? Is Gabby up?"

Jack squeezed her hand then got to his feet. "Not yet, and when she does get up, I'll take care of her, Liz. Just close your eyes and lie still." He knew this migraine was bad because his normally talkative wife didn't say a word but instead silently followed his instructions.

He returned quickly and put the ice pack into Liz's hand, knowing she preferred to position it herself. He set a glass of water along with two aspirin on the night table. "Liz, when you're ready to sit up, the aspirin are on your nightstand."

Opening her eyes, Liz reached for the meds, and Jack supported her as she lifted her head from the pillow. She'd no more than swallowed when she shook her head and sat up, swinging her legs over the edge of the bed. Seeing her expression, Jack handed her the plastic bucket he'd brought with him. She glanced at him gratefully before getting sick all over again, throwing up the water and medicine she'd just taken.

Jack could see the pain in her face and said, "Liz, I'd like to try that IV aspirin that a researcher friend at UC-San Francisco sent me. They've had very good luck with this treatment in Europe, and Stan's research study is promising, but big pharma here in the US is lobbying against its use in the States because there's no money in it. All the studies I've read, and there've been many, show it to be safe and effective with very few side effects. Otherwise, I wouldn't even suggest it. The only other choice we have with a migraine this bad is to go into the ER, and you know what they'll do. I know how much you hate narcs, so you tell me. Do we try the IV aspirin here, or shall I pack up Gabby and take you to the hospital?"

"Let's try the new stuff," Liz whispered. "We can always go to the hospital later if it doesn't work."

It took a few minutes for Jack to start the IV, and Liz just rested with her eyes closed and the ice pack on her head. After finishing, Jack thought of one more thing he could try to ease her pain. He got a tube from the refrigerator, and after squeezing some of the cool herbal gel on his fingers, he massaged her temples lightly, knowing that even his gentle touch could be causing her pain. "How does this feel, Liz?"

Liz took a deep breath. "Good," she put her hand over his, "thank you. I think I'm feeling…"

"Is Mama Liz sick?" Gabby ran into the room and jumped up on the bed, looking at Liz with fear in her eyes.

Wiping his hands on a towel, Jack lifted Gabby into his lap. "Mama Liz has a bad headache." When Gabby looked at him, clearly confused, he said, "uh, la jaqueca." He pointed to Liz's forehead. "Mama, la jaqueca."

When Gabby's look of confusion deepened, Liz took her hand. "Me duele mucho la cabeza pero estoy bien."

"Mama is okay, Papa Jack, don't worry," Gabby said reassuringly and patted Jack's cheek.

Jack was confused. "What did you tell her? Was I wrong in my translation?"

To Jack's surprise, Liz sat up and moved Gabby into her lap. Taking his hand, she explained, "Honey, you weren't wrong. La jaqueca is the clinical term that Hispanic physicians use to describe migraine headaches. Since Gabby didn't seem familiar with the word, I simply translated how I'm feeling into five-year-old parlance and told her that I have a bad headache, but I'm okay."

"Mama is okay," Gabby repeated.

"It appears we have a budding physician in the house," Liz said then looked at Jack with gratitude in her eyes. "Jack, honey, I think that Europe's way ahead of us on this one. I feel a lot better. Thank you. Um, since I'm not part of your friend's research study, did you break any laws giving me this stuff?"

Jack shrugged his shoulders. "I may be skirting an ethics violation, but no, aspirin in any form is legal in the US. It's more a matter of giving you a drug formulation that hasn't been through the FDA approval process, and of course, there's the small matter of treating my own wife."

"What you gave me really helped, so thank you. I won't say anything."

Jack smiled at Liz's comment, then asked her, "How do you feel apart from your head? Any nausea?"

Liz nodded. "A little, but it's a whole lot better than it was earlier."

"I gave you a dose of an anti-nausea medication too. I'd hoped this would be the result."

"How long before I can get up?"

"About the same amount of time as it will take me to get this young lady," Jack swept Gabby into his arms and twirled her around, smiling at her laughter, "her breakfast." He bent over and kissed Liz. "I'll be back in a few minutes. Rest some more if you can."

Liz surprised Jack by joining him and Gabby at the table. After he removed the needle from her arm, Liz drank a cup of tea with milk in it to be social while Gabby and Jack ate their breakfasts. Liz took Jack's hand. "Thank you for your care this morning, honey."

Jack smiled broadly. "You're welcome. I love spending time with my girls. I'm so glad to see you looking better. I was worried and…"

Jack stopped talking when his cell phone buzzed. Although they normally didn't answer calls during mealtimes, Jack looked up at Liz. "It's Dan, excuse me." Getting up from the table, Jack listened intently, asked several questions, then said, "Okay, I'll be ready," before he hung up. He looked at Liz worriedly. "Our team just got called out. A solo camper missed his take-out time last night, and no one's heard from him. Dan's flying over to pick me up, but I hate to leave you like this. Should I call him back and pull Zach instead? He's off today."

Liz stood up, bracing herself on the back of the chair. "No, Jack, go ahead. Gabby and I will be fine, and I promise to take it easy." Sinking back into her chair, Liz watched her husband disappear into the bedroom and wished things were different. The truth was, she felt better but a long way from well. Thankfully, both her tea and the medications Jack had given her were still in her system. Rubbing her brow, she prayed that Gabby would be in a cooperative mood today because she wasn't certain she could handle a cranky five-year-old and a migraine at the same time. She closed her eyes, trying to relax while she had a window of opportunity.

"Liz, why don't you let me call Zach? You don't look so good," Jack said as he sat down beside her, now dressed for the outdoors.

Liz squeezed his hand gently. "Why don't you quit worrying and focus on your rescue? I don't feel great, but I am lots better, thanks to you. Gabs and I will be fine, and we'll be praying for you, the team, and the guy you're trying to find."

As it turned out, Dan must have heard something in Jack's tone because when he set the chopper down in the cleared area, Beth jumped out and waved. When she got to the house, she patted Jack's shoulder and hugged Liz and Gabby. "Hi, I thought I might provide some company around here while the guys are out, so I pulled my manager in a couple of hours early to help with the breakfast crowd, and here I am."

Both Jack and Liz breathed deep sighs of relief and Liz responded, "Thanks, Beth, from all of us. It's been a migraine kind of morning, and I can use all the help I can get." Kissing Jack, Liz gave him a gentle shove. "Go on, Dr. Worrywart, Dan's waiting, and thanks to Tia Beth, Gabby and I both have a babysitter."

<hr />

Liz and Gabby were down for late-morning naps when the doorbell rang. Beth hurried to get it before it rang again and woke up both of her charges. Opening the door, she saw a woman about her own age standing there who looked vaguely familiar. Smiling, she said, "Hello."

"Hello, are Dr. and Ms. Lockwood at home? I'd like to speak with them."

"Ms. Lockwood is home, but she's resting. Can I take a message?"

"My name is Ann Nolan, and I'm from Cook County Social Services. It's really rather important that I speak with Ms. Lockwood."

Beth nodded. "Of course, come in. I'll go get..."

"Ann?" Liz walked toward the door looking sleepy and a bit confused. When she reached them, she held out her hand to Ann. "Hello. What, um, what can I do for you?"

<hr />

It was early afternoon when the sound of a car marked the men's return from the wilderness. Their short time out and the fact that they were driving meant either very good news or very bad news for the person they'd gone to find. When Jack came through the door, Liz got to her feet and hugged her husband. "How did it go?"

Jack snorted. "Well, we found the guy."

Looking at Jack, Liz tried to figure out the reason for the scowl on his face. "Okay, that's good news. Was he alive?"

"Yes, he was alive. He was in his sleeping bag, in his tent, snoring away, and drunk as the proverbial skunk. Once we managed to wake him up, he was really confused because he thought he wasn't supposed to be out until tomorrow. He didn't realize that today was tomorrow. Anyway, we brought him back to EBCH so they could check him out and give him a couple of aspirin for his wicked hangover. He'll have another headache to deal with when he gets our bill."

Beth looked surprised. "I didn't think you charged for your services."

"Typically we don't," Jack said, "but once the powers that be in the federal government get wind of the imbecilic reason for calling us out, they won't hesitate to teach a lesson that young man will never forget. He's very lucky that it's a balmy thirty-five degrees outside and that it didn't get really cold last night. Alcohol and hypothermia don't mix." He looked at Liz closely. "How are you, love? You look a little pale. I assume our daughter is napping?"

"Actually, your daughter is wide awake and, with your permission, is going to come for a sleepover at our place," Dan spoke up, coming back into the room with Gabby in one arm and her overnight bag over his shoulder.

Confused, Jack asked, "Why? We both really appreciate Beth staying here while the team went out, but I'm home now, and Liz seems to be feeling better."

Beth laid her hand on Jack's arm. "This is kind of important, trust me. Besides, Gabby wants to come and play with Buddy, don't you?"

Gabby clapped and rooted around in Dan's arms. "Yea! Perro Buddy. I wanna play with the perro! Please, Papa Jack! Lemme go to Tia Beth's, please?"

Jack looked at Liz helplessly. "What do you think?"

Liz cleared her throat, looked at Beth who nodded, and said, "I think we should let her go with them and just figure out something really nice to do for her aunt and uncle once today is over. We need to talk about something, and it would be better not to have the munchkin around, if you catch my drift."

Jack didn't catch her drift, exactly, but he turned to Dan and Beth and said, "Okay, thank you both so much. We owe you."

Dan grinned. "No, you don't. We love having Gabby, and so does Buddy. However, neither of us would object to a jambalaya dinner at your place. We need a fix of Liz's Cajun cooking."

"You got it." Jack kissed Gabby on the cheek. "Goodbye, my girl. and have fun. Be good for Dan and Beth. We'll see you tomorrow."

"Bye, Papa, bye, Mama." She patted Liz's cheek. "Don't worry about nuffin."

After watching the trio drive away, Jack turned and looked at Liz. "So what was that all about?" He grinned. "Was 'we need to talk' code for you're feeling better and want time alone with me?"

Liz giggled as she led Jack into the living room and pushed him down onto the sofa. "Yes, I want time alone with you, but it's not what you're thinking. Sorry." Sitting down beside him, she took his hand. "We had a visitor today, and you're not going to believe who it was."

"Who?" Jack asked curiously.

"Ann Nolan."

"Social services?" A worried look appeared in Jack's eyes. "What happened? Did something go wrong with our paperwork, did we get a court date, or are they going to try to take Gabby away from us for some reason?"

"Jack, honey, everything's fine with Gabby," Liz assured him. "Ann's not even involved in her case. She's Cook County, not St. Louis County, you know that. And yes, actually, we do have a court date. We got the notification today. Gabby will formally become a Lockwood in a week's time, but that didn't have anything to do with Ann's visit."

Jack smiled in relief. "Thank God, so out with it, wife. What did Ann want? Did she have an update on the boys?"

"Um, yes, you could say that." Liz twisted her hands nervously. "She wants to know if we'd still be willing to adopt the boys together. No, that's not exactly true. She asked if we'd be willing to take in the boys as emergency foster parents sometime in the next couple of days. Then she asked if we'd still be interested in adopting them together. Apparently, things with the Albertsons went sour very fast. The mom had trouble balancing her fibro issues with the needs of an infant. The dad blew through his personal time off and FMLA[4] didn't apply because the mother refused traditional medical treatment in favor of more holistic approaches. More importantly, the dad refused to apply for religious reasons—don't ask me because I have no idea. Anyways, his company finally offered him a choice between coming to work on a regular basis or losing his job. They were talking about returning custody of the baby to the state when Pete overheard them and had a meltdown. After that, he began running away—taking the baby with him. In the end, they surrendered custody of both boys. I feel so badly for everyone concerned in this."

Jack was silent for a few moments, then he took Liz's hands. "Tell me what you're thinking."

"I'm thinking we should foster the boys so they don't end up in yet another temporary home. At least they know us."

"Agreed, and what about adopting them?"

Liz's eyes brimmed with tears. "Jack, I don't know. The same thing that happened to the Albertsons could happen to us. Look at this morning. You were talking about not going on the run and staying home because I had a migraine. There aren't that many of you in the BWSRU, so what happens when Zach or one of the other doctors decide they've had enough of filling in for you? And we only have one child. How much worse might it be with three, especially when one of them is an angsty sixteen-year-old and another is an infant approaching toddlerhood?"

---

[4] The Family and Medical Leave Act of 1993 (FMLA) is a US law requiring covered employers to provide employees with job-protected and unpaid leave for qualified medical and family reasons.

Jack hugged Liz and prayed silently for wisdom. Her point was valid, but he also knew that they were in a much different situation than the boys' former adoptive parents. That was the advantage of being older, he thought wryly, they were financially stable and possibilities existed for them that didn't exist for the other couple. Watching Liz rub her forehead, a pained expression on her face, Jack asked, "Is this really a good time to talk, Liz? I can see you're still in a lot of pain. Would it be better to give you another dose of the IV aspirin, let you sleep for a bit, and then talk?"

"I'm fine!" Liz snapped. "And we need to talk about this now. There's no time."

Jack looked into her eyes. "Are you really fine?"

Liz opened her mouth then closed it again, lowering her gaze. "No."

"Then there's time for talking after you've rested for a while. We'll get Ann an answer by tomorrow morning, just as you promised. We've got all afternoon and evening, and frankly, I could use a nap and time to think about what you've told me." They stood up, and Jack put his arm around Liz, leading her into their bedroom. After medicating her, he lay down beside her and pulled her close. "Try to sleep, please."

⌒⌒

Liz woke later that afternoon to find the bed empty. Jack was in the library on his knees, his Bible open in front of him. She joined him there, putting her arm around his waist. Together, they prayed for wisdom and for God to show them the path ahead. When they got to their feet, Jack hugged Liz close, and they stood there for long moments, content to be holding one another. Kissing her on the top of her head, he asked, "How are you feeling?"

"Better," Liz answered. "Shall we make a pizza and talk?"

One of the things they loved to cook together was pizza. While Liz made the crust, roasted the garlic, and seasoned the sauce, Jack shredded the mozzarella and chopped the ham, chicken, and green olives that were their favorite toppings. Once the completed pizza was in the oven, Jack poured them each a glass of flavored seltzer while Liz made a salad. A few minutes later, they sat down together at the table.

While they missed Gabby and her chatter, they were grateful to Dan and Beth for giving them this window of quiet to talk about what the future held. After Jack prayed for their meal, he looked up. "This looks and smells wonderful, but before I can manage a bite, I'd really like to know what you're thinking about the boys, Liz."

Liz nodded. "Okay, I'm hungry, but first, thank you for having the wisdom to postpone this discussion until after I got some rest. The IV aspirin is really effective for me, and I feel much better than before. As for the boys, I want to take them, on one, actually two, conditions. First, I want to make certain that we're financially able to do this and to see to those kids' futures in our current situation, and that includes my health. Second, I can't watch social services take them away from us again, so I want to be sure that Ann understands that we're taking them on the condition that our adoption papers are put through immediately." She bit into her slice of pizza. "Yum! we've outdone ourselves, husband."

Jack smiled, both at Liz's response to his question and because she had a string of cheese hanging down over her chin. He scooped it onto his fingertips then into his mouth. "Mmm, you're right." He bit into his own slice, chewed, and swallowed before responding to her. "Liz, I know you worry when I call off and pull a replacement for the BWSR runs when you're not feeling well. However, the reality is, I do it far less frequently than anyone else on our teams, and that includes Dan. Mostly that's because you don't let me get away with it.

"Irrespective of that, we could give those boys and Gabby the financial security they deserve and retire tomorrow if we wanted to do so. I work because I love my work, and I know it's the same for you. It would also be better financially if we could wait to retire until we both hit the fifty-nine-and-a-half-year-old mark because of taxes. We're in good financial condition to do this—our home and property are paid for, we have over a year's worth of income in the bank, we have both liquid and nonliquid investments, and the money for the adoptions is still set aside in a special account. Finally, both of us have retirement funds that should, barring a disaster, see us through until we're closing in on one hundred and still give the kids a great start in life. If, God forbid, something happens to me, you won't have to worry, and neither will the kids. And the same is true if something happens to you," Jack hugged her close, "but please don't let that happen."

Liz pulled away, frowning. "Jack, most of that money is yours, this property is yours, and…"

Jack rested a finger on her lips. "Where is this coming from, Liz? We sold your house, and that money is part of the money I'm talking about. Your retirement savings are part of the money I'm talking about, but apart from all that, when we married, we agreed that nothing was to be 'yours' or 'mine' but rather ours. This property you speak of is in both our names, you are the beneficiary or co-owner on every account that was originally mine, and it is the same for me with accounts that belonged to you. All of it is for our family. Please tell me you understand that."

Liz blushed and looked down. "I do. I'm not even sure why I said what I did. I'm sorry."

Looking at her seriously, Jack said, "I love you. Are you ready to call Ann after we finish eating, or should we give it until morning?"

# CHAPTER 13

## ABUNDANT GRACE

The moment they negotiated the last stair, Jack picked Liz up in his arms and whirled her around the great room. Ignoring her startled gasp, he pinned her high against a wall, slowly raised her arms above her head with one hand and proceeded to kiss her breathless. Laughingly, he whispered, "They're ours, Liz. We're a legal family at last. Thank you for all your hard work to make this happen. I never imagined it could be this good. I love you so much."

Hanging in midair, supported only by his arms and the wall at her back, Liz cupped his face in her hands and kissed him the way he'd kissed her. "I love you too, Jack. Thank you for all you did to make this happen in the midst of the rescue runs, the hospital, and of course, caring for our kids and me."

Trusting Jack completely, Liz leaned forward and wrapped her arms around his neck, just relishing the feel of his body against hers. Closing her eyes, she replayed their mid-May morning at the courthouse and the joy and relief in everyone's expressions when the judge made their relationship with the boys permanent. Pete, Luke, and Gabby were now all officially Lockwoods. Even Pete, who'd been more withdrawn since coming to live with them again, had laughed aloud when they all embraced each other in a family hug right there in the courtroom. Gabby jumped and clapped as Pete's arms went around her. Luke, confused by all the noise, had pitched a fit, but his cries just added to the moment. They'd all gone out to lunch at Dan and Beth's coffee shop before coming home, putting the young ones down for a nap, and seeing Pete settled with his studies upstairs. He was in the midst of finals, and to get him to study after the excitement of the morning, they'd promised him something special that Jack would be sharing with him at dinner. It had been a wonderful day so far.

Liz's thoughts splintered as Jack turned his head and kissed her neck. Suddenly, a nap was the last thing on her mind as she squirmed in his arms, trying to touch him like he was touching her. "Put me down so I can…"

"Dr. Jack, Liz," Pete stood on the stairway, staring at them, "uh, can you help me? I don't get some of this stuff." He held up his pre-calculus book.

Jack didn't drop Liz, and she managed to keep her cool as he set her down. "Sure, Pete. Bring it here." She led the way into the dining room. "Jack," she waited until he looked at her, "come on, math is more your thing than mine. I'll get dinner going while you help Pete, okay?"

As she started the vegetable mix for the quesadillas they were having for dinner, Liz took a deep breath and chastised herself for getting a bit carried away. She said as much to Jack after he finished with Pete and came in to help her with dinner. He smiled and kissed her cheek on his way by with the milk. "I know, and I'm sorry. I shouldn't have started something like that at this time of day in the middle of the living room. It's just that, well, you're," he winked at her, "irresistible."

Liz patted Jack on his hindquarters. "So are you, but I don't want our kids to need therapy after they leave our nest."

When Jack returned after filling their glasses with seltzer and the kid's glasses with milk, he looked at Liz seriously. "I understand what you're saying, and I know there are things that should remain private between the two of us. However, I do think that showing our children what a good marriage relationship looks like, including at least a part of the physical side, is important. I'm talking about demonstrating touch in a context where it's not used as a weapon between spouses or between parents and children. That's as much a part of learning to love as anything else. Given Pete's experience with Mary and her father and the circumstances of Luke's conception, I think it's really important to show that the language of love includes gentle, appropriate, and fun touch."

Liz hugged Jack so hard her arms hurt. "You're amazing, you know that? I was just kidding with you before because this isn't the first time Pete's walked in on us like that. Honestly, I never thought about touch the way you just described it. I love our physical relationship but didn't think much about it in a teaching sense. I know you're not advocating inviting the kids into our bedroom, but thank you for helping me to see the value in sharing our love of touch with them."

Smiling, Jack kissed Liz on the forehead and just stood holding her, reaching behind her every now and again to stir the veggies. They stayed like that until Pete came downstairs. He looked at them and asked, "Is it time for dinner? Dr. Jack said about fifteen minutes."

Liz gently shoved Jack out of the way. "Move it, hon, so I can put these things together. Why don't the two of you go and get Gabby washed up and to the table? If Luke's still sleeping, let him be until we're finished eating, then I'll feed him."

It was late by the time Jack and Liz crawled into bed that night. The events of the day had them both wired. She was reading when he came to bed, carrying a sheaf of papers. "Do you have a minute, Liz? I have a project that I've been waiting to share with you until we finalized the adoptions."

Liz put her book on the nightstand and waved at the papers in Jack's hand. "Sure, what are those?"

"When I gave you the tour of the house, do you remember me mentioning Mike Miller?"

"Your architect friend in Duluth? Yeah. He did a great job with this place."

"When the boys came home last February and we filed for adoption, I talked with Mike because we don't have enough bedrooms on the first floor of the house to accommodate our kids. I don't want Gabby upstairs until she gets a little older and," Jack grinned, "I don't want Luke sleeping in our room much longer, for obvious reasons." He handed her the plans. "Here's what Mike came up with, and I think it looks pretty good. What do you think?"

Liz studied the designs. Mike had removed part of a wall in the great room and extended the house out to the east. On one side of the newly created hallway, there were spacious bedrooms for Luke and Gabby, each with a generously sized closet. Mike had also moved the main bath for the first floor to a location between the two bedrooms. It had a built-in linen storage cupboard and a bathtub/shower combination for ease in bathing the kids. On the other side of the hallway were two guest rooms, each with a walk-in closet and a full bath. At the far end of the addition was a large laundry room with windows overlooking the side yard. "This looks great," she said enthusiastically, "and we'll even have room for guests in the main house. But what about Pete? Will we use one of the guest rooms for him?"

Jack shook his head. "When Mike started these plans, I asked Pete where he'd like his bedroom to be, and he told me he wanted to stay upstairs. I think he kind of likes the privacy."

"Okay. Are we going to keep the study up there or move it back to Gabby's space when she moves into her new room?"

"I was thinking that room could become a dedicated family library. That way, the kids have a screen-free place to study and read. We would keep our office upstairs since that room's a bit smaller. In addition to several adult-sized chairs, Mike has some ideas for kid-friendly fixtures for the downstairs library. That way, Gabby and Luke will feel like they've got a special place designed just for them."

Liz's face lit up with excitement. "That would be wonderful. Maybe we could put an adult-sized table in there, too, so we can use it as a game room."

Jack smiled. "That's a great idea. Mike would like to meet with us in the next few days to discuss a renovation schedule and finishes. Does that work for you?"

A tiny furrow appeared between Liz's eyes. "You're comfortable spending the money to do this?"

Jack took the plans from her hands and hugged her close. "Yes, I am. Do you have other concerns or comments? It will be a little chaotic around here over the summer if we do this."

Liz kissed him. "Make our appointment with Mike. For four new bedrooms, more storage, and that gorgeous laundry room, I can live with a little chaos. Thank you for thinking of the little ones and their aging mom who doesn't want to climb stairs fifty times a day."

"Wow, Uncle Dan, do you mean it? Really? Is it okay, Dr. Jack?"

Jack smiled and saluted from the back seat of the helicopter. "Sure, Captain Pete." Watching as Dan showed the teenager how to manipulate the control stick, Jack privately wondered what painful method of death Liz was going to choose for him when she found out about this. Seeing the look on his son's face as he took control of the aircraft eased Jack's fear just a bit. All in all, it was a fair exchange, and for a few minutes anyway, he was glad that Liz was at home with Gabby and Luke.

It had been Liz's choice to stay home, and to her credit, it wasn't her dislike of helicopters that held her back but rather her desire to give Jack and Pete some bonding time. Pete had kept his promise to study hard for finals, had done exceedingly well in school despite the upheavals in his personal life, and this trip was his reward. He was riding along with Jack on the training weekend for the BWSR units. Jack was looking forward to introducing his son to his coworkers and the search and rescue team functions.

When they arrived at the staging area, Pete jumped down from the helicopter and threw his arms around Dan. "Thanks, Uncle Dan." Then he turned to Jack. "Thanks, Dad. That was awesome." Realizing what he'd called Jack, Pete looked a little uncomfortable. "Uh, I mean, Dr. Jack."

Slinging his arm around Pete's shoulder, Jack said, "Pete, whatever you're comfortable calling me is fine. I like Dr. Jack, Jack's fine, and I really like Dad too, but I know you had a dad who was a pretty special guy. I'm not trying to take his place. I just want to be here for you since he can't be anymore."

Pete leaned into him. "Thanks, um, Dad. It just feels right to say that, you know?"

The warmth in Jack's heart stayed with him all through setting up camp, introducing his son to his coworkers, and through dinner. It even lasted through bedtime when he and Pete crawled into their sleeping bags. They were talking about the day, about Pete's grades, and about how happy he was to be back with the Lockwoods. Then Pete sat up and said, "Dad, can I ask you something? It's kinda personal."

Jack nodded. "You can ask me anything you want to, Pete, anytime."

"Well, uh, it's about Liz. Or about you and Liz."

Jack nodded, feeling a niggle of discomfort. "Okay, what's your question?"

"You really love Liz, don't you?"

Maybe this isn't going to be so bad, Jack thought. "Yes, I do. She holds my heart."

Pete nodded. "Okay, so remember that night I came into your room without knocking? It was right after you took Luke and me in the first time."

Jack would probably never forget that night, so he nodded. "Yes, I remember it. It was a tough time for you."

"Yeah, it was. Um, were you and Liz having sex when I came in?"

Fortunately, Jack remembered being sixteen and the one-track mind it tended to cause in adolescent males. He'd long ago decided that if he ever had children, he was going to be honest and not turn something that was beautiful into embarrassed stammering. Looking at Pete, Jack smiled. "Yes, we were, but you're wrong about something."

"What? It sure looked like that's what you were doing."

"Liz and I never have sex. We make love to one another."

Pete smirked. "It's the same thing."

"No, it's not, Pete, and that's something a lot of people don't understand. When I touch Liz and when she touches me, it's always in love. Don't get me wrong. Our physical relationship isn't always serious, but it's something we always do in love."

"What do you mean it's not always serious?"

"We have a lot of fun when we make love."

"Is that what you were doing when I came downstairs to get help with my precalc final? You were holding her against the wall, and I was scared that you were hurting her. Then she laughed."

"See, I told you we have fun."

"But what you were doing wasn't sex or making love."

Jack reached out and squeezed Pete's shoulder. "I hope I can convince you that you're wrong. Every single time I touch Liz, I'm making love to her. Every time she looks at me with love in her beautiful eyes, she's making love to me. Sometimes our bodies are joined, and sometimes they're not. Yet every single time is special and every time builds our love for each other."

"But you guys are old. Sorry. I thought that old people didn't do it." Pete looked at Jack sheepishly.

Grinning, Jack acknowledged, "We're a lot older than you, but lovemaking doesn't end when you grow older, at least I sure hope it doesn't. It transforms into something even more wonderful. I will tell you something though. I was a little worried when I married Liz. I was fifty years old. It had been a long time since I'd been with anyone in that way, and I wondered if it would be the same or if my body or my, uh, stamina would somehow disappoint her. That didn't happen. From that first night, the physical part of our marriage bond was something beyond my experience and more wonderful than I ever thought possible. It still is."

"You guys, uh, waited until you got married?"

Jack laughed out loud. "Yes, we did, Pete. It wasn't easy even though there wasn't a lot of waiting to do. It was only a little over a month from the time we met until we got married."

"A month? You're kidding?"

"No, I knew right away, and I think Liz did too. Someday we'll tell you the whole story, but it was important to both of us to wait.

Sex outside the relationship God designed for it is a shallow experience. He created the sex act to be the deepest, richest communication you can have with another human being. It's the only time that you and the woman you're with are one person, and it's the only act in all creation in which you can form another human being that's half you, half your wife, and yet a unique God-created being. That's a miracle."

"That's not how it worked with Mary." Pete looked sad.

Jack felt the same way Pete looked. "As with every other part of God's design, Satan tries to turn lovemaking into something either profoundly shallow or profoundly evil. Mary's dad used her in a horrific way, but when you look at Luke, do you see a horror or a miracle? You and Mary were very courageous in your decision to keep him and raise him as your own. Why did you do that rather than get an abortion?"

"It just seemed wrong to both of us even though that's what my uncle wanted us to do. It wasn't Luke's fault that Mary's dad raped her."

"Exactly. Can I ask you something, Pete?"

"I guess so."

"Did you ever make love to Mary? You thought you were married. Did you ever consummate that marriage?"

Pete nodded, looking uncomfortable. "Yeah, a couple of times before she got really big."

"When you did that with her and after what we've talked about tonight, did you have sex with Mary, or did you make love to her?"

"No, Dad, I promise I made love to her. She was my wife, at least we thought she was, and I still miss her so much. There's never been anyone else, I swear."

Leaning forward, Jack looked straight into Pete's eyes. "Then do you understand what Liz and I were doing that night you walked in on us? Do you understand what I'm telling her every time I look at her with love in my eyes and every time I hold her in my arms?"

Pete nodded without saying anything. He slid into his sleeping bag. It was a long time before he responded. "Thanks, Dad. Nobody's ever explained it that way before. Mom's lucky to have you."

"And I'm blessed to have her, Pete. God's been so good to us, and we work hard to honor His gift. Is there anything else you want to talk about before we go to sleep?"

"Are you gonna stay here all night with me?"

"I am. You're my tent mate for the whole weekend. We'll be getting up when Dan announces breakfast. Then we have a busy day ahead of us. I'm glad you're here with me, and I love you."

"I love you too, g'night."

When Dan called reveille by banging on pots and singing,

*Oh, how I hate to get up in the morning,*
*Oh, how I'd love to remain in bed;*
*For the hardest blow of all, is to hear the bugler call;*
*you've got to get up, you've got to get up, you've got to*
*get up this morning!*

Jack wiped his eyes, yawned, shook Pete's shoulder, and sang,

*Some day I'm going to murder the bugler,*
*Some day they're going to find him dead;*
*I'll amputate his reveille, and step upon it heavily,*
*And spend the rest of my life in bed.*[iv]

Pete watched as Jack pulled on his pants and shirt and then unzipped the tent fly. Seeing the dim, predawn light outside, Pete mumbled, "You guys are crazy." He pulled the sleeping bag over his head and rolled over, his back facing Jack.

Jack nudged him with a stockinged foot. "C'mon, you said you wanted to see what Dan and I do for a living. Well, this is it."

"Leave me alone," Pete groaned.

Jack shook his head sadly. "Okay, you give me no choice." Sticking his head outside, Jack bellowed, "Hey, we've got a slug-a-bed here. I require some assistance."

Just a bit later, Pete sat by the campfire, shivering in his underwear. Three men, including Dan, had appeared in their tent, picked him up bodily, stripped his sleeping bag away, and deposited him on a campstool. Jack came up a few minutes later and dumped his clothes in a pile next to him. "Good morning, sunshine. You might want to put those on," he waved at the pile, "before you freeze. Breakfast is on in ten."

---

"Honest, Mom, that's what they did, dragged me out of the tent in my underwear. The sun wasn't even up yet. Uncle Dan was singing this weird song about some bugler guy the whole time. And then they all just walked away, doing stuff like nothing happened." Pete still sounded outraged. "I tried to go back in the tent, but Dad collapsed one of the poles so I couldn't get in, and when I asked him to help me put it back up, he wouldn't. He just handed me my pants again and said, 'If you want breakfast, Son, you'd better get dressed. Otherwise, you're going to be starving as well as freezing. Lunch is a long way off.' I mean, like he really was going to let me starve."

"Maybe not starve, but it would have been a long wait for lunch," Liz said, trying not to laugh.

"He wouldn't have done that, would he?"

Liz shrugged. "The Thanksgiving after we met, he threatened to make me walk back into town after," she saw Jack enter the room out of the corner of her eye, "losing an argument."

"I did not lose that argument. I merely decided to take the high road." Jack grinned and sat down. "And if you recall, I made it worth your while to stay with me rather than walk back into Ely."

Liz took Jack's hand and blushed scarlet. "Yes, you did, but you might want to explain how you made it worth my while before Pete, um, gets the wrong idea."

"I kissed Liz for the first time that night," Jack explained to Pete, his eyes on his wife, "and after that, I couldn't even remember what we were arguing about."

Pete's eyes moved from Jack, to Liz, and back to Jack. "You're making love to Mom, aren't you, Dad?"

Liz put her face in her hands. Jack just smiled and nodded. "You got it, Pete."

~~~

Crawling into bed next to Jack, Liz sat back against the head-board and shook her husband fully awake. "We need to talk!" she exclaimed. When he sat up and looked at her, she continued, "It certainly sounds like you and Pete had quite a time this weekend. I suppose I should be grateful that having to get up at zero-dark-thirty was the top headline rather than our love life. Actually, getting up early wasn't the top headline either, and to that point you, my darling, are in big trouble."

Jack gave her his best "who me" look and said, "What did I do?"

"It seems as though our son liked flying Dan's helicopter so much that he's asked his esteemed uncle to give him lessons." Liz pulled out a printed sheet of paper. "Before you deny it, I have the evidence right here. This," she waved it in front of Jack, "is a permission slip already bearing your signature, for aforementioned flying lessons. As it happens, they need my signature too because Pete is underage. Oh," she smacked Jack's shoulder, "I want so badly to be mad at you right now. When will you learn we're supposed to talk about these things before you open your mouth?"

"You mean you're not mad?" Jack eyed her hopefully.

Liz sighed morosely. "Not even close. I've never seen Pete so effusive over anything as he was over your trip, not even the day we finalized his adoption. If I'm any judge, our son had the time of his life with you last weekend. He came back determined to go to medical school so he can be on a search and rescue team, telling me how much he learned from you about how to treat a woman, and calling us 'mom' and 'dad.' I mean, how can I be mad about a few flying lessons when he was so thrilled?" Her eyes beginning to glow, Liz caressed Jack's cheek. "I love you, so much. Thank you for taking him with you and for talking with him. He's a different kid than he was a week ago."

Jack kissed Liz's palm. "Look, I'm sorry about the flying lessons. It's just that Dan let Pete take the stick for a little while on our way to the staging area, and he was so excited. I trust Dan with my life, and it's not really his fault that Pete's uncle decided to use us for target practice a year ago. I'll go up with them for every lesson if you want me to."

Liz giggled. "A fat lot of good you'll do unless Dan's giving you flying lessons too."

Jack didn't answer, but his cheeks slowly reddened.

Putting her fingertip under Jack's chin, Liz slowly tilted his head up until his eyes met hers. "Jack, do you have something to tell me?"

"Uh, let's just say Dan gave me a few pointers. We're in the chopper together a lot, and he felt that it would be a good idea if I understood the rudiments, just in case."

"How close are you to having your helicopter pilot's license, Jack?" Liz asked archly.

"I got it almost a year ago, after the crash," Jack confessed. "Guess you're mad now, huh?"

Liz rubbed her forehead with a tired sigh. "I really, really, really wish I could say yes. You don't know how badly I wish I could say yes." She opened her eyes and looked up at him. "Anything else you want to tell me? You seem to be on a roll."

"Well, there's one other thing I guess you should know."

"Okay, out with it." Liz looked as though she were bracing herself.

"I am deeply, passionately, and forever in love with you, Elizabeth Lockwood," Jack said, "and I'm sorry for all the surprises. It was one of those weekends."

"It must have been, judging from the breadth of subject matter," Liz muttered before looking at Jack, "you and Pete seem to have covered. And I'm deeply, passionately, and forever in love with you too, Jack Lockwood. However, it may be a very long time before we get frisky again. In fact, I'm not certain forever is going to be long enough."

Jack's forehead wrinkled. "You are mad."

"No, but I can't say I'm thrilled about Pete watching us, looking for signs that we are, or have been, or will be making love. What did you tell him, anyway?"

After Jack explained, Liz rested her head on his shoulder. "What a lesson you taught. I'm sorry for ever doubting you."

"When it comes to Gabby, it's your turn." Jack put his arms around Liz and kissed her. "So does all this mean that the possibility of frisky behavior has returned to this household? I really missed you last weekend."

# CHAPTER 14

## VACATION

"Gabriela Rose Lockwood, come back here this instant!" Liz ran around the bed and chased her daughter into the great room.

Jack intercepted Gabby and swung her up into his arms. "Gabby girl, it sounds as though you're in a good bit of trouble with your mama." He removed several of his t-shirts from Gabby's hand. "Are you helping Mama pack?"

"Helping Mama unpack is more like it." Taking the t-shirts from Jack, Liz sighed. "I didn't realize until she took off that she was taking things out of the suitcase I'd finished packing just as fast as I was putting more into our second suitcase."

Liz gave the little girl a kiss on the cheek. "I love you, Gabs, but you are a handful sometimes."

Gabby nodded. "Yep, but I'm a good handful, right, Mama?"

Jack laughed. "She's sure got her mother's talent for negotiation." Looking at Liz, he said, "I'll keep Gabby entertained for a while so you can finish. Then I thought I'd barbecue that chicken you took out for dinner. Does that sound good, or did you have other plans for it?"

"A barbecue sounds perfect. We can eat in the screened-in porch and have a picnic. I made potato salad earlier, and we still have a lot of fruit salad leftover from yesterday. I'll make some corn bread when I finish packing."

"That sounds great. What time do you want to eat?"

"What time is Dan supposed to drop Pete off?"

"About five."

Liz nodded. "Okay, why don't you text Dan and see if he wants to pick up Beth on their way out here and we can all have dinner together?"

Pete was full of excitement as they sat around the table. He'd had his first flying lesson today and couldn't seem to get the words out fast enough. "I did good, didn't I, Uncle Dan?"

Dan smiled. "You're a natural, Pete, and I mean that. I've taught a lot of chopper pilots in my day, and none of them did better than you did their first time out."

Seeing the questioning look in Liz's eyes, Dan held up his hands. "It's the truth, Liz, I swear. Pete did even better than Jack did his first time out and…" Looking at Jack, Dan slowly turned red. "Oops, I shouldn't have said that."

"Relax, Harrison, I've already 'fessed up." Jack took Liz's hand. "She knows."

Dan winced. "How much trouble are you in?"

"Not nearly as much as you're going to be in, Dan Harrison, if you don't teach our son to be the best helicopter pilot around." Liz grinned. "Now relax and tell me more about how brilliant Pete is up there in the wild blue yonder. Not that I'm surprised," she touched her son's hand gently, "he's pretty darn smart."

Pete managed to look both pleased and embarrassed at the same time.

"What about me, Mama, is I darn smart too?" Gabby broke in. "I helped you put our clothes in the…the…stuitcase thing today." She stumbled over the unfamiliar word.

Smiling at Dan and Beth, who'd already heard the story of the great suitcase debacle, Liz took her daughter's hand. "You're darn smart too, Gabby. Sometimes you're even too smart for your mama to handle. Thankfully, your papa helped me so we can actually leave on vacation tomorrow."

"Tomorrow, yea!" Gabby's dark eyes sparkled. "Mama, I wanna take all the gatos on vacation, Binx 'n' Sierra 'n' Lazarus. Hey, that's one for each of us kids. Can I bring 'em, Mama, please? I have room in my stuitcase. They'll be good, I promise."

Liz let Jack explain why the cats would be much happier in their own house with Dan and Beth watching over them. Jack, Liz, and the kids, along with Lloyd and Nancy, were going on an Alaskan cruise, leaving out of Seattle the day after tomorrow. They were flying out of Duluth early tomorrow afternoon. Lloyd and Nancy had booked a three-bedroom suite with a balcony. Gabby was rooming with her grandparents so that Pete could have his own stateroom. Luke would be staying with Jack and Liz.

Gabby, not happy with her father's explanation, started to sob. Liz took her to her room on a time-out that, after the challenges of the day, she was hoping would turn into bedtime. After changing Gabby into her pajamas, Liz tucked her into bed. She bent down and gave the still-crying little girl a kiss on the forehead. "I love you, dear Gabriela, but today you've been a handful. Let's say our prayers, okay?" When Liz started the familiar prayer, "Now I lay me down to sleep," Gabby just cried harder until the very end when Liz said, "God, bless Papa, and Mama, and Pete, and Luke, and Tio Dan, and Tia Beth, and Nana, and Pop-Pop, in Jesus's name, a…"

"No, Mama, you forgot one! God bless me too cuz you're mean, and my tummy hurts, and my head hurts, and you don't care cuz you love everyone else more than me."

"Jack, honey, can you come here for a minute?" Liz, looking worried, called for her husband. When he joined her, she said, "This may be nothing more than too many tears and too much excitement, but Gabby says that her tummy and her head hurt. She's kind of warm."

Jack sat down beside his daughter and tickled her stomach, something she usually loved, but tonight, she pushed his hand away. "No, Papa, my tummy hurts."

Frowning, Jack felt her head. "Liz, will you please bring me the thermometer and the children's pain reliever?"

Liz brought them and stood behind Jack as he placed the thermometer on Gabby's forehead. When it beeped, he looked at the readout and showed it to Liz. It read 101 degrees. After giving the little girl a dose of medicine, Liz and Jack kissed her good night and closed her door behind them.

"I'm so sorry, Jack," Liz apologized. "I didn't realize that she wasn't feeling well. I just thought that she was being…"

"A five-year-old?" Jack kissed Liz's forehead gently. "You've nothing to apologize for. She's been a handful today, and you responded with grace and patience. Try not to worry too much. Kids of this age tend to spike fevers and then bounce back quickly. I'll check on her in a little bit, but the medicine we gave her should help."

⁓

Morning found Gabby feeling much better, and her temperature was back to normal. As they packed the car for the trip to Duluth, Jack smiled at Liz. "See, I told you not to worry. For some strange reason, the young ones seem to shake off illness much better than us older folks. Do you need any help in here, or shall I put Luke and Gabby in their car seats?"

"I'm just about ready. We need to get on the road soon so we don't miss our flight. Lloyd and Mom assumed we'd have a car full, so they're meeting us at the airport."

When they were finally on their way to Duluth, Liz reached over and put her hand on Jack's thigh. "Thank you for all you did this morning." She smiled. "I'm pretty excited about this. How about you?"

Jack took Liz's hand and kissed her palm. "Yes, I am. I've never been to Alaska, and it will be fun to share this adventure with you and the kids." His gaze was warm as he glanced at her. "I love you."

Before Liz could respond, Pete spoke from the back seat. "You're making love to each other again, aren't you, Mom and Dad?"

Jack glanced at Liz who looked like she was trying to sink into the car seat and said to Pete, "Yes, we are, but uh, Pete, while making love is a beautiful expression of the bond your mom and I share, it's a private thing. I'm glad that you know how much we love each other, and we welcome your questions, but lovemaking in whatever form is not generally brought up in everyday conversation, especially when others are present."

"But, Dad, it's just our family, and Gabby's asleep," Pete pointed out.

"You're right, Pete," Liz spoke up. "However, even when it's just our family, lovemaking is a private matter. What your dad and I share is ours alone. Do you remember how it was with you and Mary? Did you want your lovemaking shared with others?"

Pete thought for a long moment. "Um, no, I guess not."

"Was that because you were embarrassed to be with her or thought it was wrong?"

"No! I thought it was okay because we were married, or at least we thought we were. I wasn't embarrassed about Mary. I loved her."

"And I love your dad, and I'm not embarrassed about what we share. I just want to keep it between the two of us. Do you understand what I'm saying?"

After a few moments, Pete nodded slowly. "Yeah, I guess so. Can I still ask you questions about, um, things?"

Jack smiled. "If by um, things you mean about the relationship between your mom and me, yes you can. Anytime or rather anytime we're in private. Is that okay?"

Pete looked relieved. "Yeah, that's okay. I'm sorry if what I said was wrong."

Liz reached back and grasped her son's hand. "It wasn't wrong, but let's keep discussions about it focused on your questions, and between your dad, you, and me in the future. I'm so glad that you trust us enough to talk to us about these things. We love you so much."

Gulping, Pete squeezed her hand. "I love you guys too."

The ending to their conversation set the mood for the entire two weeks of their vacation. Even little Luke seemed to understand that they were doing something special together as a family. Even though he was teething, chew toys stored on ice and children's aspirin seemed to be everything the good-natured thirteen-month-old needed to stay happy, provided that he wasn't tired, wet, or hungry. He handled the long flights by falling asleep in Liz's arms. Once aboard ship, he and Gabby were a delight to their grandparents, and the older couple happily took on childcare duties when Pete, Liz, and Jack were busy taking excursions or enjoying private time. Pete was a bit standoffish where Lloyd and Nancy were concerned and seemed to prefer spending his time with Jack and Liz, playing with the little ones, or reading. Jack explained to their parents privately that their son had been the same way with him and Liz at first. Every night, the seven of them gathered for dinner and, apart from Luke, who was just beginning to talk, reported on the day's activities. It was a time of sweet bonding for all of them.

"Honey, we've hardly had a moment alone together," Nancy said to Liz one day as they walked the promenade deck. It was late afternoon, but the temperature was only in the midfifties. They were the only two of their group who'd ventured out on deck in the blustery weather. "It's wonderful to see you looking so happy and so well."

Liz reached out and squeezed her mom's hand. "I was going to say the same thing about you. You look great. Marriage must agree with you."

Nancy smiled and nodded. "It does. In fact, I feel like a kid again, at least until I look in the mirror."

"Mom, stop it! Your doctors even say you look a good decade younger than you are. I'm just glad that things are going well."

"Lloyd is a work in progress, as am I, but it's wonderful to have someone to walk with on life's path again after so many years. Honey, I want to hear about you. I never imagined you'd be the mother of three at this time last year. That has to have been a huge adjustment for you and Jack. How are you coping?"

Liz's smile lit her whole face. "I love being a mom to these kids, and Jack loves being their dad. It's like he was born to it, and our kids are amazing. They all came from really difficult circumstances, yet they're a joy to be around. Having them has added so much depth to our marriage relationship, something I didn't really foresee. I thought having to share our time together with the kids would dilute our feelings for each other, but just the opposite is true. I've never been happier in my life."

Nancy watched her daughter as she spoke and saw the truth in her words reflected in her eyes. "I'm so glad for you. You look younger and healthier today than I remember you looking in a long time. I remember when you were in your mid-thirties and had just had open-heart surgery. I was afraid because you looked so ill before they decided to operate. The blockages just kept coming, and your prognosis kept worsening. I know you still battle health issues, but you seem to be so much better than you were just a few years ago. I guess I owe Jack a debt of gratitude because this improvement really started when you married him."

Liz nodded and confessed, "Jack's been wonderful for me, there's no question. He stays current on research for my health issues, and when necessary, he thinks outside the box." She told her mom about the IV aspirin and how it had improved her headache days. She also cautioned her mom not to say anything to anyone, as Jack was probably dodging an ethics violation by giving it to her. Nancy rolled her eyes when Liz told her the reason why that particular formulation wasn't available in the US but promised to keep it between the two of them.

All too soon, the extended family disembarked the ship and boarded a crowded flight home. It was at this point that Luke's good nature failed, and he screamed for most of the flight into Minneapolis. By the time they landed in Duluth, Liz had a migraine that was so bad she'd ended up using several of the small bags found in the seat pocket in front of her. Jack, who, unusually for him, also had a headache, grabbed a couple more bags for the trip home. Lloyd and Nancy urged them to stay in Duluth overnight, but all Jack and Liz wanted was to get home. Liz's migraine continued to worsen, Gabby was spiking another fever, and Luke was still awake and screaming on and off. Wearily, they managed to say their goodbyes to Nancy and Lloyd and got in the car. Even Pete was unhappy because Jack wouldn't let him drive, but it was dark and raining and Jack knew Liz needed the smoothest, least stressful trip home he could manage. He would explain it to Pete later.

Liz sat in the front seat with her eyes closed, praying that she wouldn't get sick on the way home. Gabby was still of an age that throwing up produced drama on a scale that Liz didn't think she could manage right now. Jack reached over and clasped her hand, "I'm so sorry, love. We're almost home."

Liz tried to smile. "I'm just sad that our wonderful vacation ended this way. I don't even know if I said a proper thank you to Mom and Lloyd."

Squeezing her hand gently, Jack said, "We did thank them, several times over. They really enjoyed getting to know the kids. Tomorrow, everything will look bet..."

Jack never got a chance to finish his sentence. He saw headlights heading for his side of the vehicle and made a desperate attempt to swerve. His last coherent impression was Liz's moan of pain and his daughter's cry.

# CHAPTER 15

## FINDING A REASON
## TO BE THANKFUL

Liz blinked her eyes, trying to orient herself. There were flashing lights outside the small window beside her, and she was wet. She was lying down but felt like she was moving. Suddenly Zach Birch bent over her. "Liz, can you hear me?"

Liz tried to nod, but her head wouldn't move. "Ye…Yes. Zach is that you?"

"Yes, it's me, Liz. Can you squeeze my hand?" When she did as he asked, he looked relieved. "Good." He took her other hand. "Now give my hand another squeeze." This time, he frowned but said, "How are you feeling?"

"Zach, where…what…" Liz was so confused and couldn't seem to remember much apart from the fun they'd had on the cruise.

"Liz, you're medicated, and that's part of the reason you're muddled. It's okay."

"Where are Jack and the kids and what happened?"

Zach's brow creased. "You were in a car accident on your way home tonight. We're transporting you, Luke, and Pete to EBCH in one of the BWSR choppers. Jack and Gabby left just before you aboard *Life Flight*. They're going directly to St. Luke's in Duluth."

Liz tried to sit up and once again found herself restrained. "What's going on, Zach? Why did you separate us? Why can't I move? What about Pete and Luke?"

Again, Zach squeezed her hand. "Take it easy, Liz, you're restrained to keep you from moving too much. I'll explain why in a moment. First, Luke's fine. His car seat protected him from anything worse than a few lacerations. However, he's a little boy who went through something traumatic. Because he has a very healthy set of lungs, I gave him a little something to help him sleep."

"Pete?" Liz asked fearfully.

"Pete is conscious, and apart from some lacerations, bruises, and a broken arm, he's fine. He's right behind you."

"Gabby and Jack? If they're going into Duluth, it must be bad." Liz kept praying she'd wake up, but the nightmare just continued.

"Jack is doing as well as can be expected, given the severity of the accident. A pickup truck broadsided you on the driver's side, so you can imagine that he is badly bruised, but the side curtain airbags saved his life. He has a concussion and possibly a skull fracture. He hadn't regained consciousness before they took off, but imaging will tell us if there's a fracture or a bleed. He also sustained damage to his rib cage, and because of the surgery on his chest a couple of years back, we made the call to send him to Duluth with your daughter. That way, Gabby won't be alone and Theresa Paschal can look at Jack's films and determine what, if anything, needs to be done."

"What about Gabby? She was in her car seat right behind Jack." Liz couldn't stop the tremor in her voice.

Zach looked sad. "The door panels on Jack's and Gabby's side of the vehicle took the brunt of the impact, and while the car seat cushioned her, her head snapped sideways. She has every indication of a brain-stem injury. We'll know more after imaging."

"Zach, tell me what that means, please?"

"It means that Gabby has a very tenuous hold on life right now, and it means she's going to need you, Jack, and the rest of your family healthy so that you can help her fight this battle. If the films show swelling in the brain stem area, her care team will artificially lower Gabby's body temperature and keep her unconscious. That treatment will give her the best chance to survive her injuries and have a normal life.

"I realize that everyone else's condition is the first thing on your mind, Liz, but before we land, I need to talk with you about your injuries."

"I feel okay, Zach. I hurt, but I would assume that's normal after what happened."

"You may think you feel okay, Liz, but that's the pain meds talking. You have a broken collarbone and left side weakness that might indicate a brain injury, a spinal cord injury, or simply some swelling in those areas from the impact and when the car rolled. From what Pete described, you were unconscious for over thirty minutes."

Liz closed her eyes, tears seeping from beneath her lashes. A few hours ago, her biggest concern was getting home before she threw up. Now her husband and daughter were fighting for their lives and she couldn't even be close to them. She knew her sons needed her to be strong, but she was terrified. She prayed that God would see them all through this night and that renewed hope would come with the sunrise.

"Good morning, honey." Dan walked into Liz's hospital room the morning after the accident. Pete sat next to her, his cheek bruised and a cast on his lower arm but otherwise looking little the worse for what had happened. "Good morning, Pete." He leaned down and kissed Liz on the cheek. "I'm so sorry about this, Liz."

Liz tried to smile. "Hey, Dan. It's good to see you. I understand we have you and Beth to thank for keeping Luke safe through the night while he was sleeping off Zach's cocktail. Is he okay?"

"He's fine, bright-eyed as ever this morning, and when I left, he was gobbling down his scrambled eggs like there was no tomorrow." Dan gulped. "Uh, sorry, that was a poor choice of words."

Squeezing Dan's hand, Liz said, "Dan, honey, you don't have to walk on, um, eggs around me when we're talking. Thank you for taking care of Luke. Pete and I are so grateful, aren't we, Pete?"

Pete, who'd spent the night in the hospital, looked up and nodded, "Yeah, thanks, Uncle Dan."

"So what's the word out of Duluth?" Dan asked Liz, worry in his eyes.

"Jack has a skull fracture, but there's no indication of a bleed. He regained consciousness a little while ago and is pretty confused. Dr. Paschal is still evaluating the extent of his chest injury, but all in all, he's doing okay. Gabby," Liz blinked back tears, "is in a medically induced coma because of swelling of the brain stem. They've also reduced her body temperature to ease the demands on her system and give her a chance to heal. But she's on a vent and critical—they don't know if she'll come out of it."

Pete reached out and took Liz's hand. He didn't say anything. Liz took comfort in his touch and his presence. Finally, she looked at Dan again. "Were you there last night?"

Dan nodded. "I heard the call over the radio. By the time I got there, they had you, Luke, and Pete out of what was left of the car. They had to cut Jack and Gabby from the wreckage. Thank God the airbags deployed." He smiled sadly. "I'm afraid you and Jack are going to have to go shopping when things get back to normal because your car was totaled."

"Who hit us, Dan? Are they okay?"

"That's what I'm here to talk to you about. Do you have any memory of the accident?"

Liz frowned, trying to remember. "Not much. One minute, Jack was telling me that we were almost home, and the next thing I knew, I was in the helicopter and Zach was there." She took a deep, calming breath, sorting through the fragmented images in her mind. "I had a migraine, so I wasn't feeling very well. I remember hoping that I wouldn't throw up in front of the kids because Gabby, especially," Liz gulped, "well, she gets frightened when anyone gets sick. Anyway, Jack told me we were almost home, and he started to say something about tomorrow being better, but...but he didn't finish his sentence. I remember headlights coming at us, out of nowhere— blinding, bluish-white light on the driver's side, Jack swerved, then... then..." Liz punched the mattress with her right hand. "That's all there is, Dan, I'm sorry."

Dan put a gentle hand on Liz's forearm. "Hey, that's fine. Every little bit of information helps."

"I don't understand. Can't you tell from the cars, the accident scene, and the statement from the occupants of the other vehicle what happened? I just remember enough to know we were broadsided on County 1 when we had the right of way."

"Liz, honey, what happened last night was a hit-and-run. When emergency services got there, your car was upside down in the ditch, and it was obvious another vehicle had been involved, but there was no sign of it or its occupants. I've got the accident reconstruction team out there today, so I'm hoping they'll find something. For now, it looks as though whoever it was drove away from the scene."

"That's impossible, Dan." Liz objected. "An accident that did that kind of damage to our car and to us had to do enough damage to keep them from driving away."

"Judging from the tire tracks in the woods, the vehicle that hit you was a one-ton or better truck, so chances are good it was still drivable, particularly if the front end was reinforced."

Her head hurting, Liz just stared at Dan. "Tire tracks in the woods? Reinforced front end? But...but that would mean this was deliberate."

Dan just held her hand and asked, "Do you mind if Pete gives me his impressions of the accident before we talk about that?"

Liz looked at her son, who'd said nothing while she and Dan were talking. "Pete, do you feel up to answering Dan's questions right now?"

"This is really important, right, Uncle Dan?"

"It is, Pete," Dan responded quietly, "but if you need some more time, I can come back later."

"No, I can do it. What do you want to know?"

"I want you to tell me about what happened just before, during, and after the accident. What you were talking about, what your mom and dad were doing, and what you saw and felt right up until you were in the helicopter with your mom and Luke heading to the hospital. Can you do that?"

"I...I think so. We were on our way home, had just gotten through town, and were on Highway 1, pretty close to the house. Dad was driving, Mom wasn't feeling good, Gabby was asleep, and Luke was crying. I found his binky and put it in his mouth so he would stop." Pete glanced at Liz. "I hope that was okay. He was kinda loud."

Liz squeezed his hand. "Thank you, Pete, for doing that. You're very thoughtful, and it did help. Tell us what happened next."

"Dad and Mom were talking about Mom's headache, and she wondered if she'd remembered to say 'thank you' to Nana and Pop-Pop, and Dad told her that she did thank them. Then Dad told her that we were almost home. I was behind Mom, just looking around, and I saw headlights in the trees. They were off to the side. I thought that was weird, you know? There's no road there. Then the lights came closer, and I saw that a pickup—it was black or dark blue—was gonna hit us. Dad saw it too, and he swerved. The truck hit on Dad's side of the car, the airbags went off, and there was all this stuff floating around. Then our car rolled over into the ditch, and my arm hurt bad when it finally stopped. Mom, Dad, and Gabby didn't move even when I yelled at them, but Luke was screaming. Then these people drove up and tried to get Dad's door open and couldn't, so I guess they called for help. Then you and the sheriff showed up, Uncle Dan, and the fire department and the helicopters. Luke and I were the only ones awake until Dr. Zach gave Luke something to help him sleep and Mom woke up in the helicopter and talked to Dr. Zach. They took Dad and Gabby away in another helicopter. Mom said they went to a hospital in Duluth."

Hearing the stress and fear in Pete's voice, Dan reached out and grasped his shoulder. "That's enough, Pete. You did really well recalling some very scary stuff, and you told me more than anyone else has been able to remember. Thank you." He could feel the tension in Pete's muscles ease, so he kept his hand where it was. "What you've told me will help us find the truck that hit you."

Pete smiled faintly. "You mean it, Uncle Dan? I really helped?"

Dan nodded. "More than even your mom because she was unconscious. And speaking of your mom," looking back at Liz, he said, "Liz, this has to have been deliberate. What we don't know is if your family was specifically targeted, which is the worst-case scenario or if this was some sicko's idea of a prank. Either way, we'll find them."

Taking Liz's hand again, Dan asked, "What about you and Pete? What do the doctors say? Any idea of when they'll release you to go to Duluth? I'll either drive you down, or fly you down, or," a ghost of a smile played on his lips, "given everything that's happened in the last few years, maybe you'd rather I walk you down. The first sixty miles are the hardest."

Liz laughed quietly. "I may take you up on that."

⌒~⌒

"Ms. Lockwood?" An older gray-haired man stepped out onto the helipad at Duluth's St. Luke's Hospital.

Dan waved to Liz from the cockpit, and the rotors sped up as he prepared to take off. She waved back then looked at the man standing beside her. "Yes, I'm Elizabeth Lockwood—Liz, please." She extended her hand and shook his, very grateful it was her left arm that was in the sling; otherwise, she'd be a lot more debilitated than she was.

"I'm George Benson, and it's a true pleasure to meet you. I'll be the one acting as your primary care physician while you're down here. Zach Birch called me and asked that I help coordinate your family's care and," he observed her warmly, "help look after everyone, especially after your boys arrive."

Liz smiled, glad that Zach had reached out to this man. She knew many of the caregivers at EBCH, but apart from the doctor who'd cared for her after she'd been shot several years ago, she knew no one at St. Luke's. "Hello, Dr. Benson. Thank you so much. I'll also be thanking Zach for thinking of us. How are my husband and my daughter?"

"George, please." He escorted her inside and into the elevator. "I thought we'd have a cup of coffee while I bring you up to speed on what's happening with Jack and Gabby and," he eyed her intently, "while you tell me how you're feeling. A trip like the one you just took had to have been painful."

"I'm fine." Liz tried to reassure George.

Bearing a remarkable resemblance to Liz's husband, George said, "I know that can't be true. Zach was against releasing you because he's still not certain why you have the left side weakness and because he knows how much movement can hurt with a broken collarbone. So why don't we start our friendship off in the right way? How are you feeling?"

Embarrassed, Liz lowered her head and told George the truth. "My shoulder really hurts. My left hand's a little funky, but that might be due to the sling, and I have a migraine, but it's a pretty mild one. I didn't even need to use the bag I brought for the flight down," she grimaced faintly, "and that's always a win."

"Thank you, Liz. I'll order up something for pain when we get to the floor."

"George, my family? Please?"

They were seated in the coffee shop before George answered, "Jack's doing well. As you know, he did sustain a concussion and a skull fracture, so he remembers nothing of the accident. He's badly bruised, has a few deep lacerations, and has three cracked ribs on his left side from the impact. However, as long as he refrains from playing tackle football for a while, he'll be fine. He's pushing for us to release him today, and Dr. Paschal and his neurologist, Dr. Laura Bagley, are getting tired of listening to him, so he might get his way. He said he was going to call you this morning, but it sounds like you failed to connect."

Liz frowned. Jack must have tried calling when she was in with Zach or after she'd left with Dan.

George continued with his update. "Gabriela, your beautiful daughter, is holding her own. She's on a vent, in a medically-induced state of hypothermia, and in an artificial coma. All pretty much standard procedure in cases like hers. They're planning to do another MRI this afternoon, and after that, they may start to bring her out of it."

Liz put her hand on her forehead, "George, my husband is the physician, not me. I know he'll explain everything when I see him, but will you tell me, straight, what Gabby's chances are?"

George nodded. "Liz, there's one thing you can depend on—I will always give it to you straight. Okay?" Seeing her nod, he went on, "Gabby's still very much alive and is responding to external stimuli. That generally means that her chance of living through this is very good. Right now, the bigger question is, will she come back to you with Gabby's essence intact, able to breathe on her own, and able to live a normal life. What happens in the next twenty-four hours will tell us a lot more. I understand from your husband that you're a praying family, so pray. Would you like to see Jack now?"

Blinking back tears, Liz nodded. "Yes, please. Thank you for the coffee and for answering my questions."

When they got to Jack's room, he wasn't there. George took her down the hall to the pediatric ICU. Jack was in with Gabby. He held his daughter's hand in his. He'd bowed his head and tears seeped from his closed eyes. When George opened the door, Liz could hear her husband's soft words of prayer. She walked over and put a gentle hand on his shoulder, and a moment later, she was in his arms. George backed out of the room and was gone without a word.

❧

As soon as George left the room, he cloistered himself with Theresa Paschal, Laura Bagley, and Zach Birch, who participated via computer. Looking at those gathered, Zach asked, "Well?"

"Liz made it down here, and she and Jack are together right now, but," George shook his head, "both of them are among the walking wounded. I've medicated Liz, but she's clearly in a lot of pain and shows pronounced left side weakness. Jack is also in a lot of pain from the bruising, the skull fracture, and the rib injuries, but is determined that we release him today. They both need rest and time to recover, but with their daughter's hold on life so tenuous, I don't think that's going to happen until one or the other or both of them fall on their faces."

Zach nodded. "I know that's the case with Liz. She keeps minimizing her injuries and frankly imaging backs her up to some degree. There's no sign of a bleed, skull fracture, or concussion, but she hit her head hard enough to put her out for over thirty minutes. I'm sure that's the cause of the weakness although, Laura, I'll certainly defer to your opinion on the matter. I emailed you her records, but I doubt Liz will let you anywhere near her. I released her but sent her down to you with our chief of police, Dan Harrison. He's a very good friend of theirs as well as a helicopter pilot. That was the only way I could think of to keep her off the road and under someone's care."

"How are their boys?" George asked.

"They're both doing well," Zach said. "The infant, Luke, sustained a few lacerations that didn't even require stitches. We didn't have to admit him. Peter, their oldest, has a broken arm and a lot of bruising. I released him today. He went home with Chief Harrison and his wife, Beth, who've been looking after Luke since the accident. Liz has asked the chief to fly the boys down tomorrow. I still don't know if that's a wise choice because of the additional strain it will put on Jack and Liz. On the other hand, Pete would certainly benefit emotionally from being with all his loved ones. His birth family died in a car accident, so he's really worried about his parents and Gabby. The separation only exacerbates that worry. What are your thoughts?" Zach looked at the group.

"There's no question that both Jack and Liz are pretty frail right now from a physical standpoint, but from what I've seen and what I know of them, they're strong folks. Laura, Theresa, what are your thoughts about releasing Jack and reuniting the family tomorrow?" George asked.

"I'll start," Theresa said. "There's no reason to keep Jack another night from a cardiovascular perspective. He's in pain from the rib injury, but he'll be in pain whether he's here or somewhere else. He doesn't need surgery. There's no bleeding into the pleural cavity, the rib cage is stable, and his sternum, lungs, and heart are undamaged. My recommendation is to release him and encourage the two of them to find a place to rest tonight, not to spend the night at the hospital. I don't see any problem with the boys coming down. Laura?"

"From a neurological perspective, there's no reason to keep Jack, if he will take it easy. He's walking around with a skull fracture and is in a lot of pain from the impact his body absorbed in the accident. As for the boys, I think seeing them will actually be an encouragement to both Jack and his wife, especially if things don't go well with their little girl tomorrow. I would recommend that the boys make the trip after noon, so Jack and Liz can be with Gabriela in the morning."

Zach pinched the bridge of his nose between his thumb and forefinger. "So what I'm hearing is that there's no real danger if we release Jack?" Seeing their nods, he continued, "I didn't clear Liz to drive, and I presume the same is true for Jack, Laura?"

Laura nodded. "That would be my call at present. It's dangerous for him to be behind the wheel right now. Jack mentioned they had parents in town who were still driving, so presumably, they can help with transportation to and from the hospital."

Zach made a face. "It's a possibility, but let's just say that when Jack's with his dad, it's not a relaxing experience—at least not for Jack. It's getting better, and I think once the boys are here as a buffer, that staying with Lloyd and Nancy will be fine. For tonight, I just don't think that's going to result in good rest for either of them, even if we can convince them to leave the hospital."

George had been listening to the interplay between his colleagues and his eyes suddenly lit up. "I have an idea of what we can do for Jack and Liz. After all, he's both a colleague and a good friend."

George opened the door to the room, paused as Jack and Liz walked in, then put the duffel Liz had brought with her on the luggage rack. Smiling at them, George said, "You two get some rest. Unless we need to talk with you beforehand, I'll pick you up at nine-thirty in the morning to go back to the hospital. Remember that little Miss Gabriela needs you both healthy. Take care." With that, he closed the door behind him.

Liz looked confused. "Jack, what just happened? We could have called Lloyd and Mom for a ride to their place once they released you. What are we doing here?"

Jack collapsed heavily onto the bed, unwilling to admit to Liz how much pain he was in or how much the walk from the parking garage to the room had taken out of him. Smiling, he said, "I think George is taking his position as appointed babysitter very seriously. Most hospitals contract with one or several hotels in town for rooms, and at a guess, we're enjoying the St. Luke's Hospital's chief of staff's hospitality tonight. George, Zach, Theresa, and Laura probably had a conference, and here we are."

"Wait, George Benson is the St. Luke's chief of staff?" Liz questioned. "I thought he was a general practitioner assigned to our family."

Jack's smile widened. "He probably told you that, didn't he? George and I go way back, all the way to my residency days. He's a superb emergency medicine doc and a good friend. I'm glad he was there when you got here." Levering himself to a standing position using the nightstand for support, Jack put his arms around Liz's waist. "I'm so sorry I didn't call you earlier this morning. If I'd known you were coming, I would have been there when Dan dropped you off." He closed his eyes and just stood holding her, taking comfort in her warmth. "I love you so much. I'm sorry for the pain you're in, for leaving you alone, and for what happened. Thank you for watching over the boys."

Liz reached up, put her hand behind Jack's neck, and gently pulled him down into a kiss. "Jack, honey, I love you, I've missed you, and am so grateful you're going to be okay. Please stop apologizing for things you have no control over. You saved all our lives by swerving like you did the other night. I know you don't remember, but Dan can show you the reconstruction. We all would have died were it not for your quick thinking."

Jack frowned. "I spoke with Dan yesterday, and I know what a miracle it was that the collision didn't kill all of us outright. I know holding you in my arms today and the fact that all our children are still alive is a God thing. Still, knowing you're in pain has been difficult, particularly when I couldn't see for myself what was going on. While I understand why Zach made the decision he did, I agree with Pete. The separation from you and the boys has been tough, and I'm glad it's coming to an end. It did Gabby good to hear your voice today, and it will do all of us good when the boys arrive tomorrow, even if it does create some logistical challenges.

"Honey," Liz said soothingly, "the boys are fine. Pete's beginning to realize that the cast on his arm is sort of a chick magnet and is gathering an impressive collection of signatures. Dan is bringing both Pete and Luke down tomorrow. As for me, I'm okay, really. My shoulder hurts, but the collarbone fracture is minor according to Zach. If this blasted headache would go away, I think I'd feel almost normal." She took Jack's hand, and they sat down on the bed. "Honestly, the worst things wrong with me are Gabby's condition and worrying about you. I can tell it's taking all your energy just to stay upright."

Jack put his arms around Liz, and together, they stretched out on the bed. "I'm not going to tell you that I'm fine, but I am better for being with you and out of the hospital for a bit. I know that for the rest of the day and night, Gabby will just be lying there in that too-big bed, terrifyingly quiet. Hopefully, this treatment will give her body time to heal, but seeing her like that is tough."

Jack rolled onto his side, so he faced Liz. "I'm glad to have time alone to rest with you tonight. If I know George, he's the architect of this evening, and I need to thank him." Studying his wife's face, he asked, "Did George or Laura give you anything for your migraine?"

Liz nodded. "A drug called Butiaceto-something. I'm supposed to take that, wait thirty minutes, then if the headache is still there, take the other med. That one is a mild vasoconstrictor. If it causes chest pain, then I'm supposed to stop taking it and call George. So far, today, I've taken both of them, as prescribed. I'm not having chest pain, but I can't say the headache has gotten much better. I guess it's better in the sense that I'm not throwing up, but," she rubbed her temple, "it's still wicked painful. I wish we had some of that IV aspirin."

Seeing Jack's gloomy face, Liz squeezed his hand. "Look, I'm telling you all this because you asked. Given what happened the other night, I think it's pretty normal for both of us to hurt, so let's not obsess about it. I've dealt with migraines for years, and while they're uncomfortable, they aren't life-threatening. I want to enjoy being with you tonight. I want us to pray together, and I want to think about our daughter coming home to all of us tomorrow. I don't know about you, but I sure could use a nap even though it's only early afternoon. Why don't we rest for a while, then get dinner and pray together?"

Looking into Liz's eyes, Jack wasn't prepared to deny her anything, especially when what she was saying made good sense. He didn't need to remind her that there was no guarantee of a good outcome where Gabby was concerned, but he also knew that God held their little girl in the palm of His hand. Talking to Him was the best way they could spend the hours after they woke up from their nap. Reaching out, he put his fingertips on Liz's temples and rubbed them. He assumed from the relieved expression on her face that the gentle massage was helping and not causing her more pain. When he finished, she'd closed her eyes, so he drew her into the curve of his body and relaxed, breathing deeply to manage his own pain. It took time, but they both slept.

When Jack woke, he found himself looking into Liz's blue eyes. As soon as she saw he was awake, she kissed him. "I love you."

Jack hugged Liz. "I love you too. How do you feel?"

"Better," Liz answered, "how about you?"

"Better too. My head and chest are less painful than before, and I'm hungry. What would you like for dinner? I thought we'd call and have something delivered or, if you feel like it, we could walk down the street to that Asian place we tried the last time we were here. When we get back to the room, we'll call the boys, make sure everything's set for tomorrow, then pray for our girl."

Liz nodded. "That sounds good. If you're up to it, let's walk to the Asian place. It's just a couple of blocks away. We both loved the food, and getting outside sounds great."

～～

By the time they returned to the hospital in the morning, Laura Bagley was already in with Gabby. So far, the little girl hadn't responded to the rise in her body temperature, but encouragingly, she hadn't gotten worse. What they were hoping for were spontaneous respirations, indicating that they could take Gabby off the vent and any sign of returning consciousness. Laura had cautioned both Jack and Liz that this process could take several days. Gabby's most recent MRI had shown improvement and much less swelling, so Laura was hopeful that she would come out of it, and with therapy for whatever brain damage she'd suffered, if any, she could live out a normal life.

After several hours, Jack and Liz let go of Gabby's hands long enough to go meet their boys up on the helipad. After watching Dan take off, they had a sweet family reunion. Pete, in particular, hugged Liz tightly then stayed close to Jack as they walked to the elevator. Liz carried Luke in her good arm. The thirteen-month-old was uncharacteristically clingy, and Liz found herself glad. She'd missed her boys. As soon as they reached the ICU, Jack took Luke from Liz. "Why don't you and Pete go in first? We don't want to crowd the room. It might confuse Gabby."

Liz nodded. "Good idea. I'll come out in a bit and take Luke so you and Pete can spend some time together with her, too. I'll call Mom and Lloyd when you're in with her." She reached out and took Pete's hand. "I know your dad talked to you about how Gabby looks. Do you want to ask any questions before we go in, or maybe I should ask, do you want to go in or just pray for her from out here? Whatever you decide is fine, Pete."

The teenager thought for several moments before responding. "I'm not a coward, Mom, I'm not."

Jack squeezed Pete's shoulder. "Both of us know that, Pete, but you've been through some very hard experiences in your life. There is no shame in praying for Gabby from here. It was hard for your mom and me to see her like she is, especially when she's usually so active." Jack took a deep breath and blinked back tears.

"Dad, are you crying?" Pete asked, clearly surprised.

Nodding, Jack replied, "Yes, as I said, this is really hard on your mom and me because we don't know if Gabby's going to get better. We love her and miss her being with us."

Pete's eyes were wide. "But…but none of us are really yours. Do you feel that way about all of us?"

Both Liz and Jack put an arm around Pete and Liz said, "Pete, whether or not you feel the same way, in our hearts, you are our children. We couldn't love all of you more if you were born to us."

Pete looked up, his expression resolute. "Then that makes Gabby my sister, and I want to go into her room with you and pray for her, please. God has to hear us. He just has to."

"God always hears us, Pete," Jack looked at his son seriously, "but He knows what's best for Gabby, and that may not be what we hope."

"How can dying be better than living?" Pete lashed out.

"What if Gabby's brain has been so badly injured that she might never walk again, or breathe on her own again, or speak again or do any of the things that you think of when you think of Gabby? Would you want her to have to go through life like that?" Liz asked sadly. "I'm not saying that any of those things are going to happen, Pete, but God does know what's going to happen, and God loves Gabby even more than we do."

Pete looked confused. "So it's okay if she dies?"

"Oh, dear Pete." Liz looked at Jack, not knowing what to say to her son.

"Pete, we all love Gabby, and no, it's not enough to say it's okay if she dies," Jack tried to explain. "We are going to love her, pray for her, and do everything we can to help her get well so that if, in the end, God takes her home, she will know that her family loved her. Remember when I asked you to talk with Mary even though she was unconscious?"

Nodding, Pete said, "Yeah. I thought that was kind of weird."

"Do you remember what I told you about that?"

"You told me that she could hear me even though she was unconscious, but how do you know that?"

"Because I was badly hurt a couple of years ago. I was unconscious for several days, yet I could hear everyone talking in the room. I know Gabby can hear us, so tell her and tell God what's in your heart."

Along with Lloyd and Nancy, they spent the day alternating between time with Gabby and time out in the waiting room. After several hours, they'd all gone out for ice cream. Pete needed a respite, and Jack and Liz had needed one even more than Pete. Their physical injuries exacerbated the emotional toll of the day. About midafternoon, Lloyd and Nancy took Luke home, leaving the three eldest Lockwoods together.

"Mom, Dad, why aren't our prayers working?" Pete asked after his grandparents left. "We've been praying all day, and Gabby still hasn't opened her eyes."

Jack put his arm around Pete's shoulder. "God works in His time, Pete, not in ours. However, I think you might be wrong about our prayers not working. Gabby isn't conscious, that's true, but yesterday, she was in a coma, a machine was breathing for her and we didn't know if her brain would ever work right again. Right now, she's breathing on her own. Her heart is beating normally. Her body is maintaining a correct temperature. Her fingers and toes move when someone touches them. That's all really good news. Do you know why?"

Pete shook his head. "No, I mean everybody breathes, right? And everyone's heart beats. Otherwise, they'd be dead."

Jack thought for a moment, then responded, "That's true, most of the time, but since the accident and before this afternoon, a machine was breathing for Gabby. The brain stem, which is the part of Gabby's brain injured in the accident, controls her breathing and her heartbeat. It also controls whether or not she's awake. The fact that she's breathing on her own and her heart is beating in a normal rhythm suggests that she's getting better and gives us hope that there wasn't much permanent damage done to her brain. It may be that the swelling caused her symptoms and that she will come back to us as the little girl we know."

"But she isn't awake, so maybe that part's still broken."

Jack put his hand to his forehead. "Look, Pete, we can either have hope or we can give up. I'm going to have hope. You do what you have to do. Just understand that these things take time and please try not to make your mom feel any worse than she already does."

Pete's eyes widened at Jack's uncharacteristically severe tone. "I, um, I'm sorry, Dad. Thanks for explaining. I'm gonna go sit with Gabby and pray some more."

Pete walked into the glass-walled room where Gabby lay. Liz waited until he was out of earshot, then looked at Jack, confusion in her eyes. "Are you okay?"

"Sure, I'm fine. My daughter is lying in there fighting God knows what kind of a brain injury while I sit here spewing platitudes, but yes, I'm fine. Just fine," Jack said cynically.

Taking Jack's hand, Liz said quietly, "Jack, honey, that's *our* daughter in there, and I know that you're hurting because of that, but one minute you were answering Pete's questions very patiently, and the next minute you kind of blew up at him and at me." Kissing him on the cheek, Liz squeezed his hand. "I think maybe it's time we all go home to Mom and Lloyd's. I'm tired and hurting. I know you must feel the same way, and Pete needs some time away from the hospital and probably away from us. We can come back later tonight, just the two of us, or, if Gabs is still unconscious, we can pray together and come back in the morning."

By the time they got to their parent's home, they were all on edge and exhausted. Nancy recognized the look in Liz's eyes and took her aside. "Honey, you look awfully tired. Did something go wrong this afternoon?"

"No, Mom, at least not with Gabby. She's still unconscious, but she's breathing on her own and is stable. It's just been a very long day, and Jack is in pain and needs to rest. Would it be okay if the two of us napped for an hour or so before dinner? I think Pete will want some time to himself too. If Luke is too much for you after having him all afternoon, we can take him to our room with us."

Her mom squeezed her hand. "Luke's fine, and we're enjoying our time with him. Right now, I'd rather you and Jack rest. Pete and I are finding our way to a good relationship too, so we'll be okay. Jack doesn't look good, and neither do you, so go take care of each other for a little while. I'll wake you when dinner's ready."

"Thanks, Mom. I'm sorry for all this, but we're so grateful for your help and for your prayers."

Jack was standing in front of the window in their room, rubbing his forehead when Liz joined him. He had his eyes closed, and it was obvious that he was in pain. Coming up behind him, she slipped her arms around his waist. "Is your headache back?"

Jack nodded. "Yes. It's a pretty standard side effect of a head injury, but," he tried to smile at her, "I'm a wimp compared to you. You deal with these things all the time, and yet as sick as you get, you're unfailingly kind to our children and to me. Today I worried you and made Pete feel even worse than he did with my attitude. Before I came in here, I apologized to him, and now it's your turn." He held her face in his palms and looked into her eyes. "I'm sorry, Liz, for my behavior and for worrying you. I know Gabby is your daughter too and that you're every bit as anxious as I am. I also know you're in pain from your own injuries. Please forgive me."

Resting her head on Jack's shoulder, Liz hugged him close with her good arm. "There's nothing to forgive. You're my earthly rock, and I'm so grateful for your strength. You said this kind of headache is normal for someone with a skull fracture?"

Jack nodded. "It is, and the pain worsens when I'm stressed or tired. In the future, I'll do my best not to take it out on you and Pete."

"And your chest and your ribs," Liz asked, "how's the pain?"

Jack smiled faintly. "You know, you're starting to sound more like me all the time, and I'll answer truthfully. My whole body's at about a thirteen right now. I just took a couple of the meds that

Laura prescribed. I may fall asleep during dinner, but the pain should ease up soon."

"Well, I have good news on that front. Mom's putting dinner back about an hour so we can rest for a while before we eat."

Taking a deep breath, Jack murmured, "Thank you, Liz, for talking with her." He led her over to the bed and pulled her down with him. "We both need the rest."

<hr />

"Thank you, Mom and Lloyd," Liz wiped her mouth on her napkin, "that was delicious. I didn't realize how hungry I was and soup was a perfect choice."

Nancy squeezed Liz's hand. "You're welcome, honey. Were you and Jack able to get some sleep?"

"We were, Nancy," Jack said. "Thank you both. It was a long day, and speaking for myself, I needed to take some medication and lay down to be good for anything, including husbanding and parenting." Jack glanced at both Pete and Liz. "Fortunately, I have a very patient family."

<hr />

After dinner, Lloyd suggested that they pray as a family for Gabby and for everyone else because he recognized that each one of the Lockwoods, even Luke, was struggling with something, even if only a change in schedule. Reaching for his son's hand, Lloyd prayed silently until the family circle was complete, then he prayed out loud and from his heart. This was no prayer for an audience but simply a conversation with the Almighty, pleading for the return of his granddaughter and for guidance, peace, and healing for each one in the room. When they finished, he handed Nancy's guitar to Liz, knowing that music soothed his daughter-in-law and was a powerful way to worship when they couldn't find the words.

<hr />

Liz slipped the sling from her shoulder, braced her left arm on a pillow, and started to play. It hurt, but it felt good too. For long moments, she didn't sing but let the familiar worship melodies soothe her loved ones. Finally, she began to sing the song that had been on her heart all day long. She remembered the long-ago night when she and Jack came back to their Lord after she'd nearly ended their marriage. That night, it had been enough to know that God loved them and that God was sovereign. Somehow, she knew that it would once again be enough.

*There is strength within the sorrow*
*There is beauty in our tears.*
*And You meet us in our mourning*
*With a love that casts out fear.*
*You are working in our waiting,*
*You're sanctifying us.*
*When beyond our understanding*
*You're teaching us to trust.*

*Your plans are still to prosper,*
*You have not forgotten us.*
*You're with us in the fire and the flood.*

*You're faithful forever,*
*Perfect in love.*
*You are sovereign over us.*

*You are wisdom unimagined,*
*Who could understand Your ways?*
*Reigning high above the Heavens,*
*Reaching down in endless grace.*
*You're the lifter of the lowly,*
*Compassionate and kind.*
*You surround and You uphold me,*
*And Your promises are my delight.*

Jack scrambled down on the floor beside Liz. Closing his eyes, he sang the harmony with her, and she could tell each word came from deep in his spirit for his Lord.

> *Your plans are still to prosper,*
> *You have not forgotten us.*
> *You're with us in the fire and the flood.*
>
> *You're faithful forever,*
> *Perfect in love.*
> *You are sovereign over us.*
>
> *Even what the enemy means for evil,*
> *You turn it for our good.*
> *You turn it for our good and for Your glory.*
> *Even in the valley, You are faithful.*
> *You're working for our good,*
> *You're working for our good and for Your glory.*

As Liz and Jack began to sing the chorus, Liz's eyes snapped open when a youthful tenor joined them. Pete sat down beside Jack, closed his eyes, and sang the familiar words. He knew them from church and their family worship.

Tonight, the words and the declaration of trust ministered to each one in the room, and Liz felt the power and the love of God touching her deep within as they sang the chorus for a final time together.

> *Your plans are still to prosper,*
> *You have not forgotten us.*
> *You're with us in the fire and the flood,*
> *You're faithful forever.*
> *Perfect in love,*
> *You are sovereign over us.*

*You're faithful forever,*
*Perfect in love.*
*You are sovereign over us.*[v]

When Liz stopped playing, the room was silent. It wasn't until Lloyd whispered "amen" that she moved. Jack smiled at her, and for a moment, the love she saw in his eyes took her breath away. Then Pete whispered, "Wow, Mom, was God just here?"

Liz nodded. "God is always here, Pete, but I think He realized that we needed a special touch tonight." She smiled at her son. "Thank you for singing with us. You have a wonderful voice."

Pete's cheeks reddened. "Thanks. Um, has what just happened, happened to you before?"

"Yes, it has, usually when something in my life is really painful. The last time was when your dad and I got hurt a couple of years back and were really struggling to find our way back to a normal life."

"You and Dad?" Pete sounded astonished. "You guys are always so together."

Jack smiled sadly. "Not always, remember this afternoon?"

Pete nodded. "I guess so, but I'm the one who asked the question that made you mad."

"I told you a long time ago that you could ask your mom and me any question that you wanted. Your question about Gabby wasn't wrong, but my response to you was wrong. I wasn't feeling well, and I took it out on you. That's why I asked for your forgiveness. It was a difficult day, but like your mom said, what happened just now was a gift from God. I feel better, do you?"

Pete nodded. "Yeah. For the first time ever, I know, I mean I *really* know that God is real. I felt Him, and I'm glad that I made my decision to follow Him a long time ago." He took his parents' hands. "He's not going to leave us, is he? Even if Gabby doesn't come home?"

Jack patted his son's shoulder encouragingly. "No, He's not going to leave us, Pete. No matter what happens. He loves Gabby, and He loves all of us here."

Pete got to his feet, bent over, and hugged Jack and Liz, being very careful of Liz's shoulder. "I love you, Mom and Dad. I'm going to bed now if that's okay. I want to think about stuff and maybe read and pray for a while." He turned to his grandparents. "Thank you for everything, Nana and Pop-Pop. I love you guys, too."

⁓

The following morning, Jack and Liz sat by Gabby's side. She looked as though she was peacefully asleep. She'd had a good night, but while she responded to touch, she hadn't regained consciousness. Liz had brought her mother's guitar, thinking that it would be a familiar sound to their daughter and would soothe her and Jack and keep them from dwelling in the shadow of fear.

Slipping out of her sling, and grabbing a pillow to support her arm, Liz set her teeth against the wash of pain and began to sing one of Gabby's favorite songs, and Jack, smiling, sang with her.

> *Jesus loves me, this I know,*
> *For the Bible tells me so.*
> *Little ones to Him belong,*
> *They are weak, but He is strong.*
>
> *Yes, Jesus loves me,*
> *Yes, Jesus loves me,*
> *Yes, Jesus loves me,*
> *The Bible tells me so.*
>
> *Jesus loves me, He who died,*
> *Heaven's gate to open wide.*
> *He will wash away my sin,*
> *Let His little child come in.*
>
> *Yes, Jesus loves me,*
> *Yes, Jesus loves me,*
> *Yes, Jesus loves me,*
> *The Bible tells me so.*[vi]

When they finished, Liz, wanting to feel close to their daughter, started the song again in Gabby's first language.

> *Jesús me ama, esto lo sé*
> *Porque la Biblia me lo dice.*
> *Le pertenecen los pequeños*
> *Ellos son débiles, pero Él es fuerte.*

> *Si Jesús me ama,*
> *Si Jesús me ama,*
> *Si Jesús me ama,*
> *La Biblia me dice eso.*

Liz suddenly gasped and stopped playing. Gabby was singing with them, and when Liz and Jack stopped, Gabby continued,

> *Si, Cristo me ama,*
> *Si, Cristo me ama,*
> *Si, Cristo me ama,*
> *La Biblia me dice eso.*

Jack and Liz watched as God answered their prayers. After Gabby finished the chorus, she opened her eyes and whispered hoarsely, "Mamá, Papá, canta un poco más, por favor."

# CHAPTER 16

## NORMAL LIFE IS HIGHLY OVERRATED

It was a peaceful early September afternoon until Liz saw a blur of movement out of the corner of her eye. Before she could move to intercept Luke, he'd pulled over the garbage can next to the kitchen island. While it missed landing on him, its contents scattered all over the wood floor and her freshly bathed son was happily playing with used cat litter, dirty paper, and old leftovers. Liz had been working with Gabby doing exercises to strengthen her leg muscles, which were still weak after her injury the June before. Finally securing her daughter in her chair so she wouldn't fall, Liz ran for Luke and lifted him free of the garbage while removing a carrot that was way past its prime from the sixteen-month-old's fist. As she'd expected, the toddler let loose a scream of displeasure.

"Mama, I wanna get down." Gabby, now six years old, yelled over her brother's wails.

"Mom, why did you tell Uncle Dan I couldn't take a flying lesson this weekend?" Pete walked into the room and chimed into the general chaos. "I finished my chores for today, and I don't have homework until school starts. Dr. Zach took off my cast last month, and my arm is all better. I'm way behind on my flying lessons, and I want to go up with Uncle Dan this weekend."

As if he knew that he was no longer the center of Liz's attention, Luke screamed louder and smacked Liz in the shoulder with his small hand. Worse, it was the same shoulder that still ached uncomfortably after the injury to her collarbone.

"Mama," Gabby yelled louder. "Mama! Listen!"

"Mom, I need to call Uncle Dan and tell him…"

"Down!" Luke screamed in one of his ought-to-be-patented single-word sentences.

"Mama!"

"Mom!"

"Stop it this instant, all of you!" Liz bellowed before ruining the effect by bursting into tears.

"Hi, love, how was your…" Jack came in the door and, taking in the scene before him, wisely stopped talking. Instead, he walked over, calmly lifted Luke out of Liz's arms, put him in his high chair, and began picking up the garbage.

When Pete started to ask him about taking a flying lesson, Jack stopped him with a glance. "I imagine your mom has already discussed this with you, but we'll talk more in a little bit. Can you please give her a hand by bringing Gabs to her room?" When Pete, looking angry, started for Gabby's chair, Jack added, "Thank you. Be nice. It's not her fault you're mad at us."

Glancing up at Liz, Jack inclined his head toward their bedroom. "Go on. I'll take care of things for a while. Close your eyes, take a deep breath, and try not to be too angry with me. I got home as quickly as I could."

Liz took a breath, then two, before kneeling on the dirty floor beside Jack and hugging him close. "Did you find them?"

Jack nodded. "Yes. A sharp rock punched a hold in their canoe, and they didn't have a patch kit. Then they tried to walk out without most of their supplies and got very lost. Thankfully, they knew enough to start a fire and used pine branches to make enough smoke to signal the chopper. They're hungry and embarrassed but didn't even require overnight hospitalization."

"That's wonderful."

"We need to figure something out so you have help when I'm called out."

"No, we don't. I'm not fragile, and I can handle solo parenting at least for several hours at a stretch. In fact, I was just working up to my 'because I'm your mother, that's why' speech when you walked in. The tears, well, they just happen sometimes." Taking another deep breath, Liz kissed Jack. "Why don't you see if Luke has to go to the big boy potty and change him into some clean clothes while I wipe up the floor, then we can both go talk with Gabby and Pete?" She grinned. "You know what I was thinking just before you walked into this craziness?"

Jack shook his head. "I don't. I hope it didn't involve some form of exquisite torture for your missing-in-action husband."

"No, I was thinking that normal life is highly overrated." Liz frowned. "I didn't mean that, though. Apart from Gabby's legs being so weak and the renovation dust, these last few months have been wonderful. We work, we play, we enjoy our children, and I'm really thankful. I'm sorry for getting grumpy and overreacting to what just happened. I was fine until Luke decided that the garbage needed his attention. I was so afraid he'd think that the used cat litter looked like a great snack."

"Trust me when I say that toddlers have survived much worse." Getting up, Jack winked at her. "This time, I promise that I really will be right back."

Liz smiled at Jack's sheepish expression. "Honey, you couldn't help what happened, and you did call to let me know, so quit apologizing." He'd left hours earlier to make a quick run into town for milk from the grocery store and to pick up a care package of goodies from Beth. He'd been visiting with Beth when Zach had called and asked if Jack could take his place on a rescue run. Since Zach was filling in for him over the coming weekend, Jack didn't want to refuse, so he'd called Liz and did the run. His quick half hour in town had turned into a five-hour absence. Liz hadn't minded and with the exception of the last five minutes of Jack's absence, things had gone well.

After they put Luke down for a nap, they went in search of Pete and Gabby and found Pete reading to her. Both of them looked content, so rather than disturb the peace, they backed out of the room, knowing that Pete had seen them and would come find them when he finished. Jack and Liz retreated to the swing in the screened-in porch. It was an early September day, and Liz cuddled against Jack, relaxing as his arm went around her. He nuzzled her temple and opened his mouth to say something.

Liz kissed Jack before he could say anything. "If you're going to apologize again, don't. Everything is fine, and you have nothing to apologize for. You did your job, and I'm very proud of you. You save lives most every time you go out. This is why you came back to Minnesota in the first place."

Jack sighed glumly. "I know, but things were a lot different for me back when we started the BWSRU. I didn't have you or the kids and work was pretty much my life."

Liz patted Jack's arm. "I know, and I understand. I struggle with my productivity these days, but I wouldn't trade a minute of it. I never thought I'd be a wife again or a mom, and now I'm married to a man I adore, and we have three great kids."

"How can you say that, Mom, especially after what happened just before Dad got back?" Pete stood in the doorway to the house, looking at Liz with astonishment in his eyes. "We made you sad enough to cry."

Liz sat up, slid over, and patted the space between her and Jack. When Pete sat down, she put her arm around his shoulders. "Honey, I'm going to keep saying this until you believe me. I love you, and your dad loves you, just as much as if I'd given birth to you. You caught me at a bad moment this afternoon, and to be honest, I'm still pretty new at this parenting stuff. I was afraid Luke was going to eat the used cat litter, I was afraid Gabby was going to fall out of her chair, and I was frustrated because I really wanted to talk with you about this weekend, but you were unhappy and didn't seem to be in a listening mood. None of that changes the fact that I love you and am happy that you're my son."

Pete just stared at her for a few seconds and then squeezed her hand. "I'm happy I'm your son too," he looked at Jack, "and yours. You guys make me feel like I did when my real mom and dad were alive." Swallowing hard, he continued, "I think they're happy that I'm here with you. I just wish…" He paused, his cheeks reddening.

"Wish what, Pete?" Liz asked.

"I sometimes wish that Mary could be with us. She never knew what it was like to have a family like I do. Mary's parents never loved her. Her mom left when Mary was only two, and you know about her dad. You guys probably wouldn't have wanted one more kid to take care of, and I'm really glad that you and Dad adopted me. Still, I just wish, you know?"

Jack squeezed his shoulder. "I wish too, Pete. If Mary had lived, she would have been welcome in our family until the two of you were of an age to legally marry and start your life together. Never doubt that."

Pete nodded. "I think I knew that, and that's why I've thought about her living here with us. I know she's happy I'm here too." He patted Liz's hand and changed the subject. "I'm sorry that I didn't help you before, Mom. I wanted to talk with you about taking a flying lesson this weekend, but I should have helped you first then talked."

Liz leaned over and rested her head on Pete's shoulder. "Thanks, Pete. Let's talk about the weekend now that your dad's home. He had a great idea that I think sounds like a lot of fun, but we'd like to know what you think."

"Your Uncle Dan and Aunt Beth have offered to watch over Gabby and Luke this weekend," Jack said. "I thought that would give you, your mom, and me time for a long weekend in the Boundary Waters. When we were there in May, you said you wanted to go canoe camping this summer. Then we were in the accident, and between the renovation and helping Gabby get well, the summer disappeared. You've been such a great help with everything we thought it would be fun for the three of us to take tomorrow, Saturday, Sunday, and part of Monday and go on one of my favorite canoe camping loops. However, if you'd rather take a flying lesson, then your mom and I can go and you can stay here with Dan and Beth."

"Or if you'd rather it just be you and your dad, I can stay home," Liz offered.

"Liz," Jack began, but she shook her head slightly, and he didn't finish his sentence.

Once again, Pete just stared at them, then he threw one arm around Liz and grabbed Jack's hand. "Wow, I didn't think you even remembered talking about that trip with me, Dad. I want to go this weekend, with both of you." He frowned, looking a little worried. "I mean, if you think that Gabby will be okay. I don't want you to worry about her or about Luke if we go."

"I think your sister will be too busy playing with Buddy to even notice we're gone. Both Dan and Beth know her exercise routine, and they're taking the weekend off so that they can enjoy being an aunt and uncle. In fact, we'd invited them to go camping with us because your grandparents also offered to come up and look after Luke and Gabby, but Dan and Beth want to stay here with the young ones. That means that the three of us will be leaving in the morning. I think your dad wants to discuss the route with you when we're finished here and," Liz smiled at Jack, "you already know he's a really good teacher. I hope you'll help him get the equipment ready this afternoon because after Gabby and Luke go to bed tonight, we're going to pack the food. Dan and Beth will be here with Buddy at eight in the morning. We'll have breakfast together and then leave for our put-in point."

Pete looked excited when he got up. "This is so cool. Thank you!"

Jack grinned. "Your mom and I are going to relax here for a little while longer, then I'll come get you, okay?"

Pete nodded then disappeared into the house. Liz moved back into Jack's arms. "Pete's not the only one who's excited. It's been a while since we've been camping, and I love autumn in the BWCA. Thank you for thinking of this." She turned in his arms and pulled him down into a long kiss. "I love you."

# CHAPTER 17

## FOR THE BEAUTY OF THE EARTH

"Pete, why don't you take the bow position and paddle for a while? You know, give your mom a rest." Jack winked at Liz as they put in after the second portage. He didn't think she needed a rest, but he wanted Pete to learn to paddle the large canoe, and this was as good a time as any.

Pete nodded and took the paddle from Liz. "Okay, Dad, but I don't really know how."

"Were you watching Mom?" Jack asked.

"Yeah, but that's not the same as doing it, and I don't remember much from when we were doing the rescue stuff back in May."

For a while, Pete's paddling was awkward and inconsistent, but thanks to Jack's instruction, by the time they reached the next portage, he was almost as smooth a paddler as his mom. Jack told him as much when they got out of the canoe, and Pete flushed with pleasure. "Thanks, it was fun. Can I keep paddling when we get to the next lake?"

"That's up to Mom, she's usually my bowman."

Liz rolled her eyes and teased, "Darlin', if you think I'm a man, we need to have your eyes examined." Both Jack and Pete laughed as she continued, "Pete, you're welcome to my paddle because after this portage, my shoulder and I will be ready for a nice nap while you guys do all the work."

As it turned out, the day's route was long enough to give both Pete and Liz a workout. When they finally beached the canoe at their campsite, it was all they could do to help Jack set up camp. Pete had asked his dad to bring the two smaller tents because he wanted to stay by himself. When they made camp, Jack showed Pete how to put up the dome tent, telling him that he was on his own the next night but also reassuring him that if he needed help, he could ask. As they readied the tents, Liz started dinner. The freeze-dried meals were easy to prepare, and by the time the men finished, wonderful smells were coming from the pots on the two-burner stove. Everything tasted as good as it smelled. Later, they made s'mores over the campfire, then Jack and Liz sipped coffee while Pete enjoyed more s'mores. Finally, after hanging the food between two trees to keep it and them safe from hungry bears, they doused the fire and said their good nights. Liz hugged Pete. "Are you sure you want to stay in your tent by yourself?"

He nodded. "Yep. I'm sixteen and a half, Mom, not a kid."

Liz smiled. "I know, but I was a lot older than you my first time out here and I was really glad your dad was there. No way did I want to stay by myself. If you get lonesome, just come on over. We'll make room."

Pete smirked. "How am I supposed to knock on a tent?"

Jack lightly smacked his son's shoulder. "You're a bright kid, you'll figure it out. I had a great day today with you and your mom. Love you."

"Love you too. Night."

When Jack and Liz settled into their tent, Liz cuddled close to him and said, "Hey, I want to ask you something before I say anything in front of Pete."

Jack eyed her curiously. "Sure, what's up?"

"Today took a lot more out of me than I expected. My shoulder's really sore after the paddling and portages and that's with Pete doing a lot of the work. I know you have plans for us to go in about four more lakes, but what would you think if we just camped here and took day trips to some of the close-by lakes? I know you want to teach Pete how to paddle and direct the canoe from the stern, but couldn't you do that from where we are?" Liz looked at Jack in the moonlit semidarkness. "I need to know if that would really disappoint you because this is probably going to be our only recreational canoe trip this year, and I can manage the complete trip if I have to. I'd just ask Pete to do more of the paddling."

Kissing Liz, Jack smiled. "I was actually going to ask you if it would be better to do something like what you've suggested. I can see that you're hurting and pretty tuckered tonight. I honestly think that your idea is a good one. It'll give me more time to work with Pete on his canoeing skills because we won't be pressing to make our next campsite. I'll use the SAT phone to call the Forest Service in the morning and advise them of our change in plans and campsite use. I'm pretty certain that Pete will be fine with the change because I think he's a bit tuckered, too."

Liz rested her head on Jack's chest and just enjoyed his touch as he stroked her back. "Thank you, honey. I love you. Sleep well."

Jack kissed her forehead. "I love you too."

A few minutes later, or so it seemed, Liz woke to a quiet slapping on the tent door. She blinked her eyes and sat up, realizing with a start that there was dim morning light filtering through the nylon sides of the tent. She shook Jack awake then unzipped the entry flap. The sun wasn't up, but it was bright enough to know that dawn wasn't far off. Pete stood there, but when she opened her mouth, he put a finger over his lips and motioned both of them to come outside. Jack and Liz slid into their moccasins and did as Pete asked.

When they all stood side by side, clad alike in sweats and long-sleeve tees, Pete whispered, "There's a bull moose down at the end of the lake." He held the digital SLR camera he'd bought with money he'd earned by helping his Uncle Dan paint the interior and exterior of the restaurant over the summer. "I got a lot of cool photos, but you guys need to see this."

Moving quietly, they followed Pete down to the lakeshore. Not fifty yards away was a large moose with an impressive rack, standing belly-deep in the water, contentedly slurping waterlily bulbs. Pete snapped a few more photos and then handed the camera to his artist mom, who also took a series of photos. Then the wind changed.

The moose raised his head and, clearly disturbed but not in a hurry, ambled out of the water and into the woods. The three Lockwoods stood still for a few more minutes to see if the moose might return, but the lake and the woods remained quiet. Jack put one arm around Liz and one around Pete. "Wow, what an amazing way to start the day. Thank you, Pete! Now I'm ready for coffee and breakfast. How about you guys?"

◦━◦━◦

Pete was fine with the change in route, especially when his dad told him that this was his favorite campsite in all the BWCA and explained that, this way, he would have more time to teach Pete how to paddle and steer the canoe from the stern. Pete put his arm around Liz's waist. "Mom, I want you to have fun on this trip, so if you need me to do something so your shoulder doesn't hurt as much, tell me, okay?"

Liz nodded. "I will, Pete. Thanks for not being too disappointed about not taking the longer route you and Dad chose. God willing, we will have many more times together out here to explore. Before you guys head out onto the water, will you show me the photos you took this morning?"

Pete got his camera and gave it to his mom. Together, they bent over the small screen, with Jack looking over their shoulders. When Liz finished scrolling through the photos Pete had taken, she said, "Pete, these are seriously good. When we get home, we should order some of them printed on canvas for the study and at least one for the living room. I think one of these would look great on the wall by the stove."

"But, Mom, that's where your Lake Superior piece hangs, and that's my favorite."

Liz patted her son's hand. "I need to move that anyway because it gets too much light where it is, especially in the winter when the sun hits it directly. I thought I'd hang it in the dining room. Does that sound okay?"

"Do you really think one of these pictures is good enough to put in the living room?" Pete asked.

Liz smiled up at Jack and he nodded and said, "We sure do, Pete."

"You know, I was thinking," Liz interjected, still focused on Pete, "we could transfer one of these photos to fabric, maybe use sepia-toned ink, then—with your help—I could embroider it with different kinds of beads and threads. I think it would be beautiful. What do you think, Pete? If we do this, it's up to you to pick the print we use because you're the artist who took the photographs."

"Wow, that would be cool. Can we choose the picture this weekend so we can get started when we get home?"

Nodding, Liz said, "I don't see why not as long as you and your dad get your canoeing lessons in and we get some time to all do a bit of paddling together. I'd like to go in as far as Rose Lake because it's gorgeous at this time of year, and that's where we saw the mink the last time we were here. Remember, Jack?"

Kissing the top of Liz's head fondly, Jack said, "I do. That was a great trip, and I'd like to go back there too. I can portage the canoe over so we can circle Rose and enjoy the scenery. We'll just need to take lunch supplies and an emergency kit, so none of the large packs need to come with us. Why don't we do that tomorrow so I can give Pete some steering lessons today? Maybe I can rest while you guys paddle tomorrow if Pete's as good at canoeing as he is at flying."

Pete flushed, once again looking both embarrassed and pleased at the same time. "I'll try, Dad. Can we start our lessons now?"

Seeing Jack hesitate, Liz waved her hand. "You guys go ahead. I'll do breakfast clean up, and I may even take a nap after I make sandwiches for lunch."

It was about three hours before the men returned, and they found Liz, curled up on her sleeping bag, napping in a patch of sunlight. It was a beautiful warm day, and Jack could see a fine sheen of sweat on her forehead. He could also see that she was resting well, and if her posture was any indicator, she was comfortable. He looked into the cooler and, true to her word, Liz had made sandwiches for all of them. "Here." He handed one to Pete. "Why don't we enjoy some quiet time too because I don't want to wake your mom just yet, okay?"

Pete looked relieved. "Yeah, that's good. Dad?"

"What?" Jack murmured absently, intent on finding the mustard.

"Um, I'm a little tired too. I think I want to take a nap before I eat." Pete handed his sandwich back to Jack. "Is that okay? I mean you told me not to take food in my tent with me, and I'm not really very hungry."

Jack reached out and fondly squeezed Pete's arm. "Yes, it's okay. You did most of the work out on the lake today. I'll take a nap too. That way, we can all eat together later."

They slept for several hours, and by the time everyone was up, it was late afternoon. It was close to eighty degrees in the sun, so Liz, ready for a little exercise, looked at her son and husband and issued a challenge. "Last one in the water cleans up after dinner." She had an advantage that Jack and Pete were unaware of until she rapidly skinned out of her jeans and t-shirt. She was wearing her swimming suit beneath her clothing. However, it was still a race because both of the men just stripped down to their skivvies and headed for the water right behind her. Liz's healthy scream as she dived in didn't deter either man, and the race between Jack and Pete ended in a tie. The water was like liquid ice. All three of them swam hard just to get warm. Liz had brought the biodegradable liquid soap in with her so they could get clean. By the time they finished, everyone was ready to get out of the lake, soak up the warm sun, and eat their long-delayed lunch.

"Wow, Mom, I can't believe you jumped in like that. The water was cold!"

"I love to swim, and I knew I'd warm up pretty quickly," Liz said nonchalantly.

"Ah, so you screamed—why is it you screamed again?" Jack teased. "Did a big Northern Pike attack your toes, or did you see a water spider, or maybe a bear on the shoreline?"

"It would serve you right if I'd actually seen a bear since making noise is what I'm supposed to do if said bear strolls into our campsite, right? You're the one who taught me that. There was no bear," Liz confessed, "but the water was a whole lot colder than I thought it would be, especially once I went under." She punched Jack lightly on the shoulder. "Thank you so much for diminishing my feat of courage in the sight of our son."

"He didn't, Mom, honest. If I'd been the first one to the water, I wouldn't have gone in past my toes. I think what you did was pretty cool."

"No pun intended," Jack quipped.

It was their last night in the BWCA. Earlier in the day, they'd paddled and portaged into Rose Lake. They'd seen a lot of wildlife, but no mink, and they'd all taken turns paddling in both positions in the canoe. Pete had caught on very quickly to the different strokes and how to steer the canoe, but he let his dad do the navigating because the shoreline all looked pretty much the same, and finding the portage location was still challenging for him. When they'd returned to camp, it was just ahead of an afternoon rainstorm, so they'd taken shelter in their tents to wait out the bad weather. Now it was early evening; the sky was dark and clear, thousands of stars glittered overhead, and they were sitting around the fire. Jack came out of the tent he shared with Liz with his Bible and her guitar. He opened the Bible and read another of his favorite passages, this one celebrating God's creation and faithfulness to mankind.

*Lord, our Lord,*
*How majestic is Your name in all the earth,*
*You who have displayed Your splendor above the*
*heavens!*

*From the mouths of infants and nursing babies You
have established strength
Because of Your enemies,
To do away with the enemy and the revengeful.*

*When I consider Your heavens, the work of Your
fingers,
The moon and the stars, which You have set in place;
What is man that You think of him,
And a son of man that You are concerned about
him?
Yet You have made him a little lower than God,
And You crown him with glory and majesty!
You have him rule over the works of Your hands;
You have put everything under his feet,
All sheep and oxen,
And also the animals of the field,
The birds of the sky, and the fish of the sea,
Whatever passes through the paths of the seas.*

*Lord, our Lord,
How majestic is Your name in all the earth!*[5]

Jack grasped his wife and son's hands and prayed, "Abba, thank You for this beautiful day and for my family. Thank You for Your magnificent creation. Thank You for our senses of sight, hearing, smell, touch, and taste that enable us to enjoy the good things You've given us. May memories of this time together strengthen the three of us when struggles come our way. Thank You for Your faithfulness. Please keep us safe as we leave our campsite tomorrow and travel home. Watch over our children, Gabby and Luke. Keep them well and safe and give Dan and Beth patience, pleasure, and wisdom as they watch over the kids. Thank You for Your Word and the love for You it ignites in us. Bless my wife and son with sound rest tonight

---

[5] Psalm 8 NASB.

and give them peace as we return home. We pray in Christ's name and for His glory, amen." Handing Liz the guitar, he asked, "Do you feel like playing tonight?"

Liz smiled happily. "I'd love to as long as you guys help me sing." Seeing their nods, she began to play. When she started to sing, both Jack and Pete sang with her.

> *Michael row the boat ashore, Hallelujah*
> *Michael row the boat ashore, Hallelujah*
>
> *Sister help to trim the sails, Hallelujah*
> *Sister help to trim the sails, Hallelujah*
>
> *The river is deep and the river is wide, Hallelujah*
> *Milk and honey on the other side, Hallelujah*
>
> *Jordan's river is chilly and cold, Hallelujah*
> *Chills the body but not the soul, Hallelujah*

When they sang the last verse, Jack mouthed, "One more time." When Liz started to sing, Jack's baritone voice wove complex harmonies around her contralto. Pete just sat there listening with his mouth slightly open.

> *Michael row the boat ashore, Hallelujah*
> *Michael row the boat ashore, Hallelujah*[vii]

When they finished, Pete whispered, "Wow, that was awesome. Dad, how did you know what to sing? I mean it was really nice when we were all singing together, but that last part sounded so different."

Jack smiled. "If you want to learn to sing harmony, your mom and I can teach you the basics, but honestly, the best way to learn is to join a choir or a singing group. You have a very nice voice, and I can guarantee you that our church would love to have you in the choir. Mom and I plan to join as soon as Luke gets a little older, so you'll be way ahead of us if you join this fall."

Pete looked down. "Uh, I'll think about it, okay, Dad? I mean, I'm a senior this year, and I don't know how busy I'll be, but I really will think about it."

Liz took his hand. "Pete, whatever you decide is fine. We'll still sing together as a family, so pray about it and think about it. It's your decision, so don't feel you have to do it because of Dad and me. You have many gifts from God, and it's up to you how you want to use them."

Pete looked relieved. "Thanks, Mom."

Sensing Pete's stress, Liz strummed a few chords and sang softly.

> *For the beauty of the earth,*
> *For the glory of the skies,*
> *For the love which from our birth*
> *Over and around us lies,*
>
> *Lord of all, to Thee we raise*
> *This our hymn of grateful praise.*
>
> *For the beauty of each hour*
> *Of the day and of the night,*
> *Hill and vale, and tree and flow'r,*
> *Sun and moon, and stars of light,*
>
> *Lord of all to Thee we raise,*
> *This our hymn of grateful praise.*

Liz stopped playing and reached out to take Jack's hand. Jack took Pete's hand, then he and Liz finished the song acapella.

> *For the joy of human love,*
> *Brother, sister, parent, child,*
> *Friends on earth, and friends above,*
> *For all gentle thoughts and mild,*
>
> *Lord of all to Thee we raise,*

*This our hymn of grateful praise.*[viii]

When they finished, Liz smiled. "That just seemed appropriate for this glorious evening." Eyeing her son, she cuddled up close to Jack, looked into his eyes, and sang.

> *By the light of the silvery moon,*
> *I want to spoon,*
> *To my honey I'll croon love's tune,*
> *Honeymoon keep a-shining in June,*
> *Your silv'ry beams will bring love dreams,*
> *We'll be cuddling soon*
> *By the silvery moon.*[ix]

Taking the guitar from Liz, Jack bent her backward and kissed her theatrically. Doing her part, she moaned ecstatically, put a hand on her forehead, and pretended to swoon in his arms, all the while keeping one eye open to see Pete's reaction.

Their son did not disappoint. He looked from one of them to the other and grimaced, "Gaah, gross! You guys told me this kind of stuff is supposed to be private. No kid should have to witness his mom and dad doing..."

"What?" Jack asked innocently, his lips twitching with a suppressed grin. "I just kissed your mom, so what's the big deal?"

"Come on, Dad. That was not an old people's kiss."

"Hey, mister, who are you calling old?" Liz abruptly sat up and eyed Pete grumpily. "I'll show you old." She picked up her guitar before he could answer and strummed a series of cords with such power that Jack's fingertips stung in empathy.

> *When He rolls up His sleeves*
> *He ain't just puttin' on the Ritz,*

Jack chimed in,

> *Our God is an Awesome God.*

Again, Liz sang.

> *There is thunder in His footsteps*
> *And lightning in His fists.*

Jack's voice took over.

> *Our God is an Awesome God.*

Together, the two of them sang,

> *Well the Lord He wasn't jokin'*
> *When He kicked 'em out of Eden*
> *It wasn't for no reason that He shed His blood*
> *His return is very close and so you better be believin'*
> *That our God is an Awesome God.*

Together, they motioned for a surprised Pete to join them on the familiar chorus.

> *Our God is an Awesome God,*
> *He reigns from heaven above,*
> *With wisdom, power, and love,*
> *Our God is an Awesome God.*

To begin the next verse, Jack sang.

> *When the sky was starless in the void of the night.*

Liz's voice took over on the next line.

> *Our God is an awesome God.*

This time Jack motioned Pete to join him.

> *He spoke into the darkness and created the light.*

Then they all sang.

*Our God is an Awesome God.*

Together, Jack and Pete finished the verse.

*Judgment and wrath He poured out on the Sodom
Mercy and grace He gave us at the cross,
I hope that we have not too quickly forgotten that.*

Then Liz joined them again.

*Our God is an Awesome God.*[x]

By the time they finished the chorus a second time, Pete was smiling broadly. Jack and Liz sat back and quietly enjoyed this perfect ending to a wonderful vacation.

# CHAPTER 18

## "OUR GOD IS AN AWESOME GOD" AIN'T JUST WORDS IN A SONG

The closer they got to home, the more Liz looked forward to seeing their two youngest children. This was the longest she'd been away from them since their family had been together.

Jack took her hand. "Excited to get home?"

Liz nodded. "I had a great time with you and Pete, but yes, it will be good to get home and see the little ones. How about you?"

"I'm ready to be home with all our kids and you." Jack grinned and inclined his head toward the back seat. "I think Pete might also be ready to get home to his own bed."

Liz glanced behind her. Pete was sound asleep. "I think you're right. But in all fairness, he didn't get very much rest last night what with the bear and getting up pretty early this morning." Liz remembered waking to growling noises and seeing her wide-awake husband putting on his moccasins. The bear ran for the forest the moment Jack started yelling and banging pots together, but it wasn't fast enough to avoid being seen by a wide-eyed Pete, crouching in the doorway of his tent. The three of them spent the remainder of the night in the larger tent.

Jack chuckled. "I loved it when you came out of our tent screaming at the bear for waking everybody up. No wonder the poor fella headed for the hills."

"Says the man who played the entire percussion section by slamming our pots together. I'm surprised they didn't hear us in Ely." Liz stretched in her seat. "I hope we can get out with all the kids next summer. I had so much fun."

Jack just squeezed her hand, feeling so blessed in this moment. When he'd turned fifty, he'd thought that he'd be alone for the rest of his life, and while part of him had resigned himself to that fate, there'd been a part of him that had cried "Is this all there is?" Now less than five years later, he was a committed follower of Christ; he had a wonderful wife who shared his dreams, hopes, and values; and he had three great kids. His relationship with his father was slowly healing, his lovely mother-in-law was now also his stepmother, and he'd even grown closer to his sister and her family thanks to gatherings engineered by Nancy and Lloyd. Jack's work was fulfilling and challenging, he and Liz had wonderful friends, and the truth was that if someone had told him back then what his life would be like today, he wouldn't have believed them—not for an instant. For things to change so completely for the better was beyond anything he could have imagined. For just a moment, Jack's expression darkened. He remembered thinking these same thoughts after the cruise they'd taken in June. Then someone had rammed their car and nearly killed Gabby. It was a thought that would plague him often in the upcoming days.

"Hey," Liz said quietly, "where did your smile go? It looked like you were thinking really happy thoughts then poof, you started to look sad. What are you thinking about?"

Jack smiled at her. "You're very good at that mind-reading thing, Liz. Sometimes you're so good at it that it scares me a little. I'm fine. I was just thinking of how much my life had changed in the space of five years. I feel so blessed."

"So why the frown?"

"I was also thinking that the last time I felt like this was on our way home from Alaska. And look how that ended."

"It ended with us being a family again, despite having an accident that could have killed all of us." Liz reached over and caressed Jack's cheek. "Don't let Satan do this to you, honey. Don't let him take away your joy or your gratitude. If you do, then you've given him exactly what he wants."

Leaning into Liz's touch, Jack nodded. "I know, but thanks for the reminder. I think I'll feel better when we're all together again. And yes," he smiled broadly, "I had a great time with you and Pete this weekend."

When they pulled into their drive, Liz woke up. She'd fallen asleep after talking with Jack. Blinking, she sat up and looked at him sheepishly. "Sorry, I didn't mean to fall asleep on you. Is everything okay?"

"Everything is great. We're home, our son is waking up, so what say we go in and greet everyone?"

Dan and Beth met them at the door with hugs and handshakes. They were both smiling. Liz was a little confused. "Where are the kids?"

"Well, Luke is down for a nap," Beth replied helpfully.

"And Gabs?" Jack asked, sensing that something was afoot, but confused as to what.

"Um, Gabby and Buddy have a surprise for you. Are you ready?"

Seeing their nods, Beth raised her voice and said, "Announcing Miss Gabby with her sidekick perro Buddy."

To her parent's astonishment, Gabby walked out of her room under her own power. She wasn't using her walker. Her hand was on Buddy's back, and the dog padded quietly beside her. Gabby walked all the way over to where her parents stood then, balancing carefully, she extended her arms. "Ta-da!"

Jack reached down and picked her up. Gabby looked at him and then touched the tear that was sliding down his cheek. "Papa, why are you sad? I wanted it to be a good surprise."

Jack hugged her close. "Gabby girl, this is one of the best surprises ever. I love you so much."

Liz was teary too, and after she hugged Gabby, Jack, and Pete, she looked at Dan and Beth. "I don't even have the words to say thank you. What you've done here…"

"Liz, we didn't do anything," Dan insisted. "Gabby did it with a little help from Buddy. We just noticed that she would lean on him rather than use her walker, so we practiced doing that, and this is the result."

Reaching down, Liz scratched Buddy's ears. "Thank you, Buddy." Looking up at Dan and Beth, she asked, "How did Buddy and the cats get along?"

"Buddy learned his lesson quickly. The first day we were here, he took off after Lazarus wanting, I think, only to make friends," Dan grinned. "Lazarus calmly turned around, hissed at Buddy, and swatted him across the nose. Now Buddy goes out of his way to avoid the cats or at least gives ground when they come into the room."

"Oh dear, Lazarus didn't hurt Buddy, did he?" Liz asked with trepidation.

"Nope, I think Lazarus knew that Buddy was still young. Laz smacked him without extending claws and there was no blood, but he was still one surprised schnoodle. He had no idea that something so little could pack such a wallop."

Dan, Beth, and Buddy left shortly thereafter, giving the Lockwoods privacy for their reunion. Gabby cried when they left, and it was clear that she'd fallen in love with Buddy. When they'd all settled in the living room, with Gabby in Jack's arms, it seemed the cats sensed something was amiss with the little girl. Binx jumped up on the sofa and curled up on Jack's lap, right next to where Gabby sat. Sierra rested in Liz's lap next to Gabby and Jack. Finally, Lazarus jumped on the arm of the sofa and head-bonked Gabby's arm. The little girl's eyes brightened, and she reached out to pet Lazarus. "El gato Lazarus, I love you, 'n' I love gata Sierra 'n' gata Binx 'n' perro Buddy 'n' Mama 'n' Papa 'n' Luke 'n' Pete 'n' Tio Dan 'n' Tia Beth." She finally laughed and threw up her arms exuberantly. "I love everyone!"

～⌒~⌒✓

The next morning, Pete left for school early. This was his senior year, and at the beginning of September, he decided, rather than being homeschooled for his senior year, he would go to the Christ Academy high school in town and graduate with his classmates, many of them friends from church. So far, the only thing Liz and Jack had heard, apart from Pete's excitement when they'd presented him with a newer model crossover SUV for his drive into town and other sorties, was that the work was easy compared to what he'd done in his homeschooling. Pete would be graduating with honors next June at seventeen, an achievement that was close to unbelievable, given that he'd missed almost two years of formal schooling as a runaway. He was set on his goal to become a physician and work in search and rescue. Liz and Jack didn't press, wanting him to find his own path, but privately, Jack was honored that Pete had chosen to follow in his footsteps.

After kissing his wife, Jack got ready to leave for the hospital. He was on staff today and would be home by 7:00 p.m. Although he was passionate about his work in the field, he appreciated the normalcy of the hospital's schedule. He also enjoyed doing surgery, using his gifts to save lives, limbs, and he grinned and confessed to Liz, who'd been listening to him wax poetic, "I almost ended that sentence with livers."

Liz wrinkled her nose and slapped Jack gently on the behind. "That's terrible. You'd best get going because you're a much better doctor than you are a poet." She put her arms around him and gave him a kiss she hoped would keep him warm all day. "I love you. Be safe and have a good day."

It was just after 6:30 a.m., and Liz was the only one awake in the quiet house. Making a pot of tea, she settled down to do her devotions. She wanted to pray, to thank God for the wonderful weekend she'd shared with Jack and Pete, and for the miracle that had awaited them when they got home. Her heart was so full. She pulled her Bible to her, intending to find her favorite Psalm and start her time with God from there. She blinked when the words refused to focus. It didn't help. The letters were blurry, and even when she could see them, they didn't seem to make sense. Rubbing her eyes, she realized that her head felt like a block of wood. "Oh God, please," she whispered, "not today. I don't want to call Jack home after he just got back from vacation. Still, I've got the little ones. Please God, not now."

She recognized the symptoms of an aural migraine, something she'd had only a few times in her adult life. Reading was out, but she could pray and hope that she could function through the symptoms. Bowing her head, she talked to God, rejoicing in the fact that the same good God who'd given them an extraordinary weekend was also her Jehovah Rapha, her master physician. He knew what her day held and about her responsibilities. She trusted He would help her find a path that would keep Luke and Gabby safe and give her the wisdom to know when to call Jack if the headache became debilitating.

Jack had just returned to his office after spending three hours putting the victim of a motorcycle accident back together. Thankfully, the young man's prognosis was good, mostly because he'd been wearing a helmet and had been with friends who'd called for help immediately. Taking a deep breath, Jack stretched, trying to get the kinks out, and was feeling a bit better when his cell phone rang. He picked it up, saw it was Pete calling, and answered, "Hey there, did you have a good day?"

"Dad, something's wrong with Mom." Pete's voice was trembling. "When I got home, I found her on the floor in the living room. Gabby was beside her, slapping her arm, and Luke was in his high chair. When I got to her, Mom tried to talk, but I couldn't understand her. She's awake, but when I tried to lift her into a chair, her legs kept giving out, and she couldn't grab my arm. What do I do? She can't tell me."

Jack swallowed his fear, knowing his son would sense it. He took a deep breath and replied levelly, "Pete, please put a quilt over her and tell her that I'm on my way with help. Make sure she's breathing okay and take care of the little ones until I can get there. Can you do that?"

"Yeah, Dad, but hurry, okay?"

Jack looked up when his colleague Andrea Barstow walked into the ER treatment room. When Jack had gotten home, hours before, Liz couldn't stand, couldn't form words, and he could tell from the terror in her eyes that she was excruciatingly aware that something was badly wrong. Once they'd gotten to EBCH and Andi had examined Liz, they'd sat alone for hours in the small room. Occasionally, nurses and techs interrupted the quiet, greeting Jack, then drawing blood for tests and checking Liz's vitals. Just over an hour ago, they'd taken Liz away to do an MRI of her brain. Grateful that Beth was staying with the kids, Jack waited and prayed through the long hours. Now he hoped that Andi had some good news to share.

Sitting down beside Jack, Andi gently squeezed his hand. "Jack, there's no evidence of a stroke or aneurysm on the scan, but Liz still can't talk, and her left side is paralyzed. Did she fall or hit her head recently? It's possible the scan missed something."

Shaking his head, Jack said, "No, apart from a twinge every now and again from when she broke her collarbone, she's been fine. She was fine this morning when I left for the hospital. She didn't call me during the day, but from the looks of things at home, she must have known something was happening because she put our son in his high chair and Gabby was on the floor where she couldn't fall. Andi, Liz looked terrified when I found her. I'm pretty certain she knows something's happened to her and that it's something she's never experienced before. I was sure she'd had a major stroke."

"There's no sign of that kind of bleed, Jack, and her vitals are normal with the exception of a slightly elevated temp—just over one hundred degrees. Can I ask you a question before I call for a complete neurological work up?"

Jack nodded. "Of course."

"You told me that Liz has suffered from migraines for years. Do you know if she's ever had something called an aural migraine— one that affects the vision without causing as much pain as a typical migraine?"

"Yes, she's had a couple of those since we've been together. Why? Her symptoms today go far beyond anything I saw when she had those migraines."

"I know," Andi said soothingly before continuing, "Do you ever remember her saying anything about something called a hemiplegic migraine?"

Jack thought for a moment, trying to remember the literature he'd read when he first started researching migraines. "No, she hasn't said anything about them, nor has she had one since we've been married. She has no family history of that kind of migraine although her father got what we would now diagnose as migraines frequently." He looked at Andi. "Do you think that could be what's wrong with her? A migraine?"

"I know it seems unlikely, but a hemiplegic migraine is a different animal from a regular migraine. Hemiplegic migraines can cause temporary symptoms ranging from slurred speech, elevated temperature, and pronounced muscle weakness or even paralysis, all the way up to coma. I'd like to have Dr. Elise Paikkala, one of our neurologists and a headache specialist take a look at Liz. Any objections?"

"No," Jack said, relieved that Andi had ruled out a stroke and aneurysm. "I still can't believe that this could just be a migraine."

Andi got up. "Have you had a migraine before, Jack? I mean an honest-to-goodness migraine?"

Jack shook his head. "Thankfully, no."

"Then never say 'just a migraine.' Elise will be in shortly." Andi walked out of the room, shutting the door behind her. Jack, properly chastened, took Liz's hand, held it to his heart, and prayed.

⁓

"You're what?" Jack raised his eyebrows in disbelief at his colleague. It was just after eight the following morning, and while his wife was awake and talking, she didn't look good at all.

"I'm releasing Liz later this morning. The nasal ketamine worked. She's conscious and aware, and the left side weakness is resolving. She doesn't need hospitalization to recover from a migraine."

"This wasn't just a migraine." Jack had all he could do to keep from shouting at Andi, who was now into her second shift, because she was filling in for him.

The door to the ER examining room behind them opened, and Liz stuck her head out, looking at Jack with a frown. "Will you please quit arguing with my doctor? I'm the one who wants to go home, and Andi is one of the few people around here willing to stand up to you." She tilted her head back toward the small room behind her. "Come back in here, and for goodness' sake, be nice. I'm not going to say I'm fine, but I feel a whole lot better."

By the time Jack lost the argument again, they were on their way home. Liz took his hand. "Honey, I'm so sorry to have scared you like this. Just after you left yesterday morning, I figured out I was having an aural migraine. I've dealt with those before and didn't see any reason to call you. The pain wasn't too bad, and I had a nice day with Gabby and Luke. Then just before Pete was due home, I had trouble getting up off the floor. When I managed to get to my feet, I put Luke in his high chair, and was intending to put Gabs down for her nap, but my legs gave out, and I fell in the living room. Gabby sat beside me the entire time I was there with the two wee ones, and then Pete came home and called you. I was sure I'd had a stroke. I could see you, hear you, talk to you even though what I thought I was saying wasn't what was coming out of my mouth. I have to tell you, I'm relieved that this was a migraine and not something worse and far more debilitating."

Jack squeezed her hand. "Me too."

Try as she would, Liz couldn't get Jack to say much more. After a while, she gave up, and uncharacteristically, they finished the trip home in silence.

It was a difficult afternoon between the kids all wanting to talk at once when they got home and Jack's silence. He helped get lunch for everyone, said a few words to the kids, and asked Liz to let him clean up so she could go lie down. Despite her best efforts, that didn't happen. Pete was worried and wanted to talk with her, and then Luke started to scream. Jack was working with Gabby on her exercises, so Liz picked up the squalling toddler, put him on the potty, and changed his clothes when he finished. After that, she put him down for a nap, which resulted in more histrionics. She'd just picked him up again when Jack came into Luke's room and frowned at her. "What are you still doing up?"

Liz smiled grimly, determined not to give in to the urge to smack her husband. "What does it look like I'm doing, Jack? We have a very unhappy young man here, and it's not just him being uncooperative. He's cutting his molars."

Jack stomped into the bathroom and reappeared a moment later with the children's liquid pain reliever. After giving Luke a dose, Jack put him down in the crib, ignoring the screams that came the moment he let go of the toddler. Whirling around, Jack held up the bottle. "Did it ever occur to you to just give him something to help with his pain?"

Liz's eyes widened at his tone. "What's going on here, Jack? You're usually the one who medicates the kids, but I knew you were busy and I was just about to go get Luke something. He was fine until I tried to put him down for a nap."

"And picking him up every time he's upset is sending him the wrong message. No wonder he screams when we put him in his crib." Jack's voice got louder with every word.

Liz looked at Jack for a long moment, her lips set in a straight line. "Okay, since you're clearly the expert, I'll leave you to it. I'll be upstairs in the study resting if any of the *kids* need me." Before he could say a word, she left the room, hoping he'd caught her emphasis on the word kids.

A few hours later, Pete tapped on the door to the study. "Mom, it's me. Can I come in, please?"

"Uh, yeah, sure."

When Pete opened the door, Liz was sitting on the sofa in the dark, a tissue wadded up in her hand, and her eyes red and watery. He sat down beside her and hugged her. "Mom, I'm sorry. I should have helped more with Luke so you could have rested like Dad wanted you to."

Patting her son's back, Liz said, "Pete, none of this is your fault. I'm fine. I told you what happened was just a different kind of migraine. I'm sorry I scared you. As for this afternoon, you did nothing wrong. I thought I was doing okay with Luke until your dad came in," Liz gulped, trying to finish, "and…and…"

"Dad yelled at you, Mom. I've never heard him do that. Maybe if I'd helped you with Luke, he wouldn't have gotten so mad. Why did he get so mad?"

Liz had no idea what was going on with Jack, her head still hurt, and all she wanted was to be left alone so she could cry in peace. Still, she couldn't leave Pete thinking this mess was his fault. Taking his hand, she looked him in the eyes. "Pete, honey, I don't know why Dad got mad, but I think, I hope, it was because he was worried about me. He loves me and got frustrated when I didn't lie down. He knows a lot more medicine than either you or I do, so maybe he was trying to get me to listen."

"Getting mad is a really stupid way to show someone that you love them. It was you and Dad who taught me that. You show someone love by helping them, not hurting them."

"Pete, honey, none of us are perfect. I'm not sure why your dad's so upset, but it must be bad for him to respond that way. Please try to forgive him."

"Have you forgiven him?" Pete asked bluntly.

Liz smiled a watery smile. "I'm working on it. Did you, Gabby, and Luke get some supper?"

Pete fidgeted. "Yeah, Dad warmed up some of that soup you made last week. It was good, thanks."

"You should thank your dad. He's the one who made your dinner."

"I don't want to talk to Dad right now. I told him I was coming up to bed, but I wanted to check on you first." A tear trickled down Pete's cheek, and he dashed it away angrily. "Mom, he was mean to you, and he wouldn't even let me come up and see if you wanted dinner. Why would he do that?"

"Because he's a very mixed-up guy right now, Pete, and he was wrong to do those things," Jack said from the open doorway. He looked at Liz. "I'm sorry for my behavior. I love you, and I was wrong to say and do what I did. Can you both forgive me?"

After Pete left, Jack sat down beside his wife and bowed his head. "I really blew it today, Liz. I don't even know what to say apart from I'm so sorry. It was like I was watching someone else open his mouth and say those things to you." He took her hand. "You know I love you, right?"

With her free hand, Liz rubbed the back of his neck. "Of course I do. Please believe that I didn't say anything negative about you to Pete."

Jack attempted a smile. "I know, I listened for a few minutes before I said something. You were far too gracious to me. Especially since Pete was right, my behavior was appalling."

"Can you tell me why? What's going on in your head? Are you angry because I didn't call you to come home or are you tired of me getting sick all the time?" Liz asked.

Jack brushed Liz's forehead with a soft kiss. "I'm not angry with you, Liz, nor am I tired of you. I love you. I hate that you have to cope with these chronic illnesses, and I want to do everything I can to help you through them, not pitch a fit like I did earlier." He rubbed his forehead. "I can't even tell you exactly what happened, except it seems like every time I get to feeling blessed, something awful happens. We had a great long weekend together, Gabby is walking on her own, getting stronger every day, then yesterday, I get a call from my scared-out-of-his-wits son telling me that you were on the floor and he couldn't get you up. I came home to find you almost unresponsive, except for the sheer terror in your eyes."

Jack put his head down on his balled fist. "Liz, do you know how scared I was that I'd lost you? At least the part of you who sings, who creates exquisite beauty with her hands, and who makes my life and our kid's lives so rich with her love. What would I have done if what I feared had really happened? I'm still terrified by the thought," he confessed, raw agony in his voice.

Liz prayed silently for wisdom, knowing she'd be every bit as scared if Jack had been the one flat out on the floor. "Jack, honey, I'm right here, and I love you. I don't know what else to say except that what you feared didn't happen. It was just a new and improved version of a migraine. As much as you may not want to hear this, my migraines are probably going to be around for as long as I am. Although," she made a face, "I could do with never having another one like this again."

Jack closed his eyes. "That makes two of us. Liz, please don't leave me without letting me say goodbye. Promise me. I can't do that again."

In a moment of clarity, Liz understood what was going on with her husband. She waited until Jack opened his eyes, then she took his hand. "Jack, honey, I can't promise you that, but what I can promise is that every day God gives me with you, I will do my best to make you happy and to love you so well that you will never doubt that what we shared is worth the grief you feel at my home going. This is about Ellie and the way she died, isn't it?"

Taking a shuddering breath, Jack shrugged. "Five minutes ago, I would have said no. Now I don't know. All I know is that when I came into this house and found you the way I did, I thought I'd lost my chance forever to tell you that I love you and to see that warmth in your eyes that's for me alone. And yes, I thought of Ellie and remembered that the one thing I regretted most of all was not being able to tell her once more that I loved her. You've no idea what that's like."

"Actually, Jack, I do."

"I thought Eric died of a heart attack in the hospital. I just assumed that you were with him. Coronaries usually leave time for goodbyes if the victim makes it to the hospital."

"Well, 'usually' didn't apply in our case. Eric and I were in the living room reading one evening. I didn't think much of it when his book slipped from his hand. When it fell on the floor, I got up, picked it up, and went to shake Eric awake so he could go to bed. That's when I realized he wasn't breathing. I called 911 and started CPR. When the EMTs arrived, they shocked him and were able to get a heart rhythm, but his heart stopped again on the way to the hospital, and he was DOA. He never regained consciousness. The last thing I said to him was that he watched too much television and I just wanted some quiet so I could read. I was stunned when they told me he was gone. I was the one with all the health issues. I weighed over three hundred pounds at the time, so we'd always assumed that if anyone was going to be dying before their time, it was going to be me. Needless to say, I carry around my own scars from that night, so, Jack, believe me when I tell you I understand."

Jack smoothed Liz's hair away from her face. "I didn't know you were alone with him when it happened. I'm so sorry I never asked for the particulars."

"That's why I hate it when we fight, especially when we go to bed angry with each other, or when I get so busy with the kids in the morning that I forget to tell you how much I love you." Liz covered his hand with hers. "Jack, honey, bad things happen to everyone. If we dwell on them, we begin to live in fear. Once that happens, we end up not living at all and not able to love because loving requires a willingness to risk loss. For us, having already lost someone dear, that's not an abstract concept. We know how tearing that pain is, we know what it's like to wake up in the morning, breathing normally, and then memory returns and with it the crushing weight of grief. I'm willing to take a chance with you and the kids because you all bring such beauty and joy to my life. What about you? Can you get past this fear?"

Instead of answering Liz, Jack took her hand and led her down the stairs and into their bedroom. He made love to her, slowly and tenderly, letting his touch heal them both. Afterward, they lay together, his head on her stomach. Kissing her soft skin, he said, "I love you, and I want you in my life forever or for as long as God gives us. Please help me move past this place. Pray with me and for me, and I will do the same for you."

Liz, worn out and glowing, ran her fingers through his hair. "I love you too, Jack, and of course we can pray together." Her stomach gurgled, and Jack raised his head, looking surprised. Giggling, Liz pushed herself upright. "After we eat, I'm starved."

A little while later, they sat at the dining table, eating the remainder of the soup. It was well past midnight, and the house was quiet. When Liz finished, she plunked herself in Jack's lap and cuddled close.

"Wow, God really works fast." Pete's voice came out of the darkness at the foot of the stairs. He walked into the dining room, his eyes moving over his parents, clad in their bathrobes, cuddled together in one chair, with empty bowls in front of them.

Jack didn't let go of Liz, but he stopped stroking her back long enough to say, "How's that, Pete?"

"I've been praying for you guys tonight and about what Mom said to me. I wanted so much to be mad at you, Dad, but Mom wouldn't let me. Still, I didn't think things would ever be right again, so I prayed. Are you guys okay?"

Liz got up and put her arms around their son. "We are, honey. I told you we would be. Your dad and I just needed time to talk."

Pete looked from one of them to the other and smiled broadly. "Our God really is awesome!"

After Pete got a glass of milk and went back upstairs, Liz sat back down in Jack's lap, her shoulders shaking with laughter. "That poor kid, he keeps walking in on us at the worst times. Do you remember thinking about your parents, um, 'doing it?' I do, and for a long time, all I could come up with was 'eew, gross.' I was convinced they'd gone out and bought my brother and me. Can you imagine what Pete is thinking after all this?"

"That his dad is one buff dude?" Jack asked hopefully.

Liz smacked his arm gently. "I'm serious."

"Liz, we're both covered from neck to ankles in flannel, you were doing nothing more than sitting in my lap, and I wasn't even touching you," Jack grinned, "much. I don't really think we ruined our eldest for life tonight, but your point is sound. Are you ready to go back to bed?"

Shaking her head, Liz wound her arms around Jack's neck. "Not really. I'm comfortable right where I am, and I want to pray with you. Still, we probably don't have much of a choice if we don't want someone walking in on us again."

Jack kissed the top of Liz's head. "Love, there are always possibilities." He tightened his hold on her, got to his feet, and walked back into their bedroom holding her, shutting off the dining room light with his elbow. Settling into the recliner in the library area, he pulled the quilt from behind him and wrapped it around her. "How's this?"

"Perfect, I love being in your arms like this."

"And I love having you so close," Jack whispered.

Putting her arms around his neck, Liz pulled Jack's head down so she could rest her forehead against his and whispered, "'*For God has not given us a spirit of timidity, but of power and love and discipline.*'[6] I believe that, Jack. I also believe that God is our refuge and that He gives us a place to shelter when we're in danger or afraid. The Psalmist says,

> '*You will not be afraid of the terror by night,*
> *Or of the arrow that flies by day;*
> *Of the pestilence that stalks in darkness…*
> *For He will give His angels charge concerning you,*
> *To guard you in all of your ways.*
> *They will bear you up in their hands,*
> *Lest you strike your foot against a stone.*'"[7]

Liz looked up, her gaze holding Jack's. "I'm so sorry that Ellie left you alone like she did, especially when you'd had so little time together. I'm certain that wasn't her choice. I love you, Jack, and I won't willingly leave you alone either through death or through some form of living death. You're my earthly joy, and I love being your wife. Still, as Reynoso said, chances are that one or the other of us is going to have to face that kind of loss. I don't want to live my life in the fear of that time, and I don't want you to live that way either. It can only sap your joy in the present and your wonderful witness of its power."

---

[6] 2 Timothy 1:7 NASB.

[7] Psalm 91:5–6a, 11–12 NASB.

Jack nodded. "I know all this in my head, Liz, but something else took over yesterday, and I forgot to follow the instructions found at the beginning of Psalm 91, you know, that part that says, *'He who dwells in the shelter of the Most High, will abide in the shadow of the Almighty. I will say to the Lord, My refuge and my fortress, My God, in whom I trust.'*[8] That's what happened earlier. After you collapsed, I thought I was going to lose you, just like I lost Ellie. I forgot to dwell in the shelter of our Most High. I let fear gain a foothold in my spirit. Once that happened, it controlled my actions to a point that I hurt you and our son last evening, and I am so sorry. Forgive me, please."

"You were forgiven before you started talking last night, Jack." Liz closed her eyes and sang quietly,

> *Amazing grace*
> *How sweet the sound*
> *That saved a wretch like me*
> *I once was lost, but now I'm found*
> *Was blind, but now I see*
>
> *'Twas grace that taught my heart to fear*
> *And grace my fears relieved*
> *How precious did that grace appear*
> *The hour I first believed*

Jack smiled at Liz. "That was one of the first songs you ever sang to me. I know God's forgiven me. It's your forgiveness I'm asking for now."

Liz reached up and caressed his cheek. "I meant what I said about forgiveness, Jack, and that includes mine. You say you know God's forgiven you. If that's true, then you are truly free from the bondage of your past, including the unreasoning fear of untimely separation from those you love. If they are in Christ, then homegoing is a cause for pain, yes, but also for celebration. You don't have to live in fear because as you told me and Pete when Gabby was in the hos-

---

[8]   Psalm 91:1–2 NASB.

pital, God holds us all in the palm of His hand and loves us beyond imagination. Your chains are gone." She grinned, "And yes, 'Amazing Grace' was one of the first songs we shared, but this is 'Amazing Grace' with a twist."

Sitting up, she sang.

*My chains are gone*
*I've been set free*
*My God, my Savior has ransomed me*
*And like a flood His mercy rains*
*Unending love, Amazing grace*

*The Lord has promised good to me*
*His word my hope secures*
*He will my shield and portion be*
*As long as life endures*

Jack listened, his mouth slightly open. Some of the verses were those of the traditional hymn he knew and loved, but the "my chains are gone" verses soared as a completion of the traditional words—the joyful promise of what God's grace does in the life of a believer.

*My chains are gone*
*I've been set free*
*My God, my Savior has ransomed me*
*And like a flood His mercy rains*
*Unending love, Amazing grace*

Liz motioned Jack to join her. Holding hands, they together sang.

*My chains are gone*
*I've been set free*
*My God, my Savior has ransomed me*
*And like a flood His mercy rains*
*Unending love, Amazing grace*

*The Earth shall soon dissolve like snow*
*The sun forbear to shine*
*But God, Who called me here below*
*Will be forever mine*
*Will be forever mine*
*You are forever mine*[xi]

When they finished, Liz squeezed Jack's hands. "Honey, God says, '*Be anxious for nothing, but in everything by prayer and supplication with thanksgiving let your requests be made known to God. And the peace of God, which surpasses all comprehension, will guard your hearts and your minds in Christ Jesus.*'[9] I know He can heal our hearts of painful yesterdays, and before you say it's just you with the problem, please remember what I almost did after I came home three years back. I was so afraid of losing you that I almost gave up on the most precious gift God's ever given me. I never want to make that mistake again." She squeezed his fingers. "I love you so much."

Bowing their heads, they prayed, minutes turning to hours and finally to sleep, right where they sat snuggled together in the chair.

---

[9]   Philippians 4:6–7 NASB.

# CHAPTER 19

## A LONG DAY'S NIGHT IN THE WILDERNESS

"Mom, Dad?"

Liz forced her eyes open and realized they'd fallen asleep in the recliner where they'd prayed through the early hours of the morning. Clearing her throat, she looked up at her eldest who was standing in the doorway of their bedroom, holding his younger siblings' hands. "Good morning, Pete. What, uh, what time is it?"

"About eight thirty. I'm sorry that I woke you up, but the door was open. I wanted to know if I should give Gabby and Luke some cereal or something? They're both kind of hungry."

Extricating herself from Jack's embrace, Liz shook him gently and then stood up. "Pete, honey, thanks, but I'll get breakfast. I just overslept, that's all. Will you please get the little ones ready and to the table? I'll make cheesy eggs. How does that sound?"

"Yummo, Mama!" Gabby yelled enthusiastically. "Cheesy eggs are my favorite!"

Liz smiled as Pete led Gabby and Luke out of the bedroom. Jack was slow waking up, so she bent and kissed him. "Hey, you, our kids caught us sleeping and are starved. How do you feel about some cheesy eggs?"

Jack wrapped his arms around Liz's waist and rested his head on her chest. "If it was just us, I'd say let's skip the eggs and go back to sleep, but," he sighed, "I don't want our kids to starve, so yeah, cheesy eggs sound great."

A short while later, Liz tried to keep her eyes open while she chewed a mouthful of her special cheesy eggs. The kids and Jack loved them, but right now, she wished she didn't have to expend the energy chewing required, it had been hard enough just to get showered and dressed. At four this morning, she'd been wide awake and enjoying praying with Jack. Now she was paying the price. How she was going to get through a full Saturday with Jack and the kids home, she had no idea. The last forty-eight hours had been a challenge, and she could feel pain curling in her muscles.

"Liz," Jack shook her gently, "love, wake up."

Liz started awake, her cheeks flushing when she realized she was napping with her head on her hand at the breakfast table. She looked up at Jack. "I'm sorry, I must have dozed off. Where are the kids?"

Smiling, Jack crouched beside her. "They finished their eggs, toast, and juice then scattered. Luke and Gabby are watching a cartoon, and Pete's up in his room, probably recovering from seeing his parents occupying the same chair for the second time in twenty-four hours. I don't think any of them noticed how uncharacteristically quiet their mother is this morning. I was afraid you were about to go face down in your eggs, so I," he winked at her, "rescued you."

Liz scooted back from the table and hugged Jack. "My hero. I'm sorry, I guess I'm too old to stay up most of the night and still function in the morning." Caressing his forehead, she said, "I don't regret a moment of our time last night. I feel a lot better."

Jack got to his feet, pulling Liz with him, then stood holding her. "Me too. Thank you for being the blessing you are to me." Cupping her chin, he studied her face. "You look beat, and when you get this tired, bad things happen. Will you please lie down and rest? I'll clean up the kitchen, and later, the kids and I will go on a discovery walk so you have some quiet time."

Liz pouted. "I love our discovery walks. I'll go lay down now, but why don't you let me know before you leave, and if I'm a bit more awake, I'll join you." She stood on tiptoe and kissed Jack. "Thank you. I love you. Wake me if you need me."

Liz woke to Jack gently shaking her shoulder. She opened her eyes. "Hey, do you need help with something?"

"No, love, I just wanted to let you know that Pete and I are heading out with the little ones for our walk. You asked me to wake you. Do you want to come with us?"

Noticing that Jack wore Gabby's backpack carrier, Liz thought for a moment then shook her head. "I'm going to pass. It looks like you're ready to go and I'm still really tired. Is that okay?"

Jack hugged her close. "Yes, it's okay. Pete and I will be fine. He's got Luke's snuggie, and I can carry Gabs when she gets tired of walking. We'll all miss you, but I," his eyes darkened as he kissed her deeply, "don't want to take any chances with you just recovering from a migraine like you had the other day. Do you need anything before we leave?"

Liz shook her head. "No, I'm fine," she smiled, "really. Just go and have a great time. Be careful."

When Liz lay back against her pillow, Jack said, "We will. I've got the SAT phone if you need us. I'll lock you in and we'll be back in a couple of hours."

Liz curled up, listening to the general hilarity and chaos as Jack and the kids got ready to leave. She was almost ready to get up and go with them when the house was suddenly quiet. She could hear them outside and had to smile when she heard Gabby say, "Giddyap, Daddy," like he was her faithful steed, which, Liz thought, he was. Gabby had her daddy wrapped around her little finger, and Jack was blissfully unaware of it.

Snuggling under the quilt, Liz relaxed in the puddle of sunshine on their bed. It was so peaceful. She was warm, and the birds chirped outside their window. She was almost asleep when she heard muffled voices outside. Frowning, she got up, intending to go see who was there when she heard glass breaking in the other room. Someone rattled the doorknob. Liz realized they'd shattered the sidelight on the front door in an effort to get to the release for the deadbolt lock.

Shutting the bedroom door, Liz quietly retrieved her pistol and SOB (small of back) holster from the locked false bottom in the nightstand drawer and then loaded a magazine from the lockbox on the bookshelf. She grabbed her emergency kit and the other SAT phone from the dresser drawer and was just about to leave through the French doors when she heard someone right outside their bedroom. Wheeling around, she ducked and crawled under the bed, just as whoever was in the living room opened the door.

Liz listened from her hiding place. The two men were having a conversation in Spanish and were clearly frustrated that the Lockwoods were nowhere around. According to what she was hearing, they'd checked the garage and found all three vehicles parked inside and so had expected to find the family at home or somewhere close by. When she heard the reason they were looking for her family, Liz knew that she had to get out of the house and warn them before they unknowingly walked into a trap.

The men did a cursory search, then retreated to the living area to wait. Liz scooted free of the bed. Hearing others outside, she elected to go out the window in their bath, emerging on the far side of the house from the garage. She ran into the trees and stopped, watching the men in their yard. That was a mistake, and one of them spotted her and yelled. Not wasting another second, Liz took off down the barely visible trail at her feet.

After about ten minutes, she slowed her pace and listened carefully. She couldn't see or hear any sign of pursuit, so she pulled the phone from her pocket and called Jack.

⁓

Jack was holding Gabby's hand as she picked wintergreen leaves from the forest floor. When she finished, she put one in her mouth and chewed vigorously. "Tastes minty," she declared with satisfaction. She handed one to Luke. "Here, try this."

Luke took it, put it in his mouth, took an experimental bite, and spit it out. "Yuck!"

Jack squeezed Gabby's hand and looked up at Pete. "You just can't please some folk. Let's go down by…" The SAT phone in Jack's daypack rang, so he gave Gabby's hand to Pete, pulled the phone free, and answered. "Hey, love, is everything…" He stopped, listening to his wife's gasping words.

"Liz, are you okay?" he asked after a few minutes. "No, I understand. We won't go home. You want to meet us where?"

"Our…our rock by the wetlands," Liz panted. "Can you do that?"

"Yes. Liz, are you sure you…" Jack stopped again, hearing the sound of a gunshot. "Liz!"

"I'm okay, they just, just…"

Jack heard the sound of another gunshot, then Liz cried out, and he could hear what sounded like crashing through the underbrush. The connection went dead, leaving him staring at the silent phone.

"Dad? Dad! What's wrong? Was that Mom?" Pete let go of Gabby's hand long enough to shake Jack's shoulder. "Dad!"

Jack blinked, trying to absorb both Liz's call and Pete's by now frightened pleas for his attention. "Yeah, Pete, that was Mom. It sounds like she's in trouble. Someone broke into the house a little while ago."

"Mom was there all by herself. Did they hurt her? Where is she?"

Jack put a hand on Pete's shoulder, trying to calm his son while forcing down his own fears. "She got out, Pete, and was calling to warn us not to go home. From what your mom overheard, someone's after Gabby and doesn't mind going through the rest of us to get to her. When we were talking, they must have found Mom and started shooting. The last thing I heard was your mom scream and then nothing. The phone cut out."

A plan started to form in Jack's scattered thoughts. Pulling Pete, who was carrying Luke, down beside him, he cuddled Gabby in his lap. "Pete, I need you to do something for all of us. I have to go after your mom and make sure she's okay."

Pete nodded vigorously. "Let's go!"

Shaking his head, Jack said calmly, "Not *us*, Pete, *me*. They're after Gabs, so I don't want any of you anywhere near them. I need you to take Gabby and Luke and head west. I'll call Dan and arrange for him to meet you where the trail crosses Snowbank Lake Road. It's a long hike, Pete, and you'll probably have to walk most of the night or rest and finish walking out in the morning. I'm going to leave the phone with you so you can stay in contact with Dan. If your mom calls, tell her what you're doing and that I'm coming for her. I'll write down some instructions for you along with the compass headings and landmarks for your hike. You also take the first aid kit, the water purification tablets, and the snacks. I know carrying these two can be really hard, so rest as you need to, but no campfires. I'll find your mom, and we'll leave a trail for these guys to follow so you can get away. Can you do this?"

Looking scared, Pete nodded. "I think so, Dad. But why can't we just stay together, find Mom, and then go meet Uncle Dan?"

"Because that's what they'll expect us to do, and as I said, I don't want these guys anywhere close to the three of you. I know you can do this. We've done similar hikes when you and I have gone out for overnights." Jack looked Pete in the eyes. "I love you, and I trust you to keep the little ones safe. Dan will be waiting for you, and actually, if I know him, he'll hike in to meet you." Jack spent the next few minutes scribbling notes and talking to Pete about the route. Then hugging all his kids close, Jack prayed for their safety and for God to give Pete the stamina he needed for the trip. Then he called Dan, pulled several items out of his daypack, including his compass and flashlight, and put them into Pete's pack. After walking back to the place where the trail forked, Jack hugged Pete, kissed Gabby and Luke, and admonished them, "You guys be good and mind your brother. I love you all. Be safe."

Pete looked at Jack. "I'll keep the kids safe, Dad, I swear. You be careful and find Mom. Love you too."

With that, Pete turned down the path, carrying Luke in front of him wrapped in his snuggie and a crying Gabby on his back in her pack. Jack watched as they walked out of sight and was relieved when his daughter's cries faded into choked hiccups. He took a deep breath, battling back fear, and prayed that he hadn't seen the last of his family. His wife was missing under frightening circumstances, and he'd just sent his son off on a grueling eight-mile hike carrying his brother and sister. Jack knew that a trek like that would challenge his own strength, and he was not at all certain that Pete could manage it on his own. Still, Dan would be coming for them from the other end of the trail. If Jack could get to Liz, and if she wasn't badly hurt, they could draw their pursuers away from the kids long enough for the three of them to reach safety. After that, things were in the hands of the Ely police department and the St. Louis County sheriff.

After praying for a few minutes, Jack moved down the trail toward their house. He was getting close to their property line, so he stayed focused, watching for any sign of movement in the woods ahead of him. The last thing he wanted was to be discovered when he was trying to find Liz.

⁓

Liz blinked, trying to orient herself. Her head hurt, and when she tried to move, searing pain shot through her right shoulder. Finally managing to roll over and sit up, she realized that her right arm was hanging limply by her side and that the back of her head was sticky with blood. She'd come to rest half in and half out of Lupine Creek at the bottom of a ravine. She frowned, trying to remember what had happened. She remembered calling Jack, her pursuers shooting at her, and then taking a step backward into nothingness. She got to her feet, gritting her teeth as pain stabbed through her again. Her back was stiff and sore, but her arm and head hurt the worst. Her emergency kit was around her waist, and her gun still rested in the holster at the small of her back. She was right-handed, so the gun wasn't going to do her much good, but she was still glad it was there. Looking around, she couldn't find the SAT phone.

Without the phone, Liz had to get to Jack and the kids. She didn't know how long she'd been out and prayed that enough of her message had gotten through that her family was still waiting for her at the rock. The sun was low in the sky, slanting through the trees. At this time of year, darkness would descend quickly once the sun dropped below the horizon. If that happened, she'd never find them. Following the creek bed, she looked for a way up the bank. It was quiet in the woods, and she didn't hear any signs of pursuit. Finally, she found a gully that appeared climbable. Struggling to the top of the bank, she found the trail. Ducking into the underbrush, she looked around but didn't see or hear anything, so she started in the direction of the rock, praying that Jack was still there with the kids.

Liz stopped to check her compass, and as she did so, a hand clapped over her mouth and dragged her into the woods. Terrified, Liz fought her captor, driving her left elbow into his gut as she stomped on his instep. The man let out a muffled groan, held her more tightly, and hissed in her ear. "Liz, it's me. Quiet."

Astonished, Liz went limp as Jack removed his hand from over her mouth. "Jack," she whispered, "you're hurting me. Can you please let go of my arm?"

Jack let go of Liz and, taking her left hand, he led her away from the trail and east. After they'd gone about a mile, the sun fell below the horizon and twilight closed in around them. After another mile, it was almost dark. He stopped, listened intently for a couple of minutes, then sank down on a rock, pulling her with him. He avoided touching or jarring her shoulder. Kissing her, he whispered, "Thank God you're okay."

"Where are the kids? Are they safe?"

Jack nodded and said, "Liz, we need to get out of the immediate vicinity. The bad guys are only a mile or so behind us, and I want them to follow us until it gets really dark. Can you walk a little further? I'll explain everything when we stop."

Looking up at Jack, Liz said wearily, "Yes, I'm fine. I'm just tired, and I did something to my right shoulder when I fell. Let's get out of here, and I'll tell you about it later."

Liz struggled to keep up with Jack, who still had a tight hold on her hand. She tripped and fell full-length on the ground but managed to get up before he had to pull her to her feet. "Jack," she whispered, "we need to slow down a little. It's getting dark, and I can't see all the obstacles in my path."

Jack didn't say anything but slowed his pace, taking more care in choosing their route through the woods. After another forty minutes or so, he stopped, stepped off the trail onto the granite shoreline of the lake that had opened in front of them. They were well into the BWCA, and by this time, Liz had no idea where they were. Pulling her down into a crouch, he said, "Rest for a minute. This is where we leave the guys behind us in the dust. Are you wearing your hiking boots?"

"Yeah, but if you're worried about me getting wet, it's too late. I landed in Lupine Creek earlier and am already drenched from my thighs down."

Jack's brow furrowed. "That's not good. I don't want you to get chilled because we'll likely be out here until morning, and it's going down to about forty-five degrees tonight."

"Don't worry. Let's just lose these guys so we can rest. Where are we heading?"

"Into the burn area. I need a clear view to the west and south. I have a place in mind where there's some shelter from the wind. To get there, we need to go wading along the shore for about one hundred yards then pick up the trail."

"The moon isn't up yet. Can you find the trail in the dark? Otherwise..." Liz smiled faintly in the rapidly fading light, pulled her pack around to her front, and clumsily unzipped it with her left hand. Triumphantly, she held up a small LED flashlight. "I have this."

Hugging her carefully, Jack grinned. "Thank you! I gave mine to Pete, so this will really help."

"Can you tell me where the kids are?" Liz asked as they got to their feet.

"Let's get to where we're going before the light gives out completely, then I promise I'll tell you the whole story. They're fine." Leading Liz by the hand, Jack quietly stepped into the shallow water and whispered under his breath, "I hope."

---

Jack found the indistinct side trail without having to turn on the flashlight. He set off at a fast pace, pulling Liz with him. He knew she was tiring quickly, and they needed to cover a lot of ground before they rested for the night.

After another three miles, Liz tugged at Jack's hand, stopping him, "I can't go any further." She was white, bent over at the waist, and gasping for air. "I need to rest. I'm sorry."

Jack led her off the trail and sat down on a fallen tree, pulling Liz with him. She had tears in her eyes. He cradled her close. "There's nothing to apologize for, Liz. You're doing great! There are only about two miles left before we get to the spot I have in mind."

"Two miles might as well be ten, Jack, I'm done. Just leave me here and do what you need to do to make sure the kids are safe. I've got my kit and I'll be okay."

"Tell me what happened to you today, Liz. I can see you dislocated your shoulder and I promise I'll fix that as soon as I'm certain the guys chasing us won't hear you when you yell. What else is going on?"

"Other than the fact I'm out of shape compared to you?" Liz sighed unhappily. "I hit my head on a rock, so I have a bad headache, my back hurts, and I'm freezing. Apart from that, I'm just so tired." She blinked away tears. "I'm sor..."

Jack kissed her forehead. "If the word 'sorry' escapes those lips again, I'm going to get irritated. Your quick thinking saved all of us today. I don't know how you got out of the house, but by calling me when you did, you kept the kids and me safe. I know we need to talk, but right now, I need to get us to shelter." He took her shoulder in his hands, and after feeling the injured joint, he asked, "How did this happen?"

"I fell backward down into the...Ow!" Liz choked, tears running down her face. Jack had taken her upper arm and in a swift, twisting move put the ball of the joint back into the socket.

Holding Liz to him, Jack rubbed her back. "I'm sorry for doing that to you without warning, love, but believe me, it's better to do it when you're least expecting it. That way, you don't tense up. Still, I know how badly that procedure hurts, and I hated surprising you like that."

Liz moved her shoulder experimentally then her arm. "What you did really hurt, but it feels better now." She leaned against Jack.

"I still don't know how much further I can make it. I think we lost the goons, so just leave me here."

Jack stood and then lifted Liz onto his back. "I'm not leaving you alone."

"Jack, put me down!" Liz hissed. "You've been out here since before noon and have to be exhausted. Besides, I'm too heavy for a piggyback ride. It's not like you're just walking across a room with me. Please."

Jack adjusted his grip on her and calmly responded, "I'm fine, you're fine, and as I told you, we're almost there. So just relax and enjoy the ride. I rescue people far heavier than you all the time."

Liz leaned forward and nipped his ear. "Lockwood! Would you listen to me? Put me down, and I will find a way to walk with you the rest of the way. You don't carry your rescues halfway across the BWCA."

"Lockwood," Jack responded calmly, "I love you, but be quiet. I'm fine and I'm not going to put you down."

"I have my gun," Liz threatened.

"No, you don't. You gave it to me after we found each other, remember?" Jack responded smugly.

Liz looked a bit chagrined, but she came back quickly, "I could kick you where it counts."

Eying her suspiciously, Jack said, "That wouldn't be very polite."

"Well then, what should I do?" Liz sniffed.

"I guess if you don't want to relax where you are for the next couple of miles, you could always try 'giddyap, Jack.'"

Liz gave up and kissed Jack's neck. "Fine, if you can't move tomorrow, you have no one to blame but yourself." Sobering, she tried again. "Seriously, honey, I can probably walk some more. I do feel better thanks to what you did to my arm."

"Liz, I can see exhaustion and pain in your face and in your posture. You've done amazingly well today, especially given the migraine you had a couple of days ago, your interrupted night's sleep last night, and the fall you took earlier. The truth of the matter is, I do a lot of lifting in my rescue work, and right now, I want to carry you. It makes me feel like I'm not a complete failure as a husband since we seem to have people shooting at us again." Feeling her tense, he squeezed her thigh. "Kidding, just kidding. But won't you please, just this once, let me be your 'he' man?"

Liz stiffened but said nothing. Instead, she cuddled close to Jack's back and relaxed. They stopped twice for brief rests, but she still didn't say anything. Each time, when he picked her up, she put her arms around him and stayed quiet. Finally, they reached the rocky shelter that they'd been heading for since darkness had fallen. When he set her on her feet, she stretched and winced, then looked at her husband. "Thank you, honey. Do you have any idea what time it is?"

Jack pushed a button on the side of his watch, and when the dial lit up, he said, "It's a few minutes before nine. We made good time."

"Wow, I would have thought it was after midnight." Liz sighed morosely in the darkness. "Now that we've arrived, Jack, what can I do? Do you want me to go in search of some firewood?"

Jack took her hand and led Liz over to the place where the land dropped away in a steep slope. "Look, over there." He turned her so they had the same view out over the valley. There was a campfire back the way they'd come. It was several miles away, but she could see two tiny figures moving around.

"Uh, I guess that's a no on the firewood, huh?" Liz said sadly. "Is there anything else you want me to do before I sit down because once I'm down, it's going to take heavy equipment to get me up again?"

Jack kissed her temple. "How are you feeling?"

Shrugging her shoulders, Liz said, "About the same, except my shoulder doesn't hurt so much. I'm cold, and I've got a wicked headache."

Jack unbuckled Liz's emergency kit from around her waist, squatted down, and used the flashlight briefly to look inside. He pulled two flat packages from the interior. Moving closer to the rock outcropping to a place more sheltered from the wind and out of the line of sight from the group behind them, he opened one of the packages and spread a green tarp over the ground. Then he sat down and took her hand. "Come on. The first rule for staying warm is shared bodily heat." When she cuddled into his lap, he took his water bottle and gave it to her. "Drink what you need. I've got one more bottle, and I can filter more in the morning." After they'd both drunk their fill, he rested his forehead against hers. "Now before we try to rest, why don't you tell me what I did or said to upset you? You've hardly said a word to me since I started carrying you. Are you that angry that I didn't set you down?"

"I'm not angry with you, Jack." Liz touched his cheek. "Thank you for helping me up here. I'm sorry that I made you feel badly."

Jack's forehead wrinkled as he whispered, "You did nothing of the sort. What are you talking about?"

"What you said about being my 'he' man. You're always doing something that makes me feel that way, whether it's carrying me to our bed when we're making love, parenting our kids, or doing extra work around the house so I can rest. I was just worried about you earlier. I still don't know the story of your day after I called you, but I know you well enough to know that you took as much on yourself as you could. Since you found me, you've been taking care of me while eluding the guys chasing us. I've felt pretty much like the ball and chain slowing us down."

Jack chuckled and hugged her close. "Liz, sometimes I feel the same way. Today, prowlers breaking into our home awakened you from sleep, yet you kept a clear head and managed to hear enough so that we know why we're targets. Then you armed yourself, grabbed your kit, got out of the house, and called me. They started shooting at you while you were trying to warn me. If you fell where I think you fell, you survived a thirty-foot tumble down a very steep gully, dislocated your right shoulder, wrenched your back, and hit your head hard enough to put you out for, from what you described, was close to twenty minutes. After all that, you still found me. Since then, we've bushwhacked over six miles through the woods, and I only carried you for the last two. You never once questioned my route. You just trusted me enough to follow. I knew that you were worried about me when I picked you up, but I was more worried about you, especially after you got the bright idea for me to leave you behind. I wouldn't—couldn't—do that. No more than you would have left the woods today before trying to find the kids and me." Bending his head, Jack kissed her tenderly.

When they finally pulled apart, Liz rested her head on his chest. "I love you. Are you okay?"

"I'm tired and worried about my family. Otherwise, I'm fine." Jack looked at Liz, concern in his eyes. "Speaking about being worried about my family, I know you're cold, your jeans are still damp, and by morning, it's going to be a whole lot colder. I came prepared for a two hour walk in the woods with our kids, not an overnight like we're going to be facing. Thankfully Pete and I both brought our emergency kits. After your fall, I'm afraid you're not going to be able to move by daybreak. I have pain meds in my pack. May I please give you a dose? Otherwise, you're in for a very difficult night."

Liz held out her arm. "I'm not going to argue. I hurt."

After Jack gave her the shot, he tore open the other pouch and unfurled a space blanket, shiny on one side and earth-toned on the other. Tucking it around them, dark side up, he gathered her close, leaned back against the rock, and asked, "How's this?"

Liz curled up in his arms. "This is wonderful, Jack. Now, please, tell me what's going on with the kids. Where are they?"

After Jack explained, he added, "That's why we're up here because Dan's going to fire a flare when he's got the three of them safely out of the woods. Once he clears our house of vermin, he'll set off another flare. Then we'll start walking out, avoiding those two down below. Dan and his party will meet us somewhere between here and our place."

"Why didn't you go with the kids," Liz asked curiously.

Jack pressed his lips to Liz's forehead, kissing her gently. "Love, the last things I heard before the phone went dead were the sounds of shots being fired, your scream, and a lot of underbrush crashing. I had to go after you, so I gave Pete the other SAT phone, the first aid kit with the exception of the narcotics, and most of my supplies. He has my compass, the bear spray, and my flashlight. I figure the earliest they'll clear the woods will be about 2:00 a.m., but I think it's far more likely that it will be closer to sunrise. He's a smart kid."

"And he's being trained in outdoor safety and survival by one of the best teachers out there," Liz added. Resting her head against Jack's chest, she said, "Thank you. I know they'll be okay, especially with Dan on the way to find them." She yawned. "I can't believe this, but I'm actually getting sleepy."

Nuzzling her neck, Jack whispered, "That's good. Rest is the best thing for you."

"What about you?"

"I'm going to keep watch," Jack said, "but I don't think I'll make it through the night. I'm pretty beat. When I get tired, I'll wake you to spell me for a while."

Liz nodded, feeling Jack's warmth seep into her cold, tired body. Putting her arms around his waist she whispered, "Good. I want to do my share, and I know we'll both feel better when we see the bat signal in the west."

Jack's chest rumbled with laughter. "Go to sleep, wife. I love you."

"Love you too," Liz murmured. She moved against Jack once more and was asleep.

⌣﹏⌣

Cold! Liz woke in the deep night, trying to figure out where she was. She was shivering and hurt so badly that her every move made her gasp. Opening her eyes, she realized she was in Jack's arms. But why was she freezing? Lifting her head, she tried to orient herself. The world around them was dark and windy, and as she sat up, large drops of liquid ice spattered her arm. No wonder she was cold. They were in the middle of a fall rain that would be coming down as snow if it were just a few degrees colder. She looked up, her eyes meeting Jack's worried gaze. "Hey. How are you doing? Have you seen a flare? What time is it?"

Jack looked exhausted as he wrapped the blanket around Liz, leaving more of his body exposed to the elements. "Hey. I'm okay, except for this front moving in about twelve hours early. I haven't seen a flare yet, but I'm actually hoping that Pete will find some shelter and wait out this storm. It's shortly after 2:00 a.m., so I don't expect they're out of the woods yet. You look cold and like you're in pain. I have two doses of meds left." He scooted out from under her, stood up, and, putting his hands around her waist, lifted her to her feet.

Liz groaned but stayed vertical. "Where are we going?"

"The wind shifted, so we're moving under the rock face over there, plus we're going to stretch our muscles a bit. This cold can be dangerous, even with the blanket, especially now that we're both soaked. Walk with me." Jack grabbed their packs, the blanket, and the tarp. "Come on, I promise you'll be happy we did this."

Liz doubted she could make it five feet, but to her surprise, each step was easier than the one before. As they navigated the burned stumps and the new primary forest growth to the other end of the rock formation, she warmed up a bit. Squeezing Jack's hand, she said, "This was a good idea. I feel better now that I'm moving. I just wish this rain would stop. That wind is cold."

When they reached the shelter of the overhang, Jack put the tarp down before he said anything. "Love, I know you're cold, but at least we won't get wetter under here. Let's stretch before we sit down." He reached out and took her sore shoulder in his hands. When she flinched away at his touch, he patted her back soothingly. "Relax, I'm just going to help you stretch the joint a little. Nothing like the last time."

"Promise?" Liz moaned. "Because what you're doing really hurts." Gritting her teeth, she tried to work with Jack, stretching her sore shoulder, then her good shoulder, her back, and finally her legs. By the time they finished, she had tears running down her cheeks, but at least she was warmer. Finally, he sat down, took her in his arms, wrapped her in the blanket, and medicated her. A few minutes later, feeling the medication fog sweeping away her pain, she murmured, "Thank you, Jack, but what about you? How will you stay warm? Please take some of the blanket and cover us both like before."

"If I do that, you're going to get really chilled, and that worries me." Jack snapped on the flashlight and looked inside her emergency kit. The first smile she'd seen since she wakened crossed his face as he pulled out two more flat packets. "Bless you, Liz, for your tendency to overpack, especially since this is your summer kit." He took one of the packets, opened it, and unfurled another blanket identical to the one wrapped around her. In just a few seconds, she cuddled into his lap with one blanket around her shoulders and the other covering both of them. Then he snapped the other packet in half and handed it to her.

Liz felt the chemical hand warmer he'd given her start to thaw her cold fingers. Resting her head against Jack's shoulder, she undid three buttons on his damp wool flannel shirt and pressed the packet inside the opening against his chest, sharing the welcome heat. "How's this? Can you feel any warmth?"

Putting his hand over Liz's, Jack murmured, "Yes, I can. Thank you."

Liz could hear the ragged edge of exhaustion in his voice. Looking up at him, she said, "Why don't you let me keep watch for a while? Just point me to the right section of the sky. I'm too cold and wet to sleep right now, even with the drugs in my system. I promise to wake you up if I get sleepy."

Jack looked at Liz gratefully and handed her his watch. "Just give me an hour or so." He rested his chin on the top of her head. "Wake me if you get tired. Straight ahead of us is west, and you should be able to see the flare without a problem. Are you sure you can do this?"

Liz leaned back and kissed Jack's chin. "I'm a lot better and more awake than I was an hour ago. Thank you for helping me move and for medicating me. It's better over here, out of the wind and a lot drier. Plus, this little hand warmer puts out a lot of heat, and that feels really good. How long do these chemical packs last?" When he didn't answer, Liz lifted her head and smiled. He was already asleep.

Settling against Jack, Liz watched the night sky, praying for her children, her husband, and Dan's search party as she kept her vigil. She could tell by Jack's deep breathing that, despite the discomfort and cold, he was asleep. She was determined to keep watch for as long as she could. He'd pushed himself to the limit since they'd found each other on the trail, and now it was her turn. She blinked suddenly as a burst of red and orange lit the sky in front of her. It took her a few seconds to process what she was seeing, then she shook his shoulder. "Jack, look. The flare!"

Jack opened his eyes in time to see the last fizzle of color and hugged her close. "They're safe! What time is it?"

Liz looked at his watch. "It's almost 4:00 a.m."

"Praise God," Jack whispered in relief. "Pete made great time. I'm sure they're wet and cold, but if I know Dan, they'll soon be comfortable and resting with Beth and Buddy watching over them. I wish I could take care of you like that." Nuzzling Liz's neck, he kissed her. When she responded by wrapping her arms around his neck and deepening the kiss, he pulled her closer, his hands caressing her back. When they finally separated, they were both breathing heavily.

Liz smiled, her face just inches from Jack's, "Wow, that got the blood flowing. I'm not sleepy anymore, and I'm definitely warmer."

Jack rubbed her nose with his, "I'm warmer too, but another kiss like that, and we'd be breaking one of the rules of wilderness survival."

"Which one?" Liz teased. "I mean, we'd definitely be sharing body heat."

"True, but rolling around in the mud sans clothing isn't a good idea when the only thing separating this rain from snow is about ten degrees. So don't tempt me." Jack kissed Liz again, this time more gently, touching her lightly until she made a soft sound of contentment, relaxing against him. Then he rubbed her back. "That's it, love, relax and try to get some more rest. I'm awake now and will keep watch for the signal that tells us that we can go home. I love you."

"Love you too, so much," Liz murmured, unable to keep her eyes open. Jack's gentle massage felt so good it was mesmerizing. She still held the hand warmer pressed against his chest and she felt its warmth spreading between them. Her eyes closed and she slept.

The next thing Liz knew, Jack was shaking her. The morning sun had cleared the horizon, and the rain had moved off. She was freezing and in pain, but she looked up at him, a happy smile on her face. "Can we go home?"

An hour later, they'd eluded the men who were looking for them and were getting close to their property line. Jack had led them cross-country, avoiding the trails and moving slowly and quietly both to avoid detection and in deference to Liz. As the sun rose in the sky, she warmed up, but exhaustion was taking its toll. She didn't have Jack's stamina, and pain was dogging her steps. She was focusing on putting one foot in front of the other when he stopped. A moment later, she could hear the sound of male voices ahead of them. She listened intently but couldn't tell what they were saying. Suddenly, Jack smiled broadly and stepped out of their hiding place. A few minutes later, she had her arms wrapped around her eldest son.

⁓⌒⌒

Dan lingered nearby, smiling. Gary Gibbs was also a member of the search party and stood next to Jack, holding his rifle. He listened intently while the Lockwoods celebrated their reunion. He was clearly uncomfortable with their position. Finally, he cautioned Dan, "Chief, we should go back to the house now before the others who were out looking for them come back."

Dan and Jack both nodded, and they turned to follow the trail back to the house. Jack put his arm around Liz, but when she stumbled and nearly fell, he picked her up and waited for the explosion. To his surprise, it didn't come. Instead, Liz looked up at him and whispered, "Thank you."

As they were walking, Pete came up beside them. He took Liz's hand. "Mom, what's wrong? I can help you too if Dad gets tired." His brow creased. "You just got out of the hospital, and I don't want you to have to go back."

Liz squeezed Pete's fingers. "Don't worry, Pete, everything's fine. I'm just really tired, and I hurt a lot. It's nothing serious."

"But, Mom, you've got blood on the back of your head."

Smiling wanly, Liz reassured him. "Yeah, but you ought to see the other guy. Honestly, Pete, I'm okay. Jack, honey, tell our eldest I'm fine."

Jack looked sideways at his son. "Mom's not fine, Pete, but there's nothing wrong with her that a little first aid, a hot shower, and a good rest won't cure."

By this time, the house was in sight. Liz tapped Jack's arm. "Hey, put me down, please. I want to walk into the house under my own power."

Jack did as Liz asked, steadying her when she staggered. "Liz, are you sure?"

Liz nodded. "Yes, I just need to get my land legs back. I've already scared Pete, and I don't want to do the same thing to the little ones."

Pete and Jack remained close beside her as Liz walked into the house. Gus and Beth got up from their seats at the dining room table. Beth hugged Liz then Jack. "I'm so glad you're both safe. It's been quiet around here since Dan, Pete, and Gary went out to find you all, and the sheriff's department team headed out to find the other guys."

Taking Beth in his arms, Dan kissed her. "Quiet is good. There's been no word from the sheriff's party yet, but that's not surprising." Calling Gary and Gus over, he gave them instructions. Then, sniffing the air happily, he strolled into the kitchen and poured himself a cup of coffee.

Liz leaned into Jack, supporting herself against his body. "Where are the kids?"

Beth smiled. "They're both asleep. From the sounds of it, neither of them got much rest last night, and I don't think Pete got any. He did a great job getting the littles out of the woods. Dan found them sheltering under a large balsam tree, just a few miles from Snowbank Lake Road."

Jack and Liz hugged Pete and Jack said, "Thank you, Pete. Your mom and I can't even find the words to tell you how proud we are of you or how grateful we are that you kept the three of you safe."

Liz kissed Pete's cheek. "Thank you, honey, for saving all my kids and then coming to help your dad and me out of the woods."

Pete turned bright red. "Mom, you and Dad would have done the same thing for our family. I wanted to go after you, but I knew

Dad would keep you safe. He just couldn't go after you unless I could get Gabby and Luke away from those guys. Why are they after her anyway? She's just a kid. Who would try to hurt a little girl?" He tried to stifle a yawn. "Oops, sorry."

Jack put his hand on Pete's shoulder. "We'll tell you the whole story after we know it, but right now, please go upstairs and get some sleep."

Pete looked from Liz to Jack. "I don't want to go upstairs by myself. I want to stay down here with everyone. I'll nap in the living room, but please, let me stay down here with everyone."

Liz looked at Jack. "I understand how he feels." Seeing Jack's small nod, she kissed Pete's cheek again. "You don't have to go upstairs, but take a hot shower, then go lay down in the living room. There are clean clothes in the laundry room. Okay?"

Pete nodded. "Thanks. What are you going to do?"

"We're going to do the same thing," Jack said. "I need to look at Mom's head. We both need to get clean and warm, and your mom needs to rest." He raised his head and looked at Dan and Beth. "Is it okay with the two of you if we disappear for a bit? It was a long, cold night."

Dan and Beth both nodded, and Dan answered, "We'll keep watch while you go take care of each other." Seeing Jack hesitate, Dan gave him a little push. "Go on, brother. Between Beth, me, and Ely's finest, we can handle this. You do what you need to do for you and your wife."

"Thanks, everyone." Jack put his arm around Liz and led her into their room, shutting the door behind them.

# CHAPTER 20

## A PERPLEXING CESSATION OF HOSTILITIES

When they were alone, Liz sat down on the bed. "Jack, will you please quit hovering. I got knocked around a bit, but I'm fine, especially since you fixed my shoulder. I just want to take a hot shower and change my clothes. I'm still a little damp."

Jack reached down and pulled Liz to her feet. "Come on, I'll stop hovering after I look at the back of your head, and the least painful way of doing that is to get some warm water involved. Is a shower okay?"

"That's fine." Stripping off her grimy clothes, Liz grinned. "I swear, you'll do anything to get clean with me."

After Jack skinned out of his clothes and turned on the water in the shower, he took Liz's hand and pulled her under the warm spray. Kissing her, he said, "Guilty as charged, but today I swear my motives are pure." Taking a washcloth from the rack, he gently turned her around, so he could look at the back of her head. Rubbing at her matted hair, he cleansed it of dried blood and winced. "Oh, love, that had to hurt."

"Actually, I didn't think too much about it at the time. I just used your diagnostic and figured I was good to go."

Jack kissed her shoulder. "What diagnostic is that?"

Leaning back into Jack, Liz said, "I remembered what had happened to me, so I figured nothing could be too badly scrambled. Do I need stitches?"

Jack squirted some shampoo into his hand and gently worked it into Liz's hair. "No. There's a large abrasion, but the laceration itself is fairly small. I'll put a Steri-Strip on it when your hair dries." He turned her in his arms, so she faced him. "Do you still have a headache?"

"A headache, yes, a migraine, no." Standing on her tiptoes, Liz kissed Jack. "I'm sorry about the 'hovering' crack. Thank you for taking such good care of me."

Once they were both out of the shower and dressed in fresh clothing, Jack came out of the bathroom with the hairdryer. "Allow me."

Liz closed her eyes as Jack dried her hair and then bandaged the cut on her head. After that, he massaged her head and shoulders. His touch was soothing, and Liz felt herself relax. "Mmm, that feels so nice."

Jack smoothed his hand over her hair then knelt in front of her and took her hand. "How's your pain, Liz?"

"Better. Between my shoulder, my head, and the fibro, about a five."

"I think you should take the breakthrough meds that Dorrene prescribed." Seeing the look on Liz's face, Jack added, "Please. Otherwise, you're going to be in for a rough twenty-four hours. I don't want you to end up back in the hospital."

Nodding, Liz sighed. "Okay. I will. I just hate how tired they make me."

"Liz, you need the rest."

Cupping his cheek with her palm, Liz said, "So do you, Jack."

"I know, but not until the others get back." Jack handed her the tablets and a glass of water and watched her take them. "Thank you. Now will you lie down and rest?"

Getting to her feet, Liz took his hand. "I'll lie down on the couch with you, but like Pete, I don't want to be alone, and I do want to see the kids when they wake up. Besides, it's just a little after noon right now, and if I sleep all day, I'll be up most of the night."

Jack smiled. "Somehow, I doubt that, but," taking her hand, he led Liz from the room, "let's go join the others."

As soon as they walked into the living room, Pete got up off the sofa. "Are you guys okay?"

Jack nodded. "We're fine. How about you?"

"Yeah, I was just resting."

"Where is everyone?" Jack asked, puzzled.

"Uncle Dan's outside, and Auntie Beth is taking a nap in Luke's room. Uncle Dan said he'd be right back. He just wanted to check in with Officer Gus. He also said that if you came out here, I should tell you both to get some rest."

Jack looked at Liz with a smile. "Another country heard from, but I say let's take his advice and relax. Want to snuggle on the sofa, wife?"

"Pete was there first, honey." Liz pointed out, her tired smile matching his.

"Mom, you and Dad take the sofa. I've got dibs on the 'foofy' chair." Pete grinned as he collapsed into the down-filled cushions of the large chair that Gabby had named.

When Dan returned, he found the three of them still awake but comfortably resting. He sat down in one of the leather recliners and said, "Well, you all look a lot more comfortable." He looked at Jack and Liz. "Is everything okay with the two of you?"

Jack nodded. "We're as okay as we can be after the night we had and with the crazies back in town and after our daughter. Has your team found them yet?"

"No," Dan answered. "Trackers picked up their trail, heading the way Pete went last night but lost it at Snowbank Lake Road. One of the sheriff's department dog teams is now on site, so maybe we'll have some good news soon. The two in custody still haven't said a word. They've lawyered up."

"What is it about us that this keeps happening?" Liz said sadly.

Jack's arms tightened around her. "I have to wonder if a specter from our past is involved given what you overheard and the language you overheard it in. I hope I'm wrong."

"I hope you're wrong too," Dan said, "but you have to admit, it fits. Yesterday makes two attempts on your lives in four months' time. But for now, everything's quiet. We've got a great team looking after us, so I think we should all follow Pete's example and get some sleep. Gus will let me know if there's any word from our guys or the sheriff's search party."

Jack and Liz looked over at Pete and found that he'd fallen asleep his long, lean form curled up in the big chair. Pulling Liz into the curve of his body, Jack nodded. "That's sound advice, brother, see that you follow it too." Kissing Liz on the temple, they both closed their eyes.

Dan watched over his friends for another minute or two then stretched out on the recliner and relaxed.

<hr />

Jack opened his eyes and found himself alone in the living area. Late afternoon sun filled the space, and he was warm to the point of discomfort. Sitting up, he listened to the sounds of conversation coming from the other room. He could hear everyone, but couldn't tell what they were talking about.

When Jack walked into the dining room, he had to smile when Gabby shouted, "Papa's awake, yea!" He loved his daughter's unfailing cheerfulness. Walking over, he bent over and kissed her on the forehead. "Hi, Gabby girl, what are you doing?"

"We're disgussin' things, Papa, 'portant things. Mama's makin' pizza, 'n' Tia Beth, perro Buddy, and Tio Dan are gonna stay with us all night long. Yea!"

Jack grinned and ruffled her hair and moved over to where Luke sat in his high chair. He squatted down beside his son and kissed his cheek. "How are you doing, buddy?"

"Da, not Buddy." Luke pointed to the dog at his feet and gave his dad an "are you stupid" look. "That Buddy, Buddy a perro."

Laughing Jack said, "You're right, Luke. I just meant that you're my pal. You know, pal?"

Luke nodded. "Pal! Da and me pal!" He looked at Jack hopefully and extended his arms. "Up, pal?"

"Sit still for now, pal, pizza's coming."

Luke frowned but didn't cry. "Pizza? Okay."

Taking a seat between Pete and Liz, Jack asked, "Why didn't you wake me? Is there any news?"

Liz squeezed his hand. "We were just letting you get as much sleep as possible. I was about to come get you for dinner, and no, there's no news. The sheriff has called off the search for now because the dogs haven't been able to pick up the trail. They'll try again in the morning. Dan sent Gary and Gus home but brought in Stew and Greta for the night. And as you already know, Dan, Beth, and Buddy are staying overnight, much to everyone's delight."

Beth laughed. "Honestly, I think Dan and I could go home, and it would be fine as long as we left Buddy here." Seeing a frown form on Pete's face, she held up a hand. "I'm kidding, and we're glad you all love Buddy. Dan and I don't want to be anyplace else until we know you're all safe."

Liz reached out and squeezed Beth's hand. "And we love having you here, but what about the restaurant? And Dan's duties?"

"My manager knows how to run the place as well as I do," Beth said, "and Dan's doing his job right here. You know as well as I do, you'd be doing the same thing for us. It's what family does for family."

As they were eating pizza, Buddy started barking and running back and forth in front of the door. Seconds later, an unfamiliar car drove onto the property. Dan looked at Jack and Liz. "Are you expecting anyone?"

Jack frowned. "No, and I don't recognize the car." He took Liz's hand. "Will you and Beth please take the kids into the other room?"

Liz didn't protest; instead, she picked up Luke, took Gabby's hand, and along with Beth and Pete, they moved out of sight into the living area. When the doorbell rang, Dan motioned Jack to stay where he was and opened the door. A silver-haired man in a suit stood there. "Yes?" Dan said.

"Is this the Lockwood residence?" The stranger asked in an accented voice.

Dan nodded, "Yes, what do you want?"

"Are you by chance Dan Harrison, the Ely Chief of Police? I was told he would be here."

"Yes, that's me. How can I help you?"

"My clients are here to surrender themselves into your custody. We understand your department has been looking for them."

Dan frowned. "Your clients?"

Handing Dan a business card, the man said, "Yes, my name is Francisco Lopez, and I'm an attorney in Duluth. My firm has been retained as counsel for these two gentlemen as well as the two you already have in custody." He turned around and nodded. Two men got out of the car with their hands held carefully in front of them. Stew and Greta were quickly at their sides, guns drawn.

Dan turned to Jack. "Can you please get Liz? She's the one who saw the guys in your house and in the woods."

It was just a few minutes before Jack and Liz returned to the room, Jack keeping Liz behind him until they reached the door. The two fugitives were standing very still in front of the car, and Liz looked at them, still able to see their faces in the fading light. She nodded at Dan. "Yes, they were both in the house, and they are the two that chased me into the woods, and that one," she pointed to the man on the left, "was the one who fired on me."

Dan motioned to Greta. "Take those two into custody." He looked at the attorney. "I assume you will follow the officers into town?"

The man nodded. "Yes, I would like to conference with all four suspects once I'm there. We will be assigning separate counsel to each of them tomorrow. I would like a word with these two men before you arrest them."

Dan nodded. "Of course, but you'll understand if we all remain where we are."

The attorney smiled broadly, "Ever cautious, but yes, I understand." He walked the few feet back to his vehicle and spoke to the two men in rapid-fire Spanish. After a minute, he turned to Dan and the officers who were standing several feet away. "They're not armed and surrender themselves to your custody, Chief."

Despite the attorney's assurances, the officers searched the two men thoroughly, then, at Dan's nod, put them into the back seat of their patrol vehicle and left, the attorney close behind them.

After they were all back around the table, Dan rubbed his forehead. "Okay, that's just plain weird. I need to make a call in a few minutes, but I want to get your take on this. Liz, you're sure those two were in the house along with the rest of them?"

Liz frowned. "Dan, I told you I could positively identify two of the four men that broke into our house yesterday. I know the two men I saw tonight were the ones who came into the bedroom and who followed me into the woods. The other two I can't identify because I got out of here before I saw them. I'm confused about a couple of things." She looked at Jack, then at Gabby. "Maybe we should talk about this later, though."

Pete, who had been watching the adults, spoke to Gabby and Luke. "Hey, guys, if you're done with your pizza, let's get some yogurt and I'll read you a story." He smiled at Jack and Liz. "May we be excused?"

Jack mouthed a "thank you" to Pete. Aloud, he said, "Yes, you may. Have fun." The three kids left with the now-quiet Buddy trailing behind them.

The room was quiet when the young ones left. Jack and Liz brought out coffee, and they settled back into their chairs. Dan looked at Liz. "You were saying?"

Liz's brow wrinkled. "I can't figure this out. Why would those guys surrender to you just like that? From the sound of things, we'd pretty much lost their trail. You said the other two refused to talk, so why give themselves up at all?"

Dan shrugged. "Like I said, it's weird. Maybe they figured the others would eventually rat on them, so they decided to gain a few points with the judge and jury by turning themselves in and, of course, assuring that our officers would arrest them peacefully, rather than as armed fugitives on the run."

"I suppose that could be it," Liz said doubtfully. "None of this explains why they came after Gabby and the rest of us in the first place. It'll be interesting to find out if they're citizens, where they live, and if any of them have an association with the Reynoso cartel."

"Why do you say that, Liz?" Jack asked, his voice low with concern.

"Well, they're Hispanic, somewhat unusual in this area. In addition, they're targeting the daughter of the man who was once the head of the Reynoso cartel. Finally, I just heard that name used twice in the conversation the attorney had with those two guys. Basically, what he told them was to plead guilty to the charges filed. He used the Reynoso name almost as a threat but then said something about taking good care of their families if they cooperate. He also said that the word was out that Reynoso's daughter and her new family were off-limits. Then he said something that I missed." Liz looked even more confused. "I don't think the guys that broke in on me were associates of Reynoso. It almost seemed like they were working for a competing group or maybe were independents looking to get in with one of the cartels. However, I do know this—those two men were scared, and I don't think it was your department, Dan, or their arrest that was scaring them. Do we know who took over running the Reynoso cartel when Eduard died?"

Dan frowned. "I think it's time we got the FBI involved in this. To answer your question, I'm not in the loop anymore. Now I'm wondering if the group we have in custody might be the same people who engineered your car accident last June." He looked at Liz with respect. "You know, I had seven years of Spanish between high school and college, and I couldn't follow a word of what Mr. Lopez said to those guys."

Liz smiled. "I did one of my legal clinics and some of my pro bono work with the Hispanic community in Minneapolis, so I've had a lot of practice. I'm just glad I was able to catch part of what they said. Anyway, it sounds as though our family is in the clear for now." She took Jack's hand, a relieved look on her face. "The baddies are in jail, and they're not going anywhere."

Jack nodded then looked at Dan and Beth. "You know you're welcome in our home, but there's no reason you need to stay the night. We know that you both have other responsibilities."

Dan looked at Beth and was silent for a few moments before responding, "I agree with your assessment of the situation, but it's getting late, and I underestimated these groups once before. That slip nearly cost you your lives. We'll stay here tonight and decide on the rest tomorrow. I want you and your family to get a good night's rest, so please," Dan took Liz's hand and grasped Jack's shoulder, "let me keep the night watch."

Beth reached out and took Dan's hand. "Let *us* keep the night watch. We'll think about the rest tomorrow."

Several hours passed and after getting Dan and Beth settled for the night in the guest room and checking on the kids, Liz and Jack retired to their room. Collapsing on the bed, Liz pulled Jack down with her. "You should never have married me," she groaned.

Holding her close, Jack grinned. "That's a silly thing to say. I adore you."

"Yeah, and look what you've been through all because I was stupid enough to take on Reynoso. You should have known better the moment I told you about how I ended up in a snowbank in your front yard."

Jack laughed quietly. "That was Dan's advice at the time. He called me the night you spent in the hospital before Thanksgiving and told me to be careful with 'this one,' meaning, of course, you and everything you'd remembered. He'd already seen what I hadn't realized until about ten minutes before he called—that I was beginning to fall hard for you. All I could tell him was that none of it mattered. I knew even then that my life would never be complete without you." He kissed Liz gently. "If I knew that back then, can you imagine how much deeper my love for you is now? No one, especially no one at our age, comes without baggage. If I'd known then what I know now, I would have made exactly the same choices. What about you? Knowing everything you know, would you have walked away from me and from what was happening between us?"

Liz's eyes sparked hot sapphire. "I should be able to say yes, but I can't because I adore you too. You've helped make my world an unspeakably beautiful place, and I knew back then that my life would never be complete without you, either. I just wish…"

Putting his arms around his wife, Jack kissed her again. "Please don't. Our lives are in God's hands, so let's not wish them away. That's what you were trying to tell me just a few nights ago. No matter where this all ends, we're so blessed, and I won't go back. I want to go forward with you in my arms and with our kids by our sides. We'll weather the storms together."

Liz cuddled closer to him. "I love you so much, Jack."

# CHAPTER 21

## WE'VE COME THIS FAR BY FAITH

Two weeks went by, life returned to normal, Dan and Beth returned home, but answers proved elusive. To a man, the group that had broken into the Lockwood's home pled guilty to the charges against them. Apart from their pleas, they said nothing, answering no questions that would have shed light on their reasons for targeting Gabby. Two of the incarcerated individuals were naturalized citizens living in Ely. When Dan executed a search warrant on their homes, he found the truck that had hit the Lockwood's car back in June, but again, other than pleading guilty to attempted vehicular manslaughter, the owner of the truck said nothing. It was as if their attorneys had some power over them that scared them more than spending years in an American prison. Dan and his team continued to work with the FBI, trying to ascertain if the cartels were involved in the events of the last few months—specifically, if the Reynoso cartel was involved.

Things were blissfully quiet for the Lockwood family, and once again, Jack and Liz began to relax. Gabby's legs grew stronger, and she was soon running around as though nothing had happened. The frequency of BWSR callouts increased, and at first, Jack was worried about leaving Liz with the kids, but nothing disturbed the peace until one morning at the beginning of October when Pete joined his parents at breakfast. Getting himself a glass of juice, he sat down at the table with them and asked, "Do you guys have a minute? There's something important I want to ask you about."

When Pete finished, Liz looked at him in surprise. "Are you sure about this, honey? I thought you wanted to graduate with your friends."

"I thought I did too, Mom, but I'm bored, and I'm not learning anything new. What I really want to do is finish up my high school requirements and apply for early graduation in December. I'm already accepted at UMD,[10] and I want to start in January if that's okay with you. I'll be seventeen by the time classes start, and that's old enough to live in the dorms. Besides, Nana and Pop-Pop live in Duluth. I know homeschooling is a lot more work for you and Dad, so if you have to say no, I get it. It's just that I'm ready to get started with college."

Liz looked at Jack and saw the same answer in his eyes that was rising in her own spirit. "Of course, we'll homeschool you and support your plans. The three of us will have to speak with your principal and the state to get approval for us to take over your schooling and for you to graduate early. We'll also have to schedule testing before you graduate. I seriously doubt you will have any difficulty with the tests, even if you took them today. We can start next week if we can get the curriculum set up for whatever requirements you have left before graduation." She leaned over and hugged Pete. "We're so proud of you."

After Pete left for school, Jack took her hand. "Are you sure about doing this, Liz? I know you've got a busy month between four receptions and the classes you've agreed to teach. I will do as much as I can to help, but the search and rescue teams are busy right now and probably won't slow down until the first major snowfalls. Plus, Dan and I have a planning session scheduled in Ontario at the middle of next month."

Squeezing Jack's hands gently, Liz smiled. "I'm sure. Pete didn't decide to go to school in town until just before the academic year started, so I'd already prepared a lot of material for this year based

---

[10] University of Minnesota–Duluth Campus.

on his few remaining requirements and his interests. You know that because you helped me with the science and math curriculums. Besides, Pete is so motivated that we just have to keep him on track. I'm happy he talked to us about it because I wouldn't want him to go through his last year of high school bored. This way we know that he'll keep up with his good study habits. You and I can sit down with your hospital schedule, when you're on call with the BWSRU, or traveling and schedule your units around when you need to be gone. When the school year ends, we'll celebrate our boy's graduation with a big party for all his friends. Does that sound okay to you?"

Jack leaned over and kissed Liz. "As long as your work won't suffer, I'm all for doing this." He grinned. "Homeschooling makes the control freak in me a happy man, but please don't tell Pete I said that. Are you still doing that meet and greet in Grand Marais on Friday?"

Liz nodded. "Yes, but it's an afternoon kind of thing, so I'll be home by six or so. I'll put dinner in the slow cooker so we won't be eating too late. Are you still off Friday, or do we need to make arrangements for someone to be here to look after Luke and Gabby?"

"I'm off, not even on call, and I'll take care of dinner Friday night. That way, you can relax when you get home. After all, we have big plans to go to Duluth for your birthday on Saturday, and I don't want you to get overtired. It would be really sad for you to have to miss your meet and greets down there." Winking at Liz, Jack added, "Not to mention keeping you healthy and happy for our first long weekend away and alone together since the kids came into our lives.

"Besides," Jack looked at Liz sheepishly, "the kids and I want to surprise you with dinner and a cake Friday night. I've already promised Gabby she can help me make the cake. So please act surprised. Dan, Beth, and Buddy will be out here bright and early on Saturday to take the reins for the weekend. I know that, for part of the time, I'll have to share you with your admiring fans, but I'll have you all to myself the rest of the weekend," he stood up and pulled her into his arms, "for three glorious days."

Liz wound her arms around Jack's neck and kissed him. "Happy birthday to us."

~⌒~

"Wow, it's a pretty evening!" Liz remarked as she sipped her seltzer water. "I haven't been to Grandma's[11] in ages." They had a table outside, overlooking the harbor. It was warm for Duluth in October, over seventy degrees even in the late afternoon hour. She grinned. "I spent a lot of time here in my last two years of college. I even made the ill-advised decision to study for my calc three final here. I wouldn't recommend that decision to anyone seriously interested in passing the course."

"So, did you?" Jack asked, a smile on his face.

"Did I what?" Liz said absently, her eyes on the harbor entry.

"Pass calculus."

"Oh, yeah." Liz was a bit embarrassed. "I did, barely. It had to have been God's providence because I pretty much hated every minute I spent in that class. I mean, if I needed to know the solution of an integrated trigonometric function, I would look it up, not calculate it."

"I'm confused." Jack looked puzzled. "Why would a business or poly-sci major have to take advanced level calculus at all?"

"You know what happens when you assume something, Jack, and that's exactly what you're doing." Liz grinned. "I wasn't a business or poly-sci major, that's why. I was premed, and my bachelor's degree is in biology, with minors in chemistry and business. I was just two classes short of a major in chemistry, but those two classes were physical and inorganic chemistry, both of which required calculus four as a prerequisite, and I was just. Not. Going. There!"

---

[11] Grandma's Saloon and Grill—the original since 1976 at Canal Park. Located in Duluth, MN, Grandma's has served up history, antiques, drinks, and fine food from their location in a former bordello. Treat yourself to a meal spent soaking up both the atmosphere and the Lake Superior scenery (https://grandmasrestaurants.com/grandmas-canal-park-3/).

Jack twined his fingers through Liz's. "So we were almost colleagues. Just when I think I know everything about you, you surprise me with something totally cool, like this. That's why you do such a great job with the science part of Pete's curriculum. I had no idea."

"'Almost colleagues' is stretching it a bit," Liz confessed. "I didn't have a gift for hard science, which is why, in my last year, I completed the business minor. It is on the strength of those grades and my GRE score that I got into my master's program, and my grad school grades plus my LSAT score got me into law school. However, I still love science, and I think if I had to do it again, I would apply myself more and go for a doctorate in bioethics and a law degree. That's a powerful combination in religious liberty law." She squeezed Jack's hand. "Don't read too much into that statement. I'm very happy doing exactly what I'm doing."

Jack grinned. "I think it's more studying in a bar for a final than not having a mind for hard science."

Liz arched her brow. "Don't knock it till you've tried it, and I'd be willing to bet you never did anything so scandalous. I may not have excelled on my calc three final, but I had fun studying for it. Besides, I knew *where* I studied wasn't going to make much of a difference. I'd studied for my calc three midterm in the library like a good little girl, and it didn't go well. So I figured, what did I have to lose? The guy I was studying with understood the material a whole lot better than I did. I'm pretty sure I passed the final thanks to the few calculus-related things he managed to cram into my mind that evening. However, if you tell Pete about this conversation, I'll deny it. I don't want him following in my footsteps."

It was Jack's turn to arch his brow. "Oh, so there was a guy involved. How did Eric feel about that?"

"For your information, Eric and I were casual daters at the time. He was already at the main U in Minneapolis, studying at the school of architecture. I saw him when he came to Duluth to visit his family, and we weren't really serious. Besides, the guy I was studying with that night was a friend. That's all." Seeing Jack's skeptical look, Liz added, "Well, mostly all. He was also the leader of my Intervarsity[12] fellow group. Now can we change the subject, please? What are you going to order?"

Jack winked at Liz. "As you wish, wife. However, we are going to revisit the subject of your mysterious gentleman friend later, even if I have to tickle the information out of you. I'm going to have a cup of wild rice soup and a turkey club. You?"

"Tickling is against the Geneva Convention. Trust me, I'm an attorney, and I know these things. I'm going to have my favorite, the Dante's Inferno sandwich." Ignoring Jack's look of disapproval, Liz added, "I'm also going to have a diet soda. With that much spice, I need the bubbles."

Jack held up her glass of seltzer water. "What do you call these bubbles, apart from better for you?"

Wrinkling her nose at Jack, Liz sighed. "Look, I worked hard all day, and I just want to indulge in one of my favorite meals at one of my favorite restaurants. Can't you please just be my husband for tonight and leave the physician in our hotel room? I promise to be good tomorrow."

Jack's smile faded. "I'm sorry, Liz. That was out of line. I was mostly teasing you and yes," he leaned over and kissed her in apology, "I want to enjoy this evening as your husband. I'm sorry that the physician in me nagged you about your choice of beverage.

"Speaking of working hard all day, how did the meet and greets turn out?" Jack continued. "I was with you, but I have no idea how things went, except that you seemed busy all day. How did your sales go, and did your book do well?"

"They were all an awful lot of fun," enthusiasm shown in Liz's eyes, "and attracted very different crowds. I sold more artwork and fewer books at the gallery reception, but I sold out of my books at the bookstore signings, took orders for more, and took orders for two commission pieces at those book signings as well. That surprised me. Altogether, I sold almost a hundred books between the three ven-

---

12 Intervarsity Christian Fellowship/USA is a non-denominational, on campus, evangelical Christian ministry established in 1941.

ues, five original art pieces, twenty framed prints, at least that many unframed prints, and took orders for four commission pieces total. Along with my orders from yesterday's reception in Grand Marais and my standing orders, that's enough work to keep me busy for at least six months. I also signed the glass on quite a few previously purchased, privately owned pieces." She grinned and waggled her fingers. "I have a bad case of writer's cramp."

"Correct me if I'm wrong, but that's a good problem to have, right?" Jack's gaze softened as he looked at his wife. "You must be beat."

"Actually, it's been a wonderful day, and I'm feeling great. I'm looking forward to a stroll on the Lake Walk together later."

They paused as their server came to the table to take their order. Once given, Liz took Jack's hand. "I love our kids, but it's nice to have you all to myself for a few days. Thank you for getting us such a beautiful hotel room." They were staying in a small family-owned inn, and their room overlooked the harbor and the Aerial Bridge. Their breakfast that morning, included in the price of the room, had been homemade and fantastic. It had also been plentiful, which was a good thing, because Liz hadn't had a chance to take a bite of the sandwich Jack had brought her for lunch. Now hungry, she was more than ready for dinner. After they ordered, they sat enjoying the view from the second-story deck seating area. The sun slanted low in the late afternoon hour, and there was enough of a breeze that sitting outside was perfect.

"You really love it here, don't you?" Jack asked quietly.

Liz nodded. "Yes, I do. I grew up in this beautiful city. The sound, sight, and smell of the water are so relaxing. I think that's why people connect with my art and my writing. It reminds those who don't live here about an idyllic moment in time. I think it also reminds those of us who live on or near Lake Superior about how blessed we are to call this place home."

"Do you miss it, living in Ely?" Jack asked. "Do you have regrets about our decision to make my place our home?"

"Jack," Liz took his hand and kissed his palm, "I have no regrets. Not about where we live, not about who I married, not about my career choices, none. I love my life. Five years ago, I was alone, and now I have you and our kids, and my life is so full. Besides, we do spend a lot of time on or near the water, either canoeing, kayaking, or staying in one of our favorite lodges along the shore. I'm a happy, blessed woman, and I truly can't think of another thing that I want or need, apart from our children growing up secure in our love, knowing the Lord, and healthy."

"Not too long ago, I was thinking about how much my life had changed in the past five years too," Jack said. "It scarcely seems possible that I went from alone to having you in my life in the space of a few short weeks." Holding tightly to Liz's hand, he shook his head. "I've no idea why you said yes to me that Christmas day, after only knowing me for a few weeks, but I am so thankful that you did."

"The answer's simple when I look back on it, Jack. I loved you. It happened almost as quickly for me as it did for you. Still, I struggled with what my answer would be if you asked me to marry you, right up until the morning of December twenty-fifth. I had a lot of trouble getting to sleep Christmas Eve, and," Liz grinned at him, "I was frustrated because I thought that you were sound asleep in the other room. It just seemed unfair, since you were the one keeping me awake. I kept remembering the morning when you came into my bedroom when I was ill. As sick as I was, there was something so intimate about you sharing my bed. I just couldn't stop thinking about how we'd be together, about us sharing intimacy far beyond you just holding me in your arms. I knew then that it would be so good, and I was confused, not to mention hot and bothered."

Jack frowned sadly. "I'm sorry. I was trying to help that morning, not add to the problem. I promise I wasn't thinking about getting into your bed when I came into your room."

"Honey, I know that," Liz acknowledged. "I'm the one who invited you into my bed. Even with a migraine, lying in your arms that morning was one of the most sublime experiences of my life. That was part of the problem along with knowing you were going to ask me to marry you, live with you, or something, sooner rather than later. A part of me was thrilled, but I was a Christian, and the Bible says that believers shouldn't yoke themselves to nonbelievers. I wanted so badly to say 'yes' wholeheartedly if you asked me to marry you. And truthfully, that was the only question I could see the man I was coming to know asking.

"That's what was keeping me up that night, fighting a battle between what I wanted and what God wanted." Seeing the look on Jack's face, Liz smiled. "Yes, I know you told me you believed in God, but I also knew that we didn't mean the same thing when you said that you did. I could tell it was more of a lifestyle with you. I could see that the idea of being a sinful creature really bothered you, but without acknowledging that sinfulness, you couldn't fully accept Christ as your Savior."

"You said 'yes' to me on Christmas morning," Jack said quietly. "Does that mean you compromised your beliefs to marry me?"

Liz shook her head. "Not at all. That night, I told God what my heart wanted—you, in my life for always—and then I acknowledged that my life belonged to Him first. I begged Him to make it very clear to me if He didn't want me to marry you. I meant that, Jack. As difficult as it would have been, I was prepared to walk away from what you and I shared, if that's what He asked of me. The thought of leaving you brought a lot of tears, but I was determined that I would be obedient in this, for my sake, yes, but also for yours."

"So why did you accept my proposal?" Jack still looked sad.

A smile blazed across Liz's face. "I'd asked God to make clear to me what I should do, and when you got down on one knee that morning and proposed, there was only one answer ringing in my heart and in my spirit. Suddenly I knew for certain that God would see you safely into His kingdom and He'd do it sooner rather than later. When I said 'yes' to you, I didn't have a single doubt. I knew it was right. I knew God would somehow redeem your past and that we'd be a household of faith. Don't ask me how. I just knew it. You made me the happiest woman in the world that morning."

"And you made me the happiest man in the world. I want you to know something, though." Jack touched Liz's face gently. "I didn't intentionally lie to you about my relationship with God. I simply didn't know that a relationship like I have with Him now was even a thing. Ellie believed as you did, and I carried that around like a talisman. Mostly, though, I thought it was about being a good person, doing good things, and somehow making up to my family for all the ways Dad had failed them."

"Was your mom a believer?" Seeing Jack's expression change, Liz said quickly, "You don't have to answer that. I'm sorry. I didn't mean to pry."

"You're not prying, but that's a discussion I would rather have in the privacy of our room. It's long past time for me to tell you about Mom, but I don't know if I can get everything out without losing it, and this is a very public place. Is that okay?"

"Jack, that's fine, but you don't have to..."

Kissing the back of Liz's hand lightly, Jack whispered, "Yes, I do, let's just wait until we've finished dinner." He scooted his chair around the table until he could put his arm around her. They sat in silence just watching the activity below them. Crowds milled around Canal Park, with many families enjoying the warm autumn day.

It wasn't until their food arrived that Jack moved back to the place where the server set his plate. Everything before him looked and smelled wonderful. He bowed his head, and together, he and Liz prayed over their meal. After they finished, Jack sampled his soup, then picked up his sandwich, He was just about to take a bite when Liz jumped to her feet and ran into the restaurant without saying a word. Jack couldn't follow her into the women's restroom, so he closed his eyes and prayed silently. When he finished, she still wasn't back. Looking at her plate, he realized that she'd taken two small bites. Curious to know if something was off with the food, he tasted her sandwich. Apart from an explosion of mild spice in his mouth, it seemed fine. He'd eaten about half his meal before Liz returned. She looked pale and a little green. He waited until she sat down before asking, "Are you okay? What happened?"

Liz grimaced. "I've no idea. I don't have a migraine, and I was feeling great right up until the time our server arrived with the food. I got one whiff of our meals, and my stomach started to churn. I thought maybe it was because I was so hungry, so I took a couple of bites and realized I was going to lose it. Thankfully, I made it to the restroom in time." She looked at Jack, sadness in her eyes. "I'm sorry, but I'm going to ask our server to pack up my meal. When you're finished eating, I need to go back to our room and lay down. I feel pretty icky."

Jack frowned and asked, "Liz, do you mind if the physician in me joins us for a few minutes? You were sick last night too, although it was a bit later in the evening. Whatever you need to do tonight is fine with me, as long as you tell me what I can do to help. But when we get home, will you please talk to Dorrene?"

Liz nodded. Dorrene Rock was their family physician and a good friend. "I'm way ahead of you. I already have an appointment for my annual physical next week, and I'll tell her about the nausea. I'm not certain what's causing it. My sugars are normal, the gastroparesis has been all but gone in the past few years, and I don't have a headache." She rolled her eyes. "It's probably just one more fun ride on the fibro merry-go-round."

"It might also be some kind of stomach virus since it's just appeared in the last week or so. Although you getting sick yesterday might have had something to do with the rather odd menu at your birthday party." Jack squeezed Liz's hand. "Sorry, I should have known better than to ask a six-year-old about the menu."

"Ah, so you're blaming our daughter, huh?" Liz had to smile. "I wondered if it was you who decided to put yogurt, fruit rollups, and crunchy fried cheese curls on the bill of fare. I had my doubts about those being Beth's contribution to the festivities. Did she help you and Gabs with the cake?"

"Yes," Jack confessed, "thankfully. My first attempt at making a cake with my daughter failed miserably, so we were really glad when Beth showed up to help. She also brought the lasagna and homemade garlic bread, so all I had to do was make a salad. We'd barely finished getting dinner ready when our guests arrived and you showed up." He eyed her. "Are you mad?"

"About what?" Liz was confused. "I had a great time."

"You usually aren't keen on surprises like that. I still remember how you reacted when Dan and Beth surprised us with a birthday party a couple of years back."

Snagging a French fry, Liz admitted, "Maybe I've mellowed a bit in my old age, but I figured that at fifty-six, I'd earned a party.

Thank you for organizing it. I can't wait to bring home my birthday gift even though I'm pretty certain that at least some members of the family, the furry ones to be exact, aren't going to be too thrilled."

Dan and Beth had decided to breed Buddy once, and when the pups were ready to leave their mother, Jack and Liz would be bringing home a female from the litter. At Liz's party, Dan and Beth had shared photos of the six-week-old schnoodle pups, and Liz had fallen in love. She'd narrowed it down to two pups of the three females and would make her final choice when they drove to Orr in two weeks to pick up their newest fur baby. Liz hoped that the cats' exposure to Buddy would help them accept the new puppy. Luke, Gabby, and Pete were, of course, thrilled. Jack just seemed to bask in the joy his gift brought everyone in his family. Blinking back tears, Liz looked at Jack. "Thank you for the party last night and for everything else. You're so good to me."

Jack took her hand and put it over his heart. "As you are to me, love." He watched Liz take a small bite of her sandwich then wash it down with a sip of soda. "Are you feeling a bit better?"

Liz's cheeks turned pink. "Yes, I am. I'm even a bit hungry again. This probably isn't the best thing for a temperamental stomach, so I'm trying to eat slowly."

"May I order you a cup of soup?" Seeing Liz's nod, Jack beckoned their server to the table, asked him to wrap up Liz's sandwich and fries, then ordered her a cup of the same wild rice soup he'd enjoyed, coffee for him and hot tea for her. He frowned when they were alone again and apologized, "I'm sorry, I should have let you order what you wanted."

"Honey, thank you for being thoughtful enough to do that for me. The soup sounds wonderful, and hot tea always settles my stomach."

They sat watching the sunset, then Jack stroked the back of her hand with his thumb. "You're looking better than you were thirty minutes ago. I'm glad. In fact, you look beautiful today. I haven't seen you in that outfit since our wedding day." He looked at her again, more intently. "Actually, I don't think I've ever seen you in that outfit. The dress is a different color, right?"

Liz nodded. "I keep the green dress that I wore when we got married put away, but I made this blue dress in a lighter weight fabric from the same pattern. I wear it when I want people to see the beauty of ethnic needlework, and yes, the collar and cuffs are the same ones I wore that day."

Jack looked at Liz with an intensity that made her blush deepen. "What are you thinking, Jack? I..."

The arrival of Liz's doggie bag, her soup, and their beverages interrupted them. When they were alone again, Liz looked at her husband, who was still staring intently at her. "What?"

Grinning, Jack took a sip of his ice water. "I just need to cool off because I was remembering what you wore underneath that beautiful dress on our wedding day."

Heat washed over Liz. She remembered Jack's reaction when he'd slipped the dress from her shoulders on their wedding night. Long before that night, she'd created everything she wore, including her undergarments, to teach an eighteenth-century heritage clothing class. She'd embroidered the white lawn chemise and pantalettes with delicate floral motifs, made the matching corset and petticoat out of silk satin and lace, with hand quilting of her own design on the front of the petticoat. She'd even knitted the thigh-high hose from silk lace-weight yarn, embroidering the garters with light pink roses. To say her new husband had been enthusiastic would be an understatement. They'd had so much fun that night as he'd undressed her, fumbling with the unfamiliar closures.

Swallowing hard, she tried to keep her voice steady as she said, "I hate to disappoint you, honey, but apart from the petticoat, I'm wearing pretty basic undergarments today. Outside of class, the only time I've worn those other things is on our wedding day."

"I remember seeing glimpses of that beautiful slip through the slit in the front of your dress at our reception," Jack reminisced. "The only reason I can think of to build that kind of peekaboo feature into a dress that covered the wearer from neck to ankles was because all those eighteenth-century lasses wanted to drive their grooms crazy. And you know what?"

Liz smiled at Jack flirtatiously. "What?"

"It worked on this twenty-first-century groom too." Jack took her hand. "Are you about ready to go back to our room? I mean, if you're feeling up to the walk across the bridge. Otherwise, I can go back to the hotel, get the car, and come pick you up."

Liz fanned herself with the wine list folder. "No, I'm feeling much better, and for some reason, I need to cool off."

Much later that evening, Jack pulled Liz closer to him. "Are you okay, love?"

Liz giggled. "Of course I'm okay." Stretching in Jack's arms, she sighed happily. "That was a lot of fun. Why are you asking if I'm okay?"

"Because you were sick earlier and said that you wanted to come back to the room and lie down."

Liz arched her brow. "Well, we came back to the room, didn't we? I'm lying down, aren't I? Can I help it if all that talk about our wedding night put something other than rest in my brain? Besides, we seem to have cured what ailed me."

Jack laughed and pulled Liz into an ardent kiss. "Well, that's good to hear. I love you."

Liz propped herself on her elbow and ran her fingers over Jack's chest. "I miss this. In fact, it is about the only thing I miss since the kids became a part of our family."

Jack looked puzzled. "We still make love, with great frequency, in fact. What is it you miss?"

"I miss cuddling with you afterward and talking. Usually, we're both so tired that we just go right to sleep. I'm not complaining, Jack. You know I love my life and our children. It's an observation, nothing more."

Jack nodded. "I agree with your observation. I love holding you like this, talking with you," he grinned, "and not worrying about whether I remembered to shut the bedroom door completely."

"Exactly." Studying Jack, Liz asked, "Are *you* okay? Especially after the breadth of subject matter we covered at dinner?"

"Well, I thoroughly enjoyed learning about your ill-advised choice to study for your calc three final at a bar. And I will enjoy hearing more about your gentleman friend who helped you study." Jack eyed Liz hopefully. "Are you, by chance, ready to talk about him?"

"Hmm, let me think. No. I would hope you'd have figured out by now that the only man I want in my bed is you. Let's not invite a guy I knew thirty-five years ago to join us."

Jack nodded sagely. "Sound reasoning. Let's see. What else did we talk about? I suppose I shouldn't have been surprised to learn you had doubts about our engagement, but I was, a little. On the other hand, I was gobsmacked when you said you loved me the night of the fire. I remember thinking that I was the luckiest guy on the face of the planet, despite what had happened that day. When you agreed to marry me that Christmas, I don't think my feet touched the ground for days." He looked at Liz fondly. "Now I'd say that I'm the most blessed guy on the face of the planet because I really don't believe in luck."

Hugging Jack close, Liz whispered, "Me either."

"Talking about our wedding night at dinner, well," Jack winked at her, "you already know how that inspired me."

Liz smirked. "I seriously doubt that Beethoven was that inspired when he wrote his Ninth Symphony. Do I take it you're good then?"

It was Jack's turn to stretch, then he turned on his side, facing Liz. "I'm great, but I want to keep the promise I made to you over dinner. It's time to talk about Mom."

"I told you, Jack, I was wrong to ask you about her. I can wait until you're ready to share that part of your life with me if that time ever comes."

Caressing Liz's cheek, Jack said quietly, "I don't think I've ever told you what your late mother-in-law's name was, have I?"

"No, but..."

"It's time, Liz," Jack interrupted her. "I want you to know. Her name was Ruth Esther Lockwood Beckett. She was a beautiful woman once—she was tall, had black wavy hair, and bright blue eyes. You know that I was the second child of three, and my earliest memories of Mom and Dad are peaceful ones. Mom loved the Lord in those days, and I think she tried to pattern our home life after another Ruth's life—a Ruth she admired, who was married to a very famous evangelist. For a while, it worked, but then Dad started to resent all her rules and began to change. He started believing his own press releases, and his values altered as his name became widely known in evangelical circles."

"So your dad was a believer, at least until Satan convinced him that he was the star of the show," Liz said, surprise in her tone.

Jack shook his head. "I honestly don't know the answer to that question. Dad says no, that he didn't come to saving faith until that Christmas Eve a few years back at our church. However, if my fuzzy memories are any indicator, I think both Mom and Dad knew the Lord at one time, and I know that Mom would say she never stopped believing. Anyway, after I came along, our happy home began to dissolve. Dad started staying out late, leaving Mom at home with two small boys. Then he started 'counseling' younger women in his church. I remember waking up night after night to the sound of Mom's sobs.

"I still don't know the circumstances of Vicki's conception since, by then, Mom and Dad weren't sleeping in the same room. I was almost five at the time, and I remember the two of them arguing about having another child because Mom thought that a baby would heal the rift in their marriage and she wanted a little girl so badly. After she got pregnant, Dad seemed to change again, this time for the better. He was home more. His church threw a baby shower for the two of them, and Mom started to smile again. When Vicki was born, they were both thrilled, but Mom had a lot of trouble losing the baby weight. In fact, she gained weight, far beyond what the pregnancy had added. Dad hated that and pressured her constantly about her appearance. All that happened was that she gained more weight, her health worsened, and she was less able to do the work around the house that Dad expected.

"Frustrated, Dad started ignoring her and instead focused on the needs of others, particularly of other women. It came to a head when I was thirteen. Dad came home one afternoon, packed a bag, and left, leaving Mom with divorce papers. In Illinois, the courts granted divorce only for cause, and he must have accused her of vile things in those papers. I don't know the specifics. I just know that Mom was never the same after that day. She withdrew into herself, and I don't think I ever saw her smile again. Still, she managed to care for us kids, loving us, and trying to be both father and mother until the day we each left the house. Walt left first, moving to New Mexico to apprentice with a journeyman electrician. He and Morgan married young and started a family. I lived at home until I got my BS in biochemistry from the University of Chicago. Because of that, Vicki and I left home within a year of each other. She went to the University of Wisconsin-Madison for her bachelor's degree, and I went to med school at Johns Hopkins. We both met and married our spouses in the course of the next few years. Neither Mom nor Dad came to any of our weddings.

"Once we were gone, Mom's bitterness consumed her. We all tried to bring light back into her life, tried to get her to engage with our spouses, and later with her grandchildren, but she just couldn't move forward. In her mind, she was the failure, not Dad. She died when I was forty-four, housebound, in pain, and alone. I was the one who found her, and it was clear she'd died several days before I arrived.

"Since then, Walt hasn't spoken to Dad, and you know the issues Dad and I have had trying to find our way back to some kind of a relationship. Vicki has been the most forbearing of all of us, and I look to her example when I'm having trouble forgiving my father for what he did to Mom. Liz," Jack blinked away tears, "more than anything I wish I could have changed those last years for Mom. I wish I'd done more, taken more time to be with her, and I wish I'd held Dad accountable for his actions instead of avoiding him. I don't even know if that would have been possible because he's also bitter about what happened. I think he's still angry at us kids for taking her side without hearing his. I think that's why he was so upset when I changed my last name to Lockwood. He might be correct because if theirs was anything like most relationships, he's not entirely to blame. If I know anything, I know a successful marriage takes two—or rather three, although it was you and Ellie, not Mom and Dad, who showed me how important that third strand is in a marriage."

Taking a deep breath, Jack finished, "So that's Mom. I'm sorry I didn't tell you about her before now. It's not something I like to think about. I try to remember her as she was when I was a boy. Kind, beautiful, and in love with life." He touched Liz's cheek. "Very much like you."

Pulling him into her arms, Liz kissed him gently. "I'm sorry, Jack. I honor you for trying to reestablish a relationship with your father after everything that's happened. I can't imagine the amount of forgiveness it's taken for you to do that. I can, however, give you another way to think about your mom. Think about her the last time she went to sleep in her home—hurting, alone, and hopeless. Then imagine her waking up to see Jesus holding out his hand, welcoming her home. Imagine her walking at her Savior's side, seeing for the first time how God has kept His promise, redeeming the years of the locust[13] for her, for you, for your brother and sister, and even for your father. Her body doesn't hurt anymore. Her eyes are alight with joy as she realizes how much she's loved by her family and by her Lord. That's the hope of everyone who dies in Christ."

Liz wiped away the single tear sliding down Jack's cheek. "Thank you for telling me about her. I think she must have been a great mom because she raised an honorable, kind, caring son. When we all meet in Glory, I'll thank her for the gift of you that she gave to me—the daughter who she never knew." Sitting up, she cradled Jack close and sang.

*There is a place more precious than any other*
*This side of heaven's door*
*A place where we love one another*
*A shelter in time of storm*
*And though it's a treasure*
*This world's not forever*
*I long for the life that's waiting beyond*

---

[13] "Then I will make up to you for the years that the swarming locust has eaten, the creeping locust, the stripping locust, and the gnawing locust. My great army which I sent among you. You will have plenty to eat and be satisfied, and praise the name of the LORD your God, who has dealt wondrously with you; then My people will never be put to shame" (Joel 2:25–26 NASB).

*Where no one will ever be hungry or cold*
*No one will hurt or will ever grow old*
*No one will die and leave someone alone*
*That's when I'll know I'm home*

*There is a place*
*Where truth will always be spoken*
*And promises can be believed*
*A place where your hearts can't be broken*
*And loved ones will never leave*
*So if you are longing for a place of belonging*
*The home you've dreamed of*
*Is waiting for you*

*When no one will ever be hungry or cold*
*No one will hurt or will ever grow old*
*No one will die and leave someone alone*
*That's when I'll know I'm home*

*I'm home forever no pain or disease*
*All will be equal, and all will be free*
*True love will come*
*And we'll fall at His feet*
*That's when I'll know I'm home.*[xii]

⁕

Driving home on Monday afternoon, Jack held tightly to Liz's hand. They'd had a wonderful weekend, and while she'd been in the shower that morning, he'd fallen to his knees and poured his heart out to God in gratitude for what he and Liz shared. They'd enjoyed three nights at the inn, spending hours walking together along the lake and talking. They shared their dreams, hopes, and plans for the next few years.

That morning, they'd gone to the UMD campus to request early admission for Pete, and as they'd anticipated, the university was happy to have both him and his tuition. They were now in possession of his password for the registration portal, allowing him to choose his spring semester classes. He also had a dorm room and a meal plan beginning in January.

Liz had been awfully quiet since they'd left Duluth, so Jack squeezed her hand and said, "A penny for them."

Her eyes dancing with mischief, Liz responded, "I doubt they're worth that much. I was just thinking about calculus guy."

"Wench." Jack took the next turn off Highway 53 and pulled into one of their favorite mom-and-pop restaurants between Duluth and home. "I was going to buy you tea and a nice piece of pie, but you can stay in the car."

"You'd miss me." Liz pouted. "You know you would."

Jack walked around the car and opened Liz's door. Helping her to her feet, he kissed her. "You're right. I'd miss you, so I guess that means you're forgiven."

Relaxing against Jack, Liz squeezed him tightly. "I love you, and I had a great time this weekend. Thank you." She grinned up at him. "Tea and pie sound wonderful."

Sitting together on the same side of an outdoor table overlooking the brightly colored autumn trees, Jack put his arm around Liz's shoulders. "Are you warm enough? That breeze is kind of chilly. We can sit inside if you prefer."

Leaning into Jack, Liz shook her head. "I'm happy right here. Besides, it gives us old fogies a reason to cuddle in public. And I'm happy to take advantage of any excuse to be close to you."

Jack brushed Liz's forehead with his lips. "I wasn't aware we needed an excuse to touch each other in public. If people don't have anything better to do than to pass judgment on our PDA's, then let them. They're all just jealous."

Liz didn't laugh; instead, she sighed sadly, "You saw the text from Dan this morning?"

Jack nodded. "I did. It seems that the four men who paid us a visit had no cartel connections, at least none that Dan's people, the CIA, NSA, or any of the other three-letter agencies could find."

"Including no connection to the Reynoso cartel." Liz frowned. "That's actually what I was thinking about when you asked me earlier. I just wasn't ready to share."

"Liz, Dan's text is good news, right?"

"Is it? Then why did four armed men break into our home? Why Gabs? Why did that lawyer even mention Reynoso in what he assumed would be a private conversation? Why did two of those men give themselves up in the first place? Why…?"

Jack squeezed her hand. "Love, take a breath. I don't know the answers to the questions you're asking, but what I do know is the four that came after us are safely in jail a long way from here. The FBI told Dan that the Reynoso cartel is in disarray after Eduard's death. It seems there's a power struggle in the family about who is going to take over for him. Drug shipments from that source have dried up, which is also good news. I don't know why Gabs was targeted, but there is strong evidence that the guys who did it are independents and they're not coming after her, or us, again."

Jack stopped talking when their server arrived at the table. He sat back so she could put their food in front of them and said, "Thank you. The pie looks great."

The teenage waitress nodded vigorously, her curls bouncing. "Homemade this morning. Enjoy!"

It wasn't until she left that Jack realized Liz was running for the restroom—again. This was the fourth time in three days. He wasn't terribly worried, her symptoms were textbook stomach virus, but he was sad for her, battling this kind of bug while on vacation. Thankfully, once she got rid of whatever was in her stomach, she recovered pretty quickly. He wondered briefly if worry had a part in her nausea, but she'd been worried many times before, and it never had caused these kinds of symptoms. He was glad she had an appointment to see Dorrene next week.

When Liz returned to the table, her pie was in a to-go box and her tea was once again hot, thanks to her husband. Pouring a bit of cream into her cup, she sipped her favorite Earl Grey brew. "Mmm, that's good." Reaching out, she squeezed Jack's hand. "I'm sorry I keep doing that to you. Thank you for getting my pie to go and a fresh cuppa for me." She glanced at his empty plate. "How was the pie?"

"Very good. I hope you'll be able to enjoy it later." Hugging Liz, Jack said, "I'm sorry this keeps happening to you. If it's a virus, it should run its course in the next few days. In the meanwhile, we'll stop on the way home and pick up some ginger ale and more loose-leaf tea. As long as you stay hydrated, you should be fine."

Liz took another sip of her tea. Then, hearing his concern, responded, "Jack, honey, I'm keeping both food and drink down. It just takes a while after this happens. I think you're right about the stomach virus. I'll bet by the time I see Dorrene, everything will be back to normal, so don't worry. I'm fine."

By the time they got home, greeted the kids, and had dinner, Liz was back to her normal self. She felt fine, and dinner stayed in her stomach. After putting the younger kids to bed, they gave Pete the information from UMD. He signed on to the registration portal and registered for his spring semester classes. Like his mother, he'd declared a biology major. Well aware that this might change, Liz was nonetheless excited for him. Her college years, especially the under-graduate years, had been so much fun. Both she and Jack hoped that Pete would have that same kind of experience. The two of them prayed for their son before they went to bed that night, grateful and looking forward to their future with each other and their family.

*There is a thread*
*running between,*
*the first and the last*
*breath that we breathe.*

*And in this strand*
*of flesh and bone,*
*reside the hopes*
*and dreams we call our own.*

*And there's a hand*
*that sews the threads together,*
*around one strand*
*of saving scarlet thread.*

*Come as you are*
*weary, worn, and tattered.*
*Come and take*
*your place among the threads.*

*There is a thread*
*sometimes unseen,*
*moving through life's tapestry.*
*And when this strand*
*enters a soul,*
*it's woven to the one that makes*
*us whole.*

*And there's a hand*
*that sews the threads together*
*around one strand*
*of saving scarlet thread.*

*Come as you are*
*weary, worn, and tattered.*
*Come and take*
*your place among the threads.*[xiii]

# ENDNOTES

i. Toby McKeehan, Geoff Moore, and Steven Curtis Chapman, "Threads" (1997), license no. 1016786, used with permission.

ii. Edward Jones, "All Through the Night" (Welsh, 1784), public domain.

iii. William J. Kirkpatrick, "Away in a Manger" (1895), public domain.

iv. Irving Berlin, "Oh, How I Hate to Get Up in the Morning" (1918), public domain.

v. Aaron Keyes, Jack Mooring, and Bryan Brown, "Sovereign over Us" (CMG Song no. 14017) (2011), license no. 1015928, used with permission.

vi. Anna Bartlett Warner, "Jesus Loves Me" (1860); William Batchelder Bradbury, 1862 (tune and chorus), public domain.

vii. "Michael Row the Boat Ashore," African American spiritual first noted during the American Civil War 1867, public domain.

viii. Folliott S. Pierpoint, "For the Beauty of the Earth" (1864), public domain.

ix. Edward Madden and Gus Edwards, "By the Light of the Silvery Moon" (1909), public domain.

x. Richard Mullins, "Awesome God" (CMG Song no. 14017) (1988), license no. 1015928, used with permission.

xi. Louise Giglio and Chris Tomlin, "Amazing Grace (My Chains Are Gone)" (CMG Song no. 40656) (2006), license no. 1016005, used with permission.

xii. Geoff Moore and Steven Curtis Chapman, "That's When I'll Know I'm Home" (CMG Song no. 5950) (1993), license no. 1015932, used with permission.

xiii. Toby McKeehan, Geoff Moore, and Steven Curtis Chapman, "Threads" (1997), License no. 1016786, used with permission.

# About the Author

Joy Harding is a Christian, a wordsmith, and a lover of books. She is committed to bringing you, her readers, exciting journeys, uplifting love stories, and family sagas that will touch your hearts. Together with her husband of almost forty years, Joy is a passionate believer in the centrality of God in the covenant marriage relationship. Her characters reflect this passion through good times and bad.

Joy lives in the beautiful state of Minnesota. Her first series, Boundary Waters Search and Rescue, is set in the north woods of her home state.

Joy loves to hear from her readers.

Please visit her website and blog at www.joyhardingauthor.com.